Jennifer Rose was born in Newbury, Berkshire, but lived most of her life in Bournemouth, Dorset with her husband John and five children. She worked in the hotel trade for over thirty years before retiring to Devon. Jennifer Rose has eleven grandchildren.

Voice From The Past

Jennifer Rose

Voice From The Past

AUSTIN & MACAULEY

A CIP catalogue record for this title is
available from the British Library.

ISBN 978 1 84963 002 3

www.austinmacauley.com

First Published (2010)
Austin & Macauley Publishers Ltd.
25 Canada Square
Canary Wharf
London
E14 5LB

Printed & Bound in Great Britain

DEDICATION

Thanks to my late mother, Ada Rose, who will be sitting on a cloud looking down at the world, knitting! The book has now been written on the laptop given to me by her. Also to my patient husband John, and for the encouragement of my five wonderful children, Lynn, Lee, Kim, Sandy and Jon.
I love you all.

ACKNOWLEDGEMENTS

My thanks to my granddaughters, Jemma and Emily for suggesting the cover. Thanks to Lynn and June who, after reading the first few chapters, encouraged me to finish the story.

Last of all but not least to the production team who professionally put it all together.

CHAPTER ONE

"Damn it," Chrissie cursed, knocking her knee against the banister, as she rushed back down the stairs to answer the phone that was ringing out in the hallway of her tranquil cottage, cursing each stair she took, as her hip bones grated together after being on her feet all day.

"Hello," she said, stifling a yawn as she waited for someone to speak, chewing on a ragged finger nail that she'd caught on the banister. Tutting, she pressed her ear closer to the phone as the sound of heavy breathing hit her ears. A shudder went down her back as her eyes darted to the front door, checking to see that it was locked.

"Look, whoever it is, speak now or the phone goes down."

If there was something Chrissie wasn't in the mood for, it was some asshole breathing down the phone at her. She had come home feeling shattered from work after running around like a lunatic all day on the so-called public, who should be locked away for their own good. (Her thoughts only, of course.) But she was feeling ratty after getting an abusive phone call at the four-star hotel, where she worked as a head housekeeper. Somebody had phoned through to her office ranting away down the phone at her, ending up by calling her a BITCH, then put the phone down on her before she could find out who it was. Left feeling shocked, she'd phoned down to reception asking if it was an internal or an outside call that had been put through to her, but they couldn't say because the phones had been manic for the last couple of hours. So Chrissie had put it down to a disgruntled guest and had thought no more of it, and all she wanted to do now was to climb into her own bed in between the cool clean sheets that were waiting for her to nestle down in, where hopefully she'd sleep the night away.

Slamming the phone down, she started back up the stairs, still cursing to herself as she tucked her newspaper under her arm. She drew the landing curtains across the window before turning to go into her bedroom, but suddenly stopped when she heard sounds coming from outside. Somebody was walking up the gravel pathway that ran along the side of the cottage. Her heart did a somersault, pounding so hard against her ribcage that she thought it would burst out at any moment as her knees started trembling.

"Now g---et a hold of yourself, Chrissie", she stuttered, trying to control her vivid imagination. "It's most probably a badger or a fox sniffing around for food," she said hopefully, taking a deep breath.

After calming herself down, she slowly lifted up the edge of the curtain to see out of the landing window. But as she stood up on her tiptoes, craning her neck to see out, the bloody phone rang again, making her jump out of her skin, as she fell back against the wall hitting her head against it, letting out a yelp that sounded like an injured animal.

Rubbing the back of her head, she grabbed hold of the banister and struggled back down the stairs with the phone still shrieking out at her as she cursed under her breath.

"HELLO," Chrissie barked out, catching her breath as she waited for someone to answer. Again, there was silence down the phone, and she had to push the panic down that was rising up in her as she went to slam the phone down, but as she took the phone away from her ear, a feeling of relief washed right through her.

"Mum … is that you?"

"DAISY…" Chrissie flopped down into the chair that was by the side of the telephone table. Who she was expecting it to be God only knows. But after the silent phone call earlier, and then the disturbance outside in the garden, her nerves were shattered, and she was so relieved to hear her daughter's voice on the other end of the phone that she started laughing.

"Mum, are you okay?"

"Yes, of course, darling."

"Then what are you laughing at? Have you got company?"

Daisy looked across at Jasmine, her girlfriend, who she was going to stay with that night. They had been out for a Chinese, and Daisy had drunk more wine than she had intended to, so decided that she would sleep over for the night, hence the phone call to her mother to let her know that she wouldn't be home until morning.

"No, there's nobody here except for me and our cat Marmalade. Why, what's up, are you okay?"

"Yeah, I'm fine. But I was going to stay over at Jasmine's tonight if that's okay? Or do you want me to come home? You don't sound yourself. Is everything okay, mum."

"I'm okay, silly," Chrissie said, now feeling much calmer in herself. "I'm feeling tired and was just on my way up to bed, and the phone rang. You know how jumpy I am on my own," she laughed, making light of it.

"Well, if you're sure."

"Of course, I'm sure." Chrissie tutted. "I've got marmalade here to protect me."

Daisy seemed happy with that explanation, knowing how tired her mother could get after a strenuous day at the hotel, so said goodnight to her, saying she'd see her tomorrow after work.

At long last Chrissie finally made it up to her bedroom. Throwing the paper onto the bed she collected her dressing gown from off the back of the door, and sauntered along to the bathroom where she cleaned her teeth and splashed warm water over her face. Having a bath had gone right out of the window tonight, it was now gone 11 o'clock and her early night was now ending up to be a late one. Making her way back to the bedroom, she paused by the landing window straining her ears for any unusual sound coming from outside, but it was silent as a graveyard, just the rustle of leaves blowing around in the warm breeze.

Shrugging her shoulders, she carried on walking along to her bedroom as she mumbled away to herself: "One wrong number dialled and you think you have a loony running around in the garden."

Switching the bedside lamp on, she went over to draw the bedroom curtains, pausing for a second to take a look around the garden. The moon was shining brightly on the weeping willow as the slender branches danced around in the breeze with a hedgehog snuffling along under it, hopefully looking for slugs that were a pet hate of Chrissie's. But just as she went to draw the curtains across, she stepped back, putting her hand across her mouth to stop herself from crying out. Through the branches of the willow tree she saw a shadow move. Her eyes darted around the room looking for her mobile. God, this night was becoming a nightmare.

She shook her head. "Now come on, Chrissie," she said to herself. "Just take a look out of the window and see what--- if anything, it is." Slowly looking behind the curtain she screwed her eyes up so she could see out in the dark. But there was nothing out there, she could see nothing, only the branches of the willow tree swaying around in the wind.

"You stupid cow!" she snapped, swishing the curtains across as she grabbed hold of her mobile and clambered into bed, still cursing herself for being such a idiot.

Stewart picked himself up from off the ground, brushing himself down. He looked up at Chrissie's bedroom window, puffing on a home-made roll-up.

"Bitch. So that's where you've been hiding," he spat out, as he watched the light go out.

Every light was against her this morning as Chrissie battled her way to work through the traffic jams. This was all she needed after getting up late, then wasting time looking for her handbag, that she'd eventually found stuffed down the back of the settee as she chewed a slice of toast. She'd run out of the cottage cursing like a trooper, putting her foot down on the pedal of her Mini, and drove like a bat out of hell, screeching to a halt at all the red lights. Usually she would have heard Daisy moving around in the bathroom, cleaning her teeth and gurgling water around her mouth. But this morning, it had been silent except for the sound of the birds chirping in the garden that had eventually woke Chrissie up. What with the fiasco of last night, it had been midnight before she'd finally got off to sleep, listening to every creak and sound as her eyes darted around the room waiting for some maniac to jump out at her. So when the alarm had gone off this morning, she'd switched it off, dozing on and off until she heard the chirping of the birds, and Marmalade meowing at the bedroom door waiting to be let out.

Turning her car into the hotel car park, she slammed the brakes on to her Mini, just missing a Jaguar that was heading out at a speed.

"Bitch," He mouthed through the window at her.

Chrissie's mouth fell open as she scrambled to wind her window down. "Who the hell are you calling a bitch?" she yelled after him, but he was gone, screeching out on two wheels. "Bloody idiot," she cursed, parking her car into her allotted spot.

Stewart blew out a cloud of blue smoke, coughing and sputtering on a roll up, as he banged his fist against the steering wheel, laughing as he headed off down towards the motorway. "This is just the beginning, bitch,"

Chrissie ran across the car park, pressing the lift button that would take her up into the hotel. As she searched around in her handbag for her office keys, she wondered who the hell had just mouthed bitch at her through their car window. As the lift jolted to a halt, she got out saying good morning to Luke who was the night porter. He yawned, nodding his head at her as he got into the lift, thankful that he was on his way home to get some shut eye. Walking through to the reception area, Chrissie stopped at the reception desk, before going up to her office, to pick up a bunch of keys that she would need for her chambermaids to get into their rooms this morning. Shelly, who was head of reception, handed over the keys to her, as she told her that one of her chambermaids had rung in sick.

"Christ, that's all I need to start the day off," Chrissie tutted, smiling as she took the keys from Shelly, thanking her. "I'll just keep on taking the tablets," she laughed.

Pushing her shoulder against the office door, she fell in cursing Darren who was head of maintenance. He still hadn't sorted out the lock on her door for her. It had been at least three months since she had asked him to take a look at it, and her shoulder was now black and blue from pushing the door in every morning...well maybe not black and blue, but her shoulder was getting sore.

Before switching the computer on she flicked the kettle switch down; a coffee was needed to start the adrenalin going before running off the departure and arrival list for her girls that day. As she savored the coffee, she waved through the office window to Daphne, her linen keeper, who was busy loading up the trolleys with linen, ready for the girls to take up on to the floors. It was a Friday, and it was going to be a mega busy day for them all as most of the hotel would be departing and filling up again with weekenders that would be coming down the coast to relax away from it all, enjoying the warmth of the weather that May had brought in. As she refilled her mug with coffee, the phone rang making her jump. She picked it up, and in her best telephone manner answered it.

"Rose Mount Hotel, Chrissie speaking, can I help you?" she said, looking at herself in the cracked mirror that hung on the wall in front of her, flicking her blonde fringe away from her large blue eyes, looking closer at the wrinkles that were forming around them.

"BITCH."

Chrissie fell back into her chair, and for a moment was so dumbstruck, that she couldn't speak. She just couldn't believe that she had been called a bitch twice in one day, and it was only 8:30 in the morning. What the hell was going on? Straightening her back, she cleared her throat ready to let rip, but before she could get a word out of her mouth, the phone was slammed down on her. She stared down the mouthpiece with her mouth wide open. She was speechless, her knuckles were white from clenching on to the phone.

"My God, who was that?" she gasped.

Dropping the phone on to its cradle, she snatched it back up and rang through to reception. Shelly answered it, laughing as she joked with a guest that had just come up from the gym asking for his room keys.

"Hi Chrissie, it's not more tablets you're needing is it?" she asked jokingly.

"Ha ha, very funny," she really was in no mood for joking, but she didn't want Shelly to know what had just happened, so she asked her as jovially as she could if she'd just put a phone call through to her? Shelly said that she hadn't but Luke the night porter might have done.

"Why, he didn't cut you off again, did he?" she laughed.

There was no time to go into it now, so Chrissie just laughed it off by saying that it didn't matter, pushing it to the back of her mind for the time being. The girls would be arriving any minute now, and she still had their day list to do.

One by one the girls began arriving, and a couple of them raised their eyebrows at seeing the departures they had that day. But the mood soon broke as Jayne came stumbling through the door, falling against the desk spilling Chrissie's coffee everywhere. Chrissie took a step back, cursing while the girls tried to suppress their smiles as the colour in Jayne's face reddened.

"Morning, Jayne," Chrissie said. "Enjoy your trip?"

By 9:30 the girls were up on the floors with their trolleys unloading their linen into piles, ready to service the rooms as the guests departed. All rooms were supposed to be vacated by 11:30, but most days there were late departures, leaving the girls running around like scalded cats trying to get the room's spick and span, ready for the next guests to go into.

Chrissie would bustle along the corridor, her keys jangling by her side as she went in and out of the rooms chivvying the girls up, ignoring their tuts and sighs as they went around with a toilet brush in one hand and a duster in the other. Then her pager would go off, and she would have to dash down to reception where she would try and rescue the poor receptionist from the verbal abuse she was getting from a guest who had arrived early, and was demanding to get into their room, asshole... God give her strength. As it was her chambermaids only had a minimum of three hours to turn around a section of ten to thirteen rooms that had to be in left in pristine condition for the next arrival, and that in itself was one hell of a mission. But it didn't stop there. Besides managing the upstairs of the hotel that had 206 bedrooms, Chrissie also had to oversee the gym area along with a large swimming pool, whilst keeping up the standards of a four-star hotel which at times proved to be one hell of a headache for her, especially when girls rang in sick at the last minute feigning illness, then to find out that they had been out on the town the night before, and it was a hangover that they had been nursing... Oh, but boy did they know all about it when they turned up for work the next morning as two extra rooms were added on to their section!

It was almost 10 o'clock, and Chrissie had to be in the Majestic suite for the daily management meeting where all heads of departments met with Mr Grey, the general manager. They would sit and listen to the complaints from the day before as they sipped on their coffee with Chrissie praying that there wouldn't be a repeat of the other day, when Annabelle, her evening housekeeper, turned down the beds in room 208, ready for the guests to slip into when they returned to their room that evening. After tidying the room and leaving fresh towels in the bathroom, she also left a chocolate on the pillow for the finishing touch! When the guest, Mrs Hastings, returned to the room later in the evening after relaxing in the cocktail lounge, she had showered before climbing into bed, switching the light off, not seeing the chocolate that had been left on her pillow. Then she woke in the morning, stretching herself as she ran her fingers through her hair. She thought she'd been shot as thick gooey red liquid dripped through her fingers. So to say she wasn't pleased was an understatement, and it had took a lot of groveling from

Chrissie to calm her down as free fruit and wine went up to her room. So now it goes without saying… Chocolates are to be left on the bedside cabinet… not on the pillows. Before coming out of the meeting, she stopped Darren and asked him once again if he could get her office door fixed.

"I shall have to take time off work if my shoulder comes out of joint from barging it open every morning," she teased, punching him playfully on the arm.

Jake, who was the duty manager that day, caught hold of Chrissie's arm as she rushed by him. There was so much work to catch up on that she had no time to hang about.

"Hey Chrissie, slow down a bit," he laughed, as his honey brown eyes pierced into hers. "Can we catch up later? I need to speak to you about the police conference coming in on Monday."

She went to pull away, but his hold on her arm tightened.

"Jake, I've got a lot on today, can't it wait until tomorrow?"

"No, it can't", he snapped.

He released his hold on her as a smile crossed her face. She could see his jaws clenching together as he tried holding back his frustration of the feelings he had for her, and for a split second there was an awkward silence between them. Chrissie knew full well that young Jake had a crush on her, but the feelings were not mutual. For a start she was going on for 45, and Jake was only in his early 30's. So when Simon the restaurant manager came bounding along the corridor, he thankfully broke the silence between them.

"Hey Chrissie, good to see you, sweetie. Where've you been? I've not seen you for a couple of days. You been on holiday?" he laughed, knowing she'd been on her days off.

She gave him a push calling him a cheeky bugger, laughing as he held his arm, pretending to be in pain. Simon was gay, and a great play actor.

"I was here yesterday running around like a loony, where were you?"

As they bantered back and forth between themselves, Jake stalked off, he was fuming with her. She could be so damn infuriating at times. All he'd wanted to do was to discuss the conference that was coming in on Monday with her. He slammed through doors, narrowly missing one of her chambermaids, apologising as he made his way over to the lift. He decided that he would catch up with her later on in the day when she wasn't so damn busy to see him!

Arriving on the ninth floor, he made his way along to the penthouse suite. The South West Farmers Association had held a two-day conference in there, and they always had a bar put in so the members could have a tipple to help them unwind after a hard day's work of discussing the ups and downs of being in the farming world. But boy... If only you'd seen them swaggering back to their rooms, sniggering like naughty schoolboys, or worst still, trying to chat up the chambermaids as they fumbled around in their pockets searching for their room keys. You could bet your bottom dollar that it was more than one tipple that they'd had! Today they were departing, so it was down to the duty manager to take stock of how much drink had been consumed before the chambermaid got in to service it... But if the girl, or girls, were lucky enough to make it into the suite before Jake or whoever else was duty manager that day, they would take a quick swig from a bottle, while somebody kept an eye out at the door, swapping over if there was time to. That's why Jake tried to make it to the suite before them. He wasn't stupid, he knew that if they got there before him they would think that Christmas had come early. Often he would call Chrissie up and confront her about her girls' behaviour, but Chrissie would stick up for them, swearing blind that her girls would never drink while on duty, as her nose twitched at the smell of mint wafting from the room as they chewed on their gum..!

Chrissie made her way back to her office after doing a spot check on a few rooms that her junior housekeeper had checked. Janie had only been working at the hotel for the last two weeks, so was still new at the job, and was being checked daily by Chrissie or Dawn, her assistant housekeeper until they were happy that the standard of the rooms were being left as should be for a four-star-hotel rating. She was still smiling from seeing Simon earlier. He was such a nutter sometimes, always play acting around, but he was a top restaurant manager, and nothing got past him. He worked with a good team, most of them as off beat as he was, but they all respected him.

She sat in front of her computer stretching over to press the switch down on the kettle. The day had flown by, and in just under an hour she would be handing over to her evening housekeeper Annabelle, and then with a bit of luck be home by six to see Daisy before going over to see her lifelong girlfriend Natasha.

She logged into the housekeeping programme, and fed the remainder of the rooms through to reception that were now ready for the rest of the day's arrivals. The only room that had not been serviced was 301, Mr Johnson's room. He was a regular, and was feeling unwell, not wanting to be disturbed. Now whether that was because he'd had punnets of strawberries sent up to his room with jugs of cream after a young attractive lady arrived late last night remained to be seen... So the chambermaid had left him in peace leaving clean towels outside of his room along with a set of clean sheets....

Chrissie smiled as she remembered back to when Jodie, one of her chambermaids, had called her up on to floors to go into the room of 301. She had tried all morning to get into the room, but the Do-Not-Disturb sign had been left out on the door, and nobody was answering when she knocked on it, and the time was getting on, so Jodie needed to get into the room to service it as it was a departure that day, and the new guest would be arriving anytime now. Chrissie arrived up on the floor with her master key, and after listening to what Jodie had to say, she went along to the room and gently tapped on the door.

"Housekeeper," she said chirpily, winking at Jodie who was stood at the end of the corridor waiting with her trolley. After no reply, she knocked the door with her fist and put her master key into the lock, slowly opening up the door. "Housekeeper," she said again, not wanting to surprise anyone if they were in the loo or something. Stepping into the room, she gasped backing back out of the door.

"Go and find a manager," she yelled down to Jodie. "NOW!" she shouted as Jodie made a move towards the room.

Jodie ran down the main staircase taking them two at a time, wondering what the hell had gone on in that room as she fell into Simon who was on his way back to the restaurant.

"Whoa…., where's the fire? Slow down."

As they both ran back up the stairs, Jodie tried explaining to him that Chrissie had told her to find a manager after she had opened up the door to room 301. "She's probably found a dead body," he muttered as they reached the third floor panting and out of breath. Simon told Jodie to stay where she was until he'd checked that everything was okay.

"Chrissie sweetie, where are you?" He shouted in a high pitched voice, as he reached the door and saw the scene that confronted him. He could see that there had been a fight of some sorts, as there was blood all over the room.

"On my bloody knees," she said, scrabbling up from off the floor where she'd knelt down to see if there was anyone lying injured under the bed.

"For God's sake, Chrissie," he yelped, jumping a mile into the air. "You almost gave me an freaking heart attack. What the hell are you doing down there?"

Chrissie gave a wry smile as she watched him flapping his hands around as his eyes darted around the room. There was blood everywhere. On the bed, on the carpet. They rang down for Mr Grey to come up, then both gingerly looked in the wardrobe, expecting a body to fall out. Chrissie jumped back stifling a scream, crashing into Simon who was close on her heels as a coat hanger sprang out at them.

"Christ," he yelled, holding onto his ticker, as he pushed her towards the bathroom poking his tongue out as she stifled her laughter.

Slowly peering around the door, they could see that it was in a worse mess than the bedroom, with blood in the bath and all up the walls.

Mr Grey arrived, sucking in a mouthful of air as he looked around the room in horror.

"What the hell has gone on here?" he asked, wiping beads of sweat from his forehead with his crisp white handkerchief.

The police arrived about 15 minutes later after Mr Grey phoning them. They took in the scene that confronted them, then started asking questions, asking Chrissie who had occupied the room last.

It turned out that two male guests had booked in late that Friday evening for the weekend. Andy the night porter had taken them both up to room 301. They had paid upfront by credit card, and it was in the early hours of Saturday morning that Andy had been called up by room 302, who were complaining of the noise that was coming from the room of 301. Somebody had been screaming, and a lot of banging had been going on, so Andy had gone and knocked on the door, telling them as quietly as he could so as not to disturb any more guests, that he was the night porter, and would they open up the door please. When a young man answered the door with just a towel wrapped around him, he asked him if everything was alright, and after reassuring him that they had just had a tiff, Andy asked him if he could please keep the noise down as it was the early hours of the morning, and he had received complaints about the noise coming from their room. The young man did apologise and promised there would be no more noise coming from the room. The police then checked with reception and found out that they had left before the receptionist had come on duty at 7:30 that morning, taking the room key with them.

A few days later the police did catch up with them in the Midlands area. Apparently, it had been a lovers' tiff that had got out of hand with one of them ending up with a right shiner to the eye, and a broken nose. Which, thank God had been contrary to the Chinese whispers that had travelled amongst the staff that there had been a murder committed in the hotel!

CHAPTER TWO

Chrissie had arrived home from work before Daisy, and knocked up a quick spaghetti Bolognese for their tea, pouring herself a rum and Coke out after feeding Marmalade, who had been meowing around her legs since she'd got in. Daisy got home ten minutes later, and ran straight upstairs to the loo, she'd been dying to go since she'd left work, and by the time she got back down again Chrissie had the meal ready and waiting on the table.

"I saw Dad today," she said, sprinkling cheese on top of her Bolognese.

Chrissie finished her mouthful before answering. She hadn't seen Freddie for a while now. In fact, the last time she had seen him was at the supermarket downtown with his new girlfriend. It was going on five years now since they had been divorced, and although sometimes she missed him being around, it had been for the best that they had made a clean break of it. She smiled to herself, wiping her mouth on a tissue as she remembered the times that Freddie had come home late from work making so many pathetic excuses to her, as perfume from another woman wafted past her nose. Sad...But there you go! The trouble was, Freddie could never keep his stick of rock inside of his trousers. She looked across at Daisy tucking into her food, thinking that at least something good had come out of it all, and there she was sat opposite her.

"Did you hear me, Mum? I saw Dad today," she tutted.

"Stop tutting, I heard you. How is he?" she asked, trying to sound interested, but not really giving a hoot about it.

Daisy went on to say that he was getting married to Jackie, who Chrissie guessed was the girl she had seen him with at the supermarket. And that there would be an invitation in the post for them to go to the wedding. Chrissie cringed inwardly. That was the last place she'd want to be at, but said nothing and sat listening, smiling when needed. Then the conversation went on to what they were doing that night. Daisy was staying in, and Jasmine was coming over with a video to stay the night if it was alright with her, which of course Chrissie thought was a great idea, seeing as she was out for the evening herself visiting Natasha, where she was going to help out with the wallpapering of her hallway. Silly as it seemed, Chrissie never felt comfortable leaving Daisy on her own in the cottage at night even though she was almost twenty, and quiet capable of looking after herself. But there you go… That's being a mother for you.

Daisy was the first to finish eating and got up from the table, getting herself an apple from out of the fruit bowl. She turned to her mother as she went through into the lounge, asking if she knew who had driven out of the lane earlier.

"No idea. Why?" Chrissie asked, joining her as she spluttered on the juice of a orange that she was sucking on.

"I thought the car had driven out of our drive, that's all."

"What type of car was it?"

"I don't know, it was driving at such a speed I had to swerve over to miss it."

Chrissie shrugged her shoulders. "Mmm, maybe it was someone who had taken the wrong turning." Then thought nothing more of it as they chatted away for a while before

Chrissie got up to get changed into her jeans before setting off to Natasha's.

All the lights were blazing from the house as Chrissie arrived at Natasha's. Parking up in the drive, she retrieved a bottle of wine from off the back seat before locking the car.

Natasha was at the door with a huge grin on her face holding a roll of wallpaper under her arm.

"About time, too," she said, grabbing the wine from Chrissie as she planted a kiss on her cheek. Chrissie followed her through to the kitchen, followed by Scamp the dog, Rosie the cat, and Bubbles the rabbit, a snowy white French lop with huge floppy ears who was almost as big as Scamp the terrier.

Natasha poured out two large glasses of white wine, handing one over to Chrissie as she shifted Bubbles out of the way with the toe of her slipper.

Chrissie laughed as she watched her squeezing through the cat flap after Rosie. "Where does she do all her poops when she's indoors?"

"After nearly skinning her alive, I've managed to train her to use a litter tray. But the moo is still lazy sometimes and plops on the bloody floor," she cursed, helping her through the flap as she got stuck halfway through.

Chrissie followed Tash, her pet name for her, through to the hallway, asking how her love life was going.

"Zilch," she sighed.

"Aren't you seeing that guy... um..." she flapped her hands in the air nearly spilling her drink trying to think of his name. "Miles... Piles... Charles... that's it, Charles."

Natasha spluttered on her wine, "Giles, you bloody fool, not Charles, and no I'm not seeing him now, got too heavy, wanted to put a ring on my finger…Yuk, no way. I'm happy as I am, thank you, with my dog, cat and rabbit."

"He was nice, Tash. It's about time you settle down, you wild thing you."

Natasha raised her eyes to the ceiling, "Yeah. Right, and it's about time that you settled down too. Now for God's sake let's get on or we'll never get the wallpapering done."

Chrissie raised her glass. "Touché," she laughed, finishing off the wine.

They went back a long way did Chrissie and Natasha. They had known one another for over twenty years now. They had met at the Rose Mount Hotel. Natasha had turned up looking for a job as a chambermaid, where Chrissie was the assistant housekeeper at the time, at the young age of 21. Natasha, who was attending college at the time, needed a weekend job to help with the expense of the cost of living, which was not cheap when you were sharing a flat with two other girls, and had to find the money for the rent plus the food to stay alive. She was studying to become a vet assistant, and was just seventeen at the time with large saucer green eyes, and honey-coloured hair that had been swept back in a ponytail. Jilly, who was then the head housekeeper at the hotel, had taken her on for weekend work, asking Chrissie to show her the ropes. Natasha had cottoned on almost straight away to the work, and Chrissie could see that she was going to be a strong worker. So after a week or two, she had given her the eight suites at the top of the hotel that were usually let to wealthy families. She had asked her if she would give the Adams Suite a spring clean while they were in a quiet period, checking first with reception that it wasn't let until later in the day, and asked her to give a good spring clean around the fireplace area. After about half an hour of leaving her, Chrissie's bleep went off. It was Natasha asking if she would go up and see her as she had a bit of a problem in the room! When Chrissie had finally gotten there, after being stopped on her way by another chambermaid who had a problem with her key that wouldn't open up the doors to let her into the rooms that needed servicing, her eyes had nearly popped out of her head when she saw what was facing her in the middle of the room. There were nuts and bolts from the electric fire all over the floor, with the elements dangling over the side of it.

"What the hell have you done?" she yelled.

"I spring cleaned the fire as you asked me to," Natasha said sheepishly, twisting the duster around her finger as Chrissie's bleep went off again… It was Shelly letting her know that the guests had arrived earlier than planned. And were now waiting at reception to get into the suite.

Chrissie chased around to find Darren to come up and sort the fire out for her. It was no surprise to Chrissie that Natasha didn't stay in the hotel trade, but went on to become the veterinary assistant instead. Hence her love of animals in the home.

After managing to put a plank across the two ladders that Natasha had propped up against the landing walls, she nervously made her way up the rungs while Chrissie stood waiting three rungs beneath her with a sheet of glued wallpaper, sipping on her wine that she had gone back in the kitchen for. As Natasha edged her way across the plank, she nervously turned around, carefully taking the sheet of wallpaper from Chrissie. Her knees wobbled as she turned to face the wall as Chrissie climbed back down and started to paste another sheet of wallpaper.

"I'll hang the next piece if you want me to," Chrissie said, slapping the paste on.

"Watch you don't make the next piece too soggy," Natasha said, nearly putting her hand through the sheet of paper that she was trying to hang onto the wall, as sprinkles of paste sprayed around in the air.

After much cursing trying to get all the air bubbles out, she eventually got the sheet of wallpaper hung up onto the wall of the stairwell, before climbing back down the ladder to let Chrissie take over. Taking a sip of her wine, Natasha lifted the wallpaper, that was dripping with paste from off the pasting table, and gingerly climbed the rungs of the ladder, handing it up to Chrissie who was holding on for grim death against the wall. Holding it out to her, Natasha started giggling as Chrissie inched herself across the plank, her knees knocking together as she took the heavy sheet of wallpaper from her. Carefully, with her hands holding on to each side of the paper, she inched it up on to the wall, ready to smooth it evenly into place. By this time, Natasha was back down the ladder, taking a sip of her wine before pasting another sheet of wallpaper, when she heard Chrissie yell out, cursing obscenities obstinately. Her hand flew across her mouth as she took in the scene above her, with Chrissie standing there with her head through the middle of the wallpaper, and paste dripping down all over her.

"My God, Chrissie…Are you alright?" she asked. But the sight of her standing there with the wallpaper stuck over her head, swearing like a trooper, was just too much for her as she fell to her knees laughing.

"Of course I'm not bloody alright," she cursed, struggling to get the wallpaper back over her head without falling off the plank.

Natasha pulled herself up from off her knees, and rushed up the ladder to help relieve her of the soggy torn wallpaper that was now hanging around her knees.

When they finally got their feet back on the ground, they took one look at each other and laughed hysterically, as Natasha gave Chrissie a shove making her lose her footing, where she landed up on the pasting table, snapping it in two… And that's when she lost control of herself as she went into fits of giggles, and ended up unable to hold her bladder any longer.

After calming down, they decided that they would give up on the wallpapering for that night, and went back to the kitchen, where they both had a strong coffee. They nattered on about this and that, and then Chrissie remembered about the car that had just missed her that morning as she drew into the hotel car park. She told Natasha about it, and of how the driver of the car had mouthed 'bitch' to her through the window. But to top all of that, of the phone calls she received when she got into her office.

"Did you call the police?"

"No, of course not."

"Why not? It could be some nutter out there stalking you."

"Oh Nats, stop exaggerating. It probably was a one-off."

"Yeah. Right, three times! Well just you keep your eyes open, you never know."

"Yes, mum."

It was after twelve before Chrissie hit the road to drive home, with Natasha nagging on to her about how it was too late to be driving home, and she should stay the night. But Chrissie reassured her that she would be okay. She was now fully awake after all the coffee they had drunk while putting the world to rights, she would ring her when she got home, to let her know she had arrived safely

As she turned into the lane, a shudder went through her. It was dark with only a solitary light left on in the porch of her cottage. As she parked up in the driveway, she thought that she saw from out the corner of her eye some movement from the hedgerow that divided her from her elderly neighbor Mr Roberts, but shook her head, cursing herself for being so pathetic as she got the torch out from the pocket of the car, and delved into her handbag for the house keys. She hurried up the driveway to the safety of her home, but before she had reached the front door, she again saw from out the corner of her eye something move by hedgerow, and started running towards the door, panicking as she struggled to get the key into the lock just as a heavy hand came down on her shoulder.

A piercing scream rang out into the silence of the night, as she swung around hitting the intruder with the full force of her handbag, screaming out obscenely like a madwomen. Lights flew on from inside of the cottage as others followed along the terrace, as Daisy fell out of her bed and came crashing down the stairs with a candlestick in her hand with Jasmine close on her heels. Tugging open the door, she was ready to swing the candlestick at whoever got in her way, but was stopped in her tracks when she saw the scene before her. There, bending over, was her mother helping up poor old Mr Roberts from off the floor, brushing him down, as she apologised profusely for knocking him to the ground. The poor old sod was struggling to catch his breath. Daisy lowered the candlestick in her hand, and was about to ask what the hell had happened, when she saw the look in her mother's eyes.

"Don't ask," she said, feeling really embarrassed with herself for attacking poor old Mr Roberts who was 80, if not older.

After he had calmed down, Chrissie took him in and gave him a large brandy as he told her why he had come round to see her so late at night. He had been putting out the milk bottles ready for the milkman in the morning, and as he'd bent down to put them on the doorstep, the front door had slammed shut on him, so he had to go round to the back of the cottage to get through a window that he knew he had left ajar in the kitchen. But as he'd climbed up on to a wooden box to climb over the window sill, he'd lost his footing and fell backwards onto the soft landing of his lawn, thank God. Then he'd seen Chrissie drive into her driveway and had scrabbled up and hobbled around for some help! After Chrissie had calmed him down, she and Daisy walked him back to his cottage, and Daisy climbed in through his kitchen window, letting him in safely inside. It was going on for two in the morning before they had all got to bed, and Chrissie was feeling wide awake, so got out her book to relax down with. But she couldn't get it out of her mind of what Daisy had said to her as they had all drank a mug of drinking chocolate before going to bed. She told her that she thought she'd seen somebody lurking around under the willow tree as she'd gone to pull the kitchen curtains across earlier. A shudder had gone through Chrissie, but she didn't say to Daisy that she thought she had seen the same thing the night before, as she was pulling across the curtains in her bedroom! She didn't want to worry her.

CHAPTER THREE

"Thank God you're here," Dawn said, pressing the lift button.

"Why? Is there a fire or something?"

Chrissie looked around the hotel foyer, catching sight of Mr Grey going into his office with a bundle of papers tucked under his arm.

"Nooo, nothing like that," she said, clicking her tongue. "But two of our girls have already rang in sick this morning and it's only 8:30, and....," she gasped, coming up for air. "We've got the hotel owners visiting us today."

"Calm down, Dawn," Chrissie laughed. "Stop flapping, we'll be fine. Let me get through the office door before we start panicking. Then after we've put the kettle on, we'll take a look and see who we have in today... Then we'll start panicking," she said, nudging her towards the kettle. She waved to Daphne through the office window as she breathed out a sigh of relief to see at least the linen keeper was in.

Dawn put the room keys on to the hooks ready for the girls to take along with their rooming list as they arrived in one by one. Some would be stifling their yawns, others would be moaning on about the amount of rooms they were expected to clean that day. But - hey... that's what it was all about working in hotels. You either loved it, or you hated it. There was no in between.

Simon popped his head around the door after collecting a few tablecloths from the linen room. "Christ, Chrissie, do I really have to go through a Spanish Inquisition every time I want a few extra cloths from your bloody linen keeper?"

"And good morning to you too, Simon," Chrissie said. "And the day only gets better," she muttered to herself, as she turned her back on him running her eyes down over the rota, then glancing up at the computer in front of her to see the amount of departures for that day.

"I hope you haven't upset Daphne this morning. We have a long day ahead of us, so can we please all keep our cool... or at least until the working day starts."

"Hmm," he said, standing with his hand on his hip. "Mine started at 6:30 this morning. Where were you?" he snapped, flouncing out of the office like the spoilt queen that he was.

God, there were times when she could quite cheerfully wring his bloody neck. Damn big wussy. Dawn drank her coffee, suppressing a smile, saying nothing.

"Well we have eight girls due in if nobody else rings in sick, with ten sections to cover, and half of the hotel departing today. Sooo... it looks like you'll have to take a section on, Dawn, and I'll check the rooms the best I can until you've got through the cleaning of your rooms. I'll give you a section with the least departures on so you can whizz through them," Chrissie smiled, winking at her.

"Gee thanks," Dawn said, pulling a face.

All the girls were in by nine and up on the floors with their trolleys by 9:30. Some cursing at the amount of the rooms they had to do, but on the whole, they were okay, especially when they found out that one of the housekeepers was cleaning rooms as well as themselves. For some reason, that always put a smile on their faces!

Chrissie glanced at her watch as she made her way along the second corridor. My God, it was 12:30 already, where had the morning gone? She smiled at Sue and Diane, two of her strongest chambermaids, as they made their way towards the staff lift that would take them down to the staff canteen. That was the in place for catching up on all the gossip that was going around the hotel as they ate their lunch.

"Morning, Chrissie, or afternoon is it? Missed you at the meeting this morning. Everything okay?"

Chrissie jumped out of her skin, as she swung around coming face to face with Jake.

"For Christ sake, Jake, you gave me the fright of my life creeping up on me like that," she snapped, bending down to pick up some papers that had slid off her clipboard.

"God, she looks so sexy when she loses her cool like that," he thought, helping her pick up her paperwork. Her wild blue eyes sparkled as she tucked wispy strands of hair behind her sexy small ears, straightening the bun at the back of her head. Jake had grown very fond of Chrissie over the last three years they had worked together, more than fond if he was to tell the truth. But he knew it was only friendship on Chrissie's part, because he had tried to take it further, but she was having none of it… But it didn't mean he was going to give up!

"I hear you're short-staffed today, do you need any help?"

Chrissie's back bristled. Just because the family were due down today, everyone started panicking. How the bloody hell did they ever manage to get through the rest of the year when they were not around. She was there all year round running the upstairs of the hotel and had always got through, even if it was by

39

the skin of her teeth at times. And nobody was ever around to offer her help then.

"We will get through it, thanks." She smiled tightly as she carried on down the corridor.

"Now what have I said?" Jake muttered as he watched her troop off down the corridor with her shoulders as straight as a beanpole. "God help anyone who crosses her today in that mood," he smirked. She was ready to do battle with anyone who got in her way.

Dawn came down the corridor smiling to herself, she had just seen the conflict between her boss and Jake. They often clashed with each other, more so on Chrissie's part than Jake's because of the sexual attraction between them, even though Chrissie had not realised that yet!

"Thank God for that," Chrissie sighed, plonking herself down into the office chair. It was 3:30, and all of the rooms had been serviced and checked. She had sent Dawn off on a late lunch break, taking over the checking of the corridors for any breakfast trays that had not been collected by the room service team that day. You would think that it would be easy just to check that all trays had been collected by midday, but there wasn't a day that passed that room service didn't have to be chased up to collect trays from off the floors. She really would have to have a word with Simon about it, but she'd wait until he wasn't in such a hissy mood. Mind you, her girls were just as bad. She was always tripping over tins of polish that were left outside of bedroom doors.

Chrissie fed all the departure rooms into the computer for reception to pick up for letting that day, then looked at her watch for the time. Only another hour before Annabelle came on duty to cover the evening shift, then she would be off like a bolt of lightning for home, kicking her shoes off and relaxing with a glass of cool wine before Natasha arrived for the evening. Daisy was going out with friends tonight, and staying over with Jasmine, so Chrissie and Natasha would enjoy the leftovers of the cottage pie from the night before, with some greens. Nats was going to stay over, but Giles her brother couldn't babysit Rosie, Scamp and Bubbles. Chrissie did suggest that she lock them in the outhouse for the night... She will not repeat her reply!

She'd let Dawn go early for being a star today. She had really worked hard servicing rooms, then going on to check the rooms that had been serviced which Chrissie had not managed to get to.

The phone rang as Chrissie was finishing off her daily report on the maintenance that needed to be done in the bedrooms, ready for Darren to pick up the following day. Reception was flashing up on the phone.

"Hi reception, how can I help you?" she chirped, looking at her watch with only now ten minutes to go before clocking off time.

"You're needed down here now Chrissie....URGENTLY."

It was Rachael who was on duty in reception, she was shaking. Somebody had just gone face down onto the marble floor in the foyer.

"Shit," Chrissie cursed, slamming the phone down as she grabbed the first aid box running out of the door. She never wanted to be a first aider in the first place. For a start she couldn't stand the sight of blood. But would they listen to her... Oh no.

She raced down the stairs, trying to remember what she had to do if she had to give a mouth-to-mouth, but the scene that she ran into stopped her in her tracks. God the poor woman, she must be in absolute agony from the angle her arm was in. It looked well and truly broken to Chrissie. She could see the bone jutting out of the skin. Rushing across to her, she swallowed hard, trying to keep the bile down that was rising up at the back of her throat. Tripping over what she thought looked like a wig that the poor woman must have lost when she crashed to the floor, she knelt down asking the elderly gentleman that was kneeling beside her to please move over so she could take in the situation.

Ricardo, a young Italian lad who had only started as a porter at the hotel a week ago, was stood with his mouth wide open, and his eyes popped out, wondering what to do next. Chrissie told him to get a blanket and pillow from the porter's office, then checked with Rachael that a ambulance had been called. Then she asked, who she took to be the husband, what was her name?

"Hello Hannah, I'm Chrissie, and I'm just going to make you as comfortable as I can until the ambulance arrives." She smiled warmly down at her, looking across to Rachael, then over to the husband who had gone as white as a sheet, with tears running down his whiskery cheeks. Rachael picked up the eye contact message and went over to him, putting her arm around his shoulder, leading him over to a seat, asking Ricardo to get a weak sweet tea.

Chrissie had gently slipped the pillow that Ricardo had brought over to her under Hannah's head, trying very hard not to move her to much, placing the blanket over her legs. The poor woman was in so much pain, and was shivering with shock, but through all the pain that she was suffering she'd managed to whisper to Chrissie if she could please retrieve her wig from off the floor and give it to Mr Leven, her husband.

As Chrissie soothed Hannah, it seemed like a lifetime before the ambulance arrived, but it was only fifteen minutes later that it parked up outside at the front of the hotel, and the first paramedic came through the swing doors.

His name was Colin, and as he took in the scene before him, he knelt down on the floor beside Hannah, knowing already that

42

it was going to be a visit to the hospital. He turned and signalled out to Joe, the other paramedic with him, to bring in the medic bag. He could see that Hannah was really suffering, her bone was jutting out at the elbow, so he would have to give her some drugs to dull the pain before he could cut away the cardigan she was wearing, and take a closer look at the injury. Chrissie took in his handsome face and smoldering dark eyes as he asked his patient what her name was. Then he listened to Chrissie as she explained how Hannah had tripped up the steps coming into the foyer, falling face down onto the marble floor. It was a miracle that she didn't smash her face in. Joe handed the medic bag over to him, then went back out to the ambulance to get the stretcher ready.

As Chrissie went to get up to stretch her legs, Colin asked her if she would help him by supporting the injured arm while he injected into it to give Hannah some relief from the pain she was in. Chrissie paled as she knelt back down behind Hannah, gently taking hold of her tangled arm in one hand, while she soothed her forehead with the other. As Colin came closer with the needle, Chrissie squeezed her eyes up tight, her stomach was doing somersaults. If he didn't get that needle into her arm soon, she was going to keel over... For if there was one thing that Chrissie feared most, it was the sight of needles! Giving it a minute or two for the drug to take affect, Colin talked softly to Hannah, reassuring her that everything would be alright. Then he smiled at Chrissie, making her toes curl. He really was a handsome man.

As Chrissie saw the ambulance off, she came up the steps rubbing her knees. They had gone numb from kneeling on them for so long.

"Good God, you look pasty, what's been going on?"

"Very funny, Jake," she said over her shoulder as she walked across to the lift. "Where were you when needed?"

"Bloody typical for a manager to turn up when it's all over," she cursed under her breath, pressing the lift button.

Jake shook his head. "Hey Chrissie, just hold on a minute, what the hell's a matter with you today?" he asked angrily, striding across the foyer as she got into the lift holding the door open with his foot so it wouldn't close on him. "Every time I open my mouth to you just lately you snap my head off. You got a problem with me?"

Chrissie had to smile to herself, Jake didn't usually get this wound up with her. And he looked quite sexy when his heckles were up.

"I've no problem with you, Jake, it's just annoying when you keep asking me if I can cope with what I'm doing. Now if you don't mind," she said, pressing the lift button.

Annabelle was waiting in the office when Chrissie finally got back, checking on the computer to see how many turn downs she had to do that evening.

Chrissie filled her in on what had happened to Mrs Leven, and asked her to do a turn down in her room, and also to put in a bowl of fruit and a bottle of water. Even if she was kept in hospital overnight, which she thought she possibly would be, Mr Leven could enjoy the fruit when he got back to the hotel after being with his wife.

Waving across to Shelly, who had just come on duty for the evening shift, Chrissie hurried across to the lift that would take her up to the hotel car park. She could see from out the corner of her eye that Jake was coming out of his office, and he was looking across at her. She didn't want to leave with bad feelings between them, so she waved, saying good night before jumping into the lift.

As she zoomed out of the car park, she didn't take note of the Jaguar that passed her at speed on the road. Or of the driver that had an evil smirk on his face!

"We'll be meeting up soon, Bitch."

CHAPTER FOUR

As she turned into the lane leading down to the cottage, Chrissie slowed up in the car as she saw somebody coming out of her driveway. She pulled up the handbrake and put her nose up against the window, straining her eyes to see if she could make out who was hanging around the bottom of her driveway. Was it a male or female? Her senses became alert as the figure, who she thought was a male with short dark hair, and was wearing a long dark coat with the collar pulled up around his ears, moved away from the end of the drive and started walking down the lane, craning his neck over the neighbors hedge to see into their garden. Putting her foot down, she raced down the lane swerving into the driveway as the gravel sprayed up underneath the car. She jumped out looking around her, straining her ears for any sound of movement. But it was eerily silent, except for the sound of the countryside, where she heard the birds twittering, and the sheep bleating. Whoever she thought she had seen had vanished into thin air, as Marmalade strolled down the gravel pathway to great her.

"That's strange," she mumbled, bending down to pick Marmalade up as he purred around her legs. She tickled him under the chin as she walked back down towards the end of the drive, peering out along the lane. She looked all around her to see if she could see anybody walking around, but the lane was deserted. There wasn't a soul around. But she knew that she had seen somebody at the end of her driveway as she'd driven into the lane. But who? She wished she knew. It could have been old Mr Roberts from next door looking for her. But then again, she would have seen him walking back up his drive. The old boy wasn't that spritely to have got back to the door of his cottage in the time that it had taken her to get to her drive. She looked around once more along the lane, but whatever she thought she had seen, was no longer there… Not a soul.

"Strange," she thought, shrugging her shoulders as she walked back up to the cottage, still hanging onto Marmalade who was purring away quite contented with being in Chrissie's arms. But then, just as she went to unlock the front door, she had this feeling that somebody was watching her. As she swung around, dropping Marmalade on to the doorstep as she saw a car reversing out of the lane at such a speed that it was gone before she could see who it was.

"Where the hell did that come from?" she said aloud, running back down the driveway and out into the lane. But by the time she had got there, there was no sign of any car. That was long gone. She shook her head with frustration as she walked back up to the driveway. She just knew that she had seen somebody hanging around the cottage. But who?

Marmalade licked himself as he watched Chrissie walk slowly back up to the cottage. He was not impressed with being dropped down onto the doorstep, and scooted through her legs, meowing as soon the door was opened, leaving Chrissie gingerly looking around her for any sign of tampering in her home. But everything seemed to be in order. Nothing looked as though it'd been touched. So once again she put it all down to her vivid imagination.

She kicked her shoes off across the kitchen floor as she stretched out her toes, sipping on a cool glass of wine that she'd poured out for herself. Deep in thought, she tried racking her brain as to who it could have been that she had seen hanging around in the lane earlier. It could have been someone from the farm, maybe Farmer Brown was looking around, checking that his fences were all intact, keeping his animals safely in the fields. But then thinking about it, Farmer Brown would never reverse out of the lane at a hundred miles an hour. Then she thought about all of the phone calls she'd had. What was that all about? She drank the remains of her wine as a chill went down her spine.

Sighing deeply, she sauntered into the small dining area, throwing open the patio doors. The warm air of the evening breeze hit her, as she walked out into the garden where all of the rose bushes were waiting to burst open. Oh, how she loved this time of year. June was just around the corner with the foxgloves waiting to burst out, and the pansies stood in clusters around the willow tree, holding their heads up high. On the weekend she would have to get the lawn mower out. The grass was getting long, and the clumps of daisies were gradually taking over. As she sauntered on down the garden, she smiled as she thought of the times that Daisy had teased her about them, telling her that they were only weeds, and needed digging out. But Chrissie always argued back, saying that they were flowers, and she would mow around them, completely ignoring her as Daisy strode off still insisting that they were weeds, threatening to use some weed killer on them. She was joking of course. Her mother would brain her if she'd done that. They were one of Chrissie's favorite flowers, and she would often stop mowing the grass, and sit in the middle of the lawn on a warm summer's day making daisy chains, much to Daisy's disgust. She would shake her head, telling her mother that she was getting eccentric, and that she was going to bring in the men with the white coats on to cart her away. But Chrissie's answer to that was to put a daisy chain around her neck, much to Daisy's annoyance, then go on to mow around the clumps of daisies with the daisy chain swinging around her neck. It used to drive Freddie mad when they were together... And thinking of Freddie, that was the next thing she had to sort out with Daisy. She really didn't want to go to his wedding, but Daisy was so insistent on it.

Chrissie was laying the table up when the phone rang, making her jump out of her skin as she went out into the hallway to answer it, cursing under her breath, hoping that it wasn't Nats ringing up to say she wasn't coming over because either Rosie, Scamp or Bubbles were feeling ill, and she wouldn't be able to leave them! But it was Jake calling from the hotel, apologising for disturbing her while she was off duty, but Simon had been to see him with steam coming out of his ears, looking for Annabelle to open up the linen room so he could get some clean tablecloths out. Chrissie asked him why the hell he wanted tablecloths at this time of the day, then wished she hadn't, she really didn't want to know. But Jake said that he was flapping around looking for the linen room keys and couldn't find them, also Annabelle wasn't answering her bleep either. Chrissie smiled to herself. She didn't blame her, she was probably trying to get some supper down her before she started her evening rounds. "He shouldn't need more cloths," Chrissie said. "So why's he looking for some now?" He had already taken his quota earlier on in the day. Jake started laughing. It was a nervous laugh as he told her of what had happened in the restaurant, and of how angry Simon had been as he filled Jake in about the sauce bottle. He really thought he was going to burst a blood vessel. Apparently, a guest had had an accident in the dining room with the sauce bottle, as they were shaking the bottle up and down, the top flew off, and the sauce had landed everywhere, except for on the plate. Chrissie started to laugh, she could just imagine Simon flying around the restaurant. Panicking as he does, growling like a lion at his staff to get it cleaned up, while he went back to the guests that were still sat at the tables, probably seething underneath, thinking how much they could sue the hotel for, as they cleaned off the sauce from their clothes in their crisp white napkins. But really Jake was far from amused. Why the hell was a sauce bottle put on the table in the first place, instead of being served up in a silver dish? He meant to find out, as a call came through to him on his phone that a guest was already demanding to see a manager, with refunds in mind, I bet. Chrissie couldn't help smiling to herself as she came off the phone. She'd told Jake to go and see Shelly in reception. She would find him a spare key in the safe for the linen room.

Going back into the kitchen, Chrissie put the leftover cottage pie into the oven before refilling her glass with wine, and just as she went to take a sip from the glass, the phone rang again. It was Daisy. She was calling to see how her mother was, and had Natasha arrived yet? Chrissie told her that she should be there anytime now, and asked her how her day had been. After catching up with what they'd done that day, Chrissie said that she would have to hang up, as Natasha would be there anytime now, and she still had the table to lay up, so Daisy said goodbye, but not before asking her mother if she had remembered that it was Dad's wedding in a few weeks' time, and were they going out to shop for an outfit for it. Not committing herself to anything, Chrissie blew a kiss down the phone, saying that they would talk about it tomorrow when she got home.

She was still smiling as she let Natasha through the door, relieving her of the bottle of wine she'd brought with her, putting it into the fridge.

"We're eating in here tonight," Chrissie said, waving her hand around the kitchen. "It's cosier." Handing a glass of wine over to Nats, she lit the gas ring under the greens as Natasha sniffed into the air, smelling the waft of the cottage pie filling the room.

"Mmm. I'm starving, when do we eat?"

"It'll be five minutes," Chrissie said, shooing Marmalade off the draining board as she reached up to the cupboard to get some plates out.

"Ah, come here," Natasha cooed, picking him up and smoothing his hair down. "Don't you worry," she purred. "I'll protect you."

Chrissie tutted, raising her eyes to the ceiling, the woman was mad. She sat down waiting for the greens to come to the boil, while telling Natasha about the call she'd got from Jake. Nats fell into fits of laughter. She knew Simon well, and she could just see him running around like a cat on a hot tin roof, scolding all his staff like children, while putting a smile on his face as he apologised to his guest, wondering why a bottle of sauce was put on the table in a four-star restaurant, instead of being served up in a silver dish. Probably it was a new waiter that hadn't been there that long, and wouldn't be there for much longer if she knew Simon. Still chuckling, Natasha was just about to ask how Daisy was, when Chrissie leaped up in the air flapping her hands around. The fire alarm had just gone off, and smoke was billowing out from the oven.

"SHIT!" she yelled, yanking open the oven door as the smoke spewed out.

Natasha jumped up grabbing hold of a tea towel. She ran around like a maniac with the towel in her hand, flapping it around the alarm trying to clear the smoke away.

"For Christ sake, instead off dancing around the alarm, open the bloody door," Chrissie yelled at her, swinging the windows open as Marmalade scooted out of the cat flap. He was well gone, no way was he staying around these crazy humans.

Throwing the charred remains of the dinner into the sink, Chrissie was still cursing, blowing on her fingers that were stinging from the heat that had come through the tea towel that she'd grabbed hold of to retrieve the burning dish from the oven.

"Whoa… We can save some of that," Natasha yelled, whipping it back onto the draining board.

"We can't eat that," Chrissie said, wiping her eyes that were still stinging from the smoke that had bellowed out of the oven as she retrieved the cottage pie.

"Oh yes we can," Natasha started, scrapping the burnt cheese from off the pie. "Drain the peas off, this will go down well with a bottle of wine, trust me," she winked, laughing.

The evening went well after all the drama of the burnt dinner and smoked-filled kitchen. They ate the burnt cottage pie after taking a good couple gulps of wine, and after that it didn't seem to taste so bad. They caught up on all the gossip putting the world to rights, then finished off with a black coffee, well Natasha did, she was driving, but Chrissie stuck with the wine.

Natasha half jokingly asked Chrissie if she had had any more of those weird phone calls, or seen any more shadows lurking around in the garden, pulling a face as she put two fingers up at the back of her head, mimicking the devil. But the smile soon faded as Chrissie filled her in on what she thought she had seen tonight when she had arrived home from work. Natasha again said she should report it to the police. She really didn't have a good feeling about this. If it was just the once that it had happened, then fair enough. But for it to happen two or three times was beyond a joke, and it was time that she reported it to the police. Then at least it would go down on record, and if, God forbid, something was to come of it, the police would at least be aware of it.

"Oh, it's probably something and nothing," Chrissie said, playfully punching her arm. "Now be quiet up or I'll never sleep tonight," she laughed.

Natasha left around 11:30, but only after making sure that Chrissie had all her doors and windows locked, and even as Chrissie was pushing her out of the door telling her to go home, she wouldn't start her car up until she had shut and locked up the door behind her, telling her to wave goodbye through the window. Now that was a friend for you, even if she had frightened the living daylights out of Chrissie.

Chrissie read her book until well after midnight, it was one of those books that she couldn't put down. It was about the supernatural, and even though it frightened the living daylight out of her, she had to read it. She looked around the bedroom before switching off the bedside light, checking that her mobile was under her pillow. Listening to Natasha tonight had unnerved her so much that she had gone into the cupboard under the stairs, and taken out the old rounders bat that belonged to Daisy, putting it under her bed – in case! Switching the bedside light off, she snuggled down into bed, and it wasn't long before she was asleep.

Something had disturbed Chrissie from her sleep, and as she turned over to click her light on, she looked towards the bedroom door half expecting at any minute for somebody to barge through it. Rubbing her eyes, she reached over to the alarm clock to see what time it was. It was 1:30 in the morning, so she hadn't been asleep that long. Just over an hour or so, but she had slept soundly. Not daring to move, she strained her ears trying to listen for any sound of movement coming from the landing outside of her bedroom door, but it was eerily silent except for the ticking of the clock. So after listening for awhile to the silence of the cottage, she turned over and switched the light off, putting it down to her overactive imagination, as she nestled down again into the warm bed, dozing on and off. But all of a sudden she sat bolt upright in the bed. She could hear the floorboards creak outside of her bedroom door. Someone was trying to get in, and as she fumbled around the light switch trying to turn the bedside light on, her eyes popped out on stalks as she watched the bedroom door handle turn. She was so scared that she felt physically sick as she reached out for the alarm clock, throwing it across the room with all the force she could muster up as the door opened. Screaming out like a banshee, she put her hand across her mouth when she saw who it was.

"FOR GOD'S SAKE MOTHER," Daisy yelled out, rubbing her shin as she hopped over to the bed. "What on earth's the matter with you?"

"DAISY!" Chrissie yelled back. "What the hell are you doing home? You frightened the freaking life out of me. Let alone almost giving me a damn heart attack."

Chrissie calmed herself as she watched Daisy's shin swell up, feeling guilty for throwing the alarm clock at her. But at the time she had been defending herself against the intruder outside of her bedroom door. How was she to know that it was her daughter who had returned home at this ungodly hour? Now wide awake, she took Daisy downstairs to put a damp cloth over her shin, then put the kettle on as she asked Daisy why she had decided to come home at such a late hour instead of staying over with Jasmine as planned. At first Daisy didn't want to stress her mother out any further, especially if it was over something and nothing. But then again if she didn't mention what had happened to her tonight, her mother would flip her lid if she was to find out later. So she decided to tell her about the stranger, who had bumped into her as she was walking along to the hole in the wall with Jasmine after coming out from the cinema. Jasmine needed to get some cash out before they made their way home, and as they walked along towards the bank, a middle-aged man bumped into her, nearly knocking her over. As he helped steady her on her feet, he asked if she lived locally, and did she know of anyone called Rosie Grimes. Chrissie's face paled at the mention of the woman's name. And it didn't go amiss with Daisy either, but she carried on telling her mother of how he said he had lost contact with her a few years ago, and now wanted to catch up with her. She had told him that she didn't know of anyone by that name in the village. Then asked Jasmine if she knew of anyone by that name, sending a chill down her spine as he ran his eyes down over her long lanky body. Jasmine said that she hadn't heard of anyone by that name either, as they'd hurried along to the bus stop after he had asked them if they would like a lift home. Thank God the bus arrived just as they got there, so they jumped straight on it and lost him. Then when Daisy had got back to Jasmine's, she decided that she would go home. She was feeling unsettled, but she'd also forgotten to bring some books with her that she would need for uni tomorrow. So had ordered a taxi, and let herself in quietly, not giving it a thought that she would scare the living daylights out of her mother, as she crept up the stairs to her room. Chrissie didn't say anything to Daisy, she didn't want to worry her. But there was only one person who knew Chrissie by the name of Rosie Grimes, and Chrissie prayed to God that it wasn't him. But she knew that she would have to report this to the police now. She couldn't risk him approaching Daisy again, who knew nothing of her mothers past. So she decided that she would go first thing in the morning, after she had phoned in at work to say she wouldn't be in.

When she finally got to bed after reassuring Daisy that everything was okay with her, Chrissie had tried to settle down to sleep. But sleep evaded her, her mind was in alert mode, every sound she heard she was up in the bed with her hands wrapped around the rounders bat, her eyes searching around the room for an intruder. She had now put all the mystery phone calls and the feeling of somebody watching her down to him. She couldn't think of anyone who would wish her any harm, and as far as she knew, she had no enemies. So it had to be him… But why would he want to see her now? He had served his sentence, she knew that. He had been jailed for five years, but as far as she was concerned, they should have kept him in there and thrown away the bloody key. God how she hated that man, shuddering at the very thought of him.

Phoning into work the next morning, Shelly answered the phone, asking Chrissie if everything was alright after she had told her that she wouldn't be into work that day. It was unheard of for Chrissie to take a day off, so Shelly knew something must be up for her to not to make it into work. Jake came on the line sounding concerned after Shelly had told him that Chrissie was on the phone, and that she wasn't coming into work. The first thing he asked her was, was she unwell, and was there anything he could do for her? Smiling at his concern for her, she reassured him that she wasn't feeling ill, but something had cropped up last night, and she needed to attend to it straight away.

As she walked along towards the police station, she hung around outside for awhile, watching all the people from all walks of life walk by her, seemingly without a care in the world. She was struggling with her inner self whether to go into the police station or not. Did she really want to drag up all the past that she had left behind all those years ago?

"Now come on, Chrissie, pull yourself together. Don't be such a bloody coward." She cursed under her breath, pulling her shoulders back as she took a deep breath and went into the station. She nervously looked around her, and came eyeball to eyeball with a tall robust man that frightened the bloody life out of her as he staggered towards her cursing, waving his arms around in the air. As she took a step back, two police officers came forward, jerking his arms up behind him as they led him away, still cursing and spitting, as they dodged out of the way of the spit that flew out of his mouth, landing up on the floor. Mustering up all of her willpower not to run back outside, and hotfoot it back home, Chrissie took another deep breath, and went straight up to the desk where a young police officer was stood writing in a logbook. As she stood waiting for him to look up, she felt her knees knock together. He seemed so engrossed with what he was doing, that it took a moment or two to realise that she was standing there. Apologising, he asked how he could help her, pushing his book to one side. And for a moment Chrissie was struck dumb. Her mouth had gone dry, and she couldn't get the words out. Then, all of as sudden, out of nowhere, she blurted out everything to this young officer who looked no older than Daisy. She told him that somebody had been stalking her. Then wondered why the hell she had she said that. She didn't even know whether she was being stalked or not. It could just all be in her imagination. "Get a hold of yourself," her inner voice yelled at her. "Why?" her mind argued back. Somebody was looking for her by the name of Rosie Grimes! A name that nobody would know her by around here.

After an hour of grueling questions being fired at her, she came out feeling drained. The first thing they had wanted to know was: Why did she think she was being stalked? Did she have any evidence to back it up? Had anyone ever approached her? Could it be a disgruntled guest from the hotel? So many questions... Why? She had already told them about the attack on her when she was seventeen, and of the court case that had followed, ending up with him going to prison for five years. And still they asked her the dumb questions.

"Who was he?" they asked. "What was his name?" They would need to know his name so they could bring it up on the computer and search for his files. Chrissie had felt physically sick at the thought of having to say his name through her lips. She had never called him anything but 'HIM' since the attack on her, and she really had to swallow hard to stem the bile that was rising up in her stomach, as she spat his name. 'STEWART!'

57

Bringing up the information onto the screen, they could see that he had gone down for five years for rape, serving only two and half. He had been out for a good few years now, and they couldn't trace anything else against him since he'd been released. So they asked her why she thought that he would want to look her up now? Had he tried to contact her over the last few years? The hairs started to bristle up on the back of Chrissie neck at the tone of their questioning, and she began to wish that she had never stepped inside of the damn place. Raking up the past was still very raw to her. Even though it had happened long ago now, it would stay with her for the rest of her life. Up until now, she had managed to lock away all of the sad memories of giving her daughter away into the deepest recess of her mind. She'd also taken on her mother's maiden name to start a new life for herself. But there was no getting away from it. Deep down she always knew it would raise its ugly head again. So again, taking another deep breath, she told them. No, she hadn't heard a thing from him over the years. And didn't want to either.

So in the end, it ended up with them telling her to be more vigilant when she was out. And if she did received any more abusive phone calls, or anything thing out of the ordinary happened, then contact them straight away, and they would then take further action. But at this moment in time, they had nothing sound to go on.

Chrissie was left feeling so frustrated, that she had to control herself from screaming out at the young Sergeant, who was smiling at her from behind his desk. "Why don't you bloody well listen to me? I'm being bloody stalked…"

But she bit on her tongue instead, even though she knew if she retaliated, it would have relieved some of the frustration that she was feeling right now.

Chrissie somehow managed to make it back to her car before breaking down. And as she dabbed away the mascara from around her eyes, she couldn't remember the last time she had been feeling this low, and would have given anything for a drag on a cigarette right now. As she drove home, she knew somehow she was going to have to push all of this to the back of her mind once again. She wasn't going to let him back into her life and rule it like he had all those years ago, when she had been that hotheaded teenager. But she also knew that she was going to have to stay alert, just in case he was out there watching her, or more importantly… Watching Daisy.

As she drove away, she didn't see the Jaguar that was parked on the side of the road, puffing on a roll up.

"So the bitch has gone to the police," Stewart cursed, watching her drive out of sight. "But it can wait. Time is on my side. You will not stop me from seeing my daughter…"

CHAPTER FIVE

"If anyone else mentions about the black rings under my eyes today, I'll bop them one."

Since Chrissie had arrived at work, already two of her colleagues had mention to her about the black rings under her eyes. It was Chrissie's first day back at work after taking off another couple of days to get her head around the ordeal she had experienced the other day at the police station. To say that it had been an experience to go through would have been an understatement. After she had stopped blubbering, and had pulled herself together to drive home, the first thing she'd done when she got through the door of the cottage, was to pour herself out a large glass of wine to calm her nerves down. She couldn't believe that she had come away from the police station feeling guilty for wasting their time. Which was the impression she'd got from the young Sergeant, after telling him about her fears of being stalked. She had thought on long and hard about the phone call she'd received at work, with somebody calling her a bitch over the line. Then of the driver who'd drove at such a speed out of the car park, almost hitting her as she'd braked hard to miss him, as he mouthed "bitch" at her through the window. Then to top it all, Daisy coming home and telling her about the stranger who had bumped into her, and asking her if she knew a Rosie Grimes. All of this had really set her nerves on edge. But now she'd had time to think about it. Maybe she had gone over the top a bit! But then again. Who was that out there asking around for Rosie Grimes..? Finally she came to the decision that there was nothing that she could do about it. She would just have to wait and see if anything else happened. God forbid if it did. But in the meantime, she had to get on with her life. So to put her mind at rest, she did ask Daisy to be more vigilant when she was out and about at night. And if anyone was to approach her again when she was out, would she please let her know. Daisy had asked her why? Was there something she should be worried about? But when Chrissie had brushed it off by saying that you could never be too careful these days, she'd just put it down to her mother being overprotective. Like all parents could be at times.

Saying good morning to Shelly, Chrissie picked up the housekeeping keys from reception.

"It's good to see you back Chrissie. How are you feeling now?" Shelly asked, looking closely at her as she noticed the black rings under her eyes. "Have you not been sleeping too well?"

Chrissie tutted, backing away from her. "Why? Do I really look that bad?"

"No, of course not. You'd look good wearing a black bin bag… Bitch." She laughed, quite oblivious to word she'd just used, and what it would mean to Chrissie, as it sent shivers down her spine, albeit in fun. Chrissie couldn't and wouldn't say why she had the black rings under her eyes. And of why she'd hardly slept over the last few nights. Laying awake, worrying about what could happen if Stewart was out there somewhere, still lurking around looking for her. She had agonised over whether to tell Daisy or not about her past life, crying into her pillow, praying that it would all go away. But then in the morning, when everything always seems to look so different from the night before, she decided that she wouldn't tell her. She would wait to see if anything else happened, and if it did then that would be the time to tell her about her past life. As it was, it had taken a lot of reassuring from Chrissie that she wasn't dying, and it was just a bug that she'd picked up from work, when Daisy had insisted that she went to see the doctor. She told her that she would be tickety-boo in a couple of days time. But even then, Daisy wasn't convinced. Her mother would have to be at death's door before she took any time off from work. But in the end, Chrissie finally convinced her that she was okay, and she would be back to work within a couple of days. Hoping to God that Daisy had believed her, not wanting to alarm her in any way. Life still had to go on, and she didn't want Daisy being dragged into her past unnecessarily.

On the way up to the office, Chrissie stood looking in the lift mirrors, pinching her cheeks to give her more colour in her face so the dark rings under her eyes wouldn't look so stark. She said good morning to Daphne who was filling up the trolleys with linen, ready for the chambermaids to take up on to the floors today.

Saying good morning back to Chrissie, Daphne asked her if she was feeling better now. "You look as though you've had no sleep," she said, noticing the dark rings under her eyes. "Are you sure you're okay to be back at work?"

Chrissie just smiled, letting herself into the office, going straight over to look at herself in the cracked mirror that was hanging up on the wall. "God, do I really look that bad," she muttered, searching around in the desk draw for her spare compact.

At 12:30 today there was going to be a fire drill in the hotel, and Chrissie was dreading it. She had twelve girls on duty, plus a linen keeper, two housekeepers and a floor porter, so she was going to have to keep her fingers crossed that they all took note of the alarm going off, and not ignore it, thinking that it was just maintenance testing the alarms. As soon as the alarm went off they 'should' drop whatever they're doing at the time, and make for the assembly point at the back of the hotel, where one of her housekeepers would be waiting for them with their clipboard with a rota clipped on to it, ticking them all off as they came out of the fire exits. But before Chrissie could vacate herself, she would have to go along with the help of another housekeeper, and knock on all of the doors that were let that day, opening them up to check that there was nobody in the rooms who hadn't heard the alarm go off, because of being in the shower at the time, or who were still sleeping.

Picking up the clipboard with the rooming list on, she left the office to start her rounds on the floors, smiling to herself as she thought of the family of five who were staying in room 416 the last time there had been a fire practice in the hotel. She was rushing along the corridor opening up all the doors checking that all the rooms had been vacated, when she came across a family of five sat out on the balcony eating their lunch. The father had looked around at her, frowning as if to say, "What's the problem?" Then went on to ask her if it was really a fire, and was it necessary for them to vacate the room right away as they'd just started their lunch! Chrissie wouldn't be able to repeat the thoughts that had gone through her head, as she'd told them in a professional manner... "The FIRE ALARM has gone off, SIR, and YES, they did have to vacate their room. But even then she'd had to wait while the parents picked up all of the food, and put it into a bag before they ushered the children out and followed Chrissie along to the fire escape.

As she went to close the office door behind her, the phone rang, and she debated whether to stop and answer it. Dawn had bleeped her earlier to say that she had a problem getting into a room, and could she go up with her master key to open it up for her. So she hesitated for a moment or two whether to answer it or not, but was pleased that she did because it was Natasha on the line.

"Hi, it's me."

"Hello me," she laughed.

"You've been off from work sick, why didn't you phone me, I would have left the animals and come across to you."

"Oh for God sake, Nats, I've had a bug that's all," she tutted. "And as you can see, I'm now back at work fit and healthy."

"No, I can't see you, you're on the other end of the phone. Duh, but you sound chirpy enough. I spoke to Daisy just as she was leaving to go to college. She said that you'd been down in the dumps for a few days. What's up?"

"Nothing's up," Chrissie lied.

Chrissie really hated lying to her best friend. But now wasn't the time for Natasha to hear about her visit to the police station, because knowing her as she does, she would be straight over to see her, demanding to know what was going on. And anyway, it was just her imagination that had run away with her. She hadn't experienced anymore weird phone calls, or even had any sightings of mysterious people hanging around the cottage.

"I'm free tonight, fancy going out for a couple of hours? We could go to the Ship Inn for a couple of drinks, then back to my place with a takeaway. Sounds good, yeah?"

"Oh, Nats it sounds really good, but I wish you had phoned me minutes earlier. I've just said that I would meet Jake after work."

"Oh that's great," Natasha squealed. "You meet up with Jake, we can catch up any time."

64

"Now don't go reading anything into this, Nats." Chrissie sighed, knowing how her friend's brain worked. "We're only meeting up to catch up on what's been going on over the last couple of days I've been off."

"Yeah, yeah, whatever. I'll phone you tomorrow."

The phone went down before Chrissie could say anymore to her, and her bleep was sounding off again. It was Dawn. She'd forgotten all about her not being able to get into the room on the second floor, and raced up the stairs taking them two at a time, totally puffed out by the time she reached her.

"How many times have you knocked on the door?" Chrissie asked, catching her breath as she looked on the rooming list for the guest name.

"Twice, and I've phoned from the other room, but no reply."

"Have you tried opening the door?"

"Yes," Dawn said raising her eyebrows at Chrissie. She wasn't that thick, "But the double lock is on, and my key will not open it. But yours will!"

Chrissie didn't bite back, stupid question to have asked her in the first place, so as Dawn carried on checking other rooms, she knocked again on the door shouting out "housekeeper," as she put the key into the lock and let herself in. The room was in darkness with the curtains still drawn, and it felt eerily quiet to her as she went over to draw the curtains, calling out Mrs Jacks' name. Turning towards the bed, she let out a gasp, as she caught sight of an elderly lady sat up in bed holding a knife to her wrist. Not wanting to startle Mrs Jacks into doing anything drastic, she smiled across at her as she mentally took in the situation that the poor woman was in. Sat bolt upright in bed was a sweet-looking elderly lady staring out into space, holding a knife against her wrist. For a moment, Chrissie just froze in her tracks. She didn't know what to do or say next. But slowly, she made her way across the room as she spoke softly to her, gently edging herself down onto the edge of the bed, as Mrs Jacks pressed the tip of the knife that she was still holding across her wrist down into the vein that was protruding like a black grape, still staring ahead off her, not seeming to notice that Chrissie had come into the room. Chrissie's adrenalin was pumping so fast through her veins that she thought they would burst, as she tried to think of what to do next. Slowly, she edged her way up the bed, gently resting her hand on Mrs Jacks' shoulder, and it took a few seconds before she registered that there was somebody else in the room with her. Blinking back the tears from her brown speckled eyes, she started apologising to Chrissie for being such a nuisance.

"You're not a nuisance," Chrissie said, putting her arm around her shoulder. At that point Chrissie could have cried for her. She looked so vulnerable sat there in her white nightie, clasping on to a knife that she held against her frail arm. Gently, Chrissie asked what her first name was.

"Edith," she said, taking in a deep shuddering breath before going on to tell her that she'd been at the hotel for over a week now. But had rarely come out of her room, using the room service for most of her meals. She had travelled down from Bath to spend a few days at the hotel after the funeral of her husband, who she had been married to for forty years. He had died a short while ago after suffering a stroke. And they had spent many holidays together at this hotel. Chrissie cuddled her in closer to her as she started to cry again, asking Edith what his name was, as she tried to think how she could get the knife away from her without alarming her. Edith told her that his name was Sam, and that she really missed him.

"Well you know, Edith," Chrissie said softly, gently taking her arm away from her, as she knelt down on the floor beside the bed, so she could be on the same level as her, "Sam would be very sad to see you like this." She smiled. "He would want you to be happy, and to keep him alive with all of the memories that you hold of him. And also, all of the wonderful times that you've spent together over the years."

This seemed to touch a point with Edith as she handed over the knife to Chrissie, sobbing her heart out, and as Chrissie soothed her, she asked if there was anyone that she could get in touch with for her. But Edith was acting very confused, so Chrissie thought the best thing to do was to phone for a doctor, so she could be checked over before deciding what was to be done with her. She sat with her until the doctor arrived, then left him with her as she made her way back down to the office, still holding onto the knife in her hand. As she calmed herself down with a mug of coffee, she looked closely at the knife that Mrs Jacks had been holding against her wrist. It was a fruit knife that had a blunt blade, thank God. So she didn't think that Mrs Jacks really wanted to harm herself. She was just crying out for help, like we all do at sometime or another through our lives. Sighing, she sipped her coffee, answering the phone to reception. It was Dawn telling her that Mrs Jacks was being taken into hospital so she could be checked over, and that the doctor had managed to get hold of her sister who lived in Bath, and she was coming down tomorrow to see her. Chrissie was really relieved about that, she didn't like the thought of her having nobody out there.

"Coooee. How are you today, my sweetie? I've heard you've not been too well, darling."

Simon closed the office door behind him as he planted a kiss on Chrissie's cheek, sitting himself down onto the spare chair in the office with the wobbly leg and tattered upholstery.

"God, it's time you got rid of this chair, Chrissie, it's a death trap," he tutted, steadying himself as the chair tipped sideways as he settled himself into it, making Chrissie laugh for the first time today. He was a breath of fresh air. Well... sometimes he was.

67

He took the coffee that Chrissie had made for him, taking a glance at the watch on her arm. He would have to make a move soon to open up the restaurant for lunch. But first he wanted to know why Chrissie had been off for the last couple of days. It wasn't like her to be off work. And going by the dark rings under her eyes, she hadn't slept that much either.

"Okay, darling, are you going to let Simon know what's going on?"

Chrissie looked at him, flicking her fringe away from her face, her blue eyes stretched wide open, feigning innocence.

"And don't go fobbing me off by saying it was just a bug you had," he tutted, waving his finger at her as the coffee spilled over him. "It's me you're talking to, remember! Simon. To me you look as though you've got something on your mind. Now come on, spill it all out to Uncle Simon. I'm all ears."

"Surely I don't look that bad," she laughed.

"Yup, you do. Now spill the beans, Sweetie, I'm listening."

Oh how Chrissie would love to spill the beans out to Simon. Get it all off her chest. He was right, she had had sleepless nights since Daisy had come home telling her about the meeting she'd had with a complete stranger who had, 'SUPPOSEDLY,' bumped into her, asking her if she lived locally, and did she know of anyone living around here by the name of Rosie Grimes. A name that nobody else would know her by but 'HIM'. She really thought that she had left behind the heartache she had gone through all those years ago. But it was still with her today. Still as raw in her heart as though it had only been yesterday, when she had been raped at the age of 17 by a very evil person.

Chrissie had known Stewart from the age of 15. He had been five years older than her, and her parents had not been happy with her seeing him because of the bad reputation he had around the area, plus that he was five years older than Chrissie.

But Chrissie had found him fun to be with. He was mature compared to all the other boys that hung around the haunts where they all used to meet up in the evenings. He treated her like a lady, taking her to the pictures, and out for meals. She was really taken by him, and in fact thought she was in love with him. But then he had started to become obsessive with her. Not wanting her to go out with friends. Wanting to see her every night. But Chrissie was young, and still wanted to meet up with her other friends, even though she loved his company, she still wanted some freedom to do her own thing. But Stewart was having none of that. He was really jealous, saying that if she really loved him, she would want to be with him all the time. Not hang around with those stupid immature kids. So after awhile, Chrissie got tired of his demanding ways, especially when he wanted to take their petting further. Wanting to make love to her. Marry her even. But Chrissie was not ready for marriage, she was only 17, much too young to settle down. But Stewart had kept on and on, trying to wear her down. So in the end, she finished with him by letter because she had been too scared to finish with him face to face. Whenever she had mentioned it to him that she wanted some space, and perhaps they should only see each other a couple of times a week, he had gone ballistic, calling her all the names under the sun. Bitch, Whore. So she finished with him. And it was after that, that her life had changed forever.

They had been finished for over two months, although Chrissie used to get the occasional phone call from him, asking her to forgive him, and would she please give him another chance. But she had stuck to her guns. He had frightened the life out of her when he had turned on her, verbally abusing her, shaking her by the shoulders. But unbeknown to Chrissie, Stewart had been following her, still simmering after being rebuffed by her. She had bruised his male ego, and he hated her for it. So much so, that he wanted to hurt her as she had hurt him. He had followed her one night to the cinema where she had gone with some of her friends. Then he'd waited for her to come out, and followed her along to the bus stop, jumping on to the bus just as it started off, so she wouldn't see him slip up on to the top deck. He then got off at the same stop as hers, after hanging around on the stairs so she wouldn't see him jump off and follow behind her to the corner of the street, where he called out to her as he ran up grabbing hold of her arm, pulling her roughly around to him.

"Stewart," she gasped.

"Rosie, how are you?" he asked menacingly, staring at her with eyes that were as cold as steel.

"You can't drop me like a bag of shit," he sneered, dragging her around the corner that led into a small park area. Chrissie opened her mouth to scream as one hand came around her mouth, while the other tightened around her neck. So tight that it caused her to gag. Sheer terror ran through her as he released his hand from around her neck, and started to rip at her clothes. Cursing her as he forced his slimy tongue down her throat, calling her everything under the sun, from a slag, to a tart, to a bitch, among many other things that she'd never heard of before. Again she tried to scream out as he threw her to the floor, but he quickly gagged her again with one of his hands, as he ripped away her clothes with the other. By this time she was in fear of her life as she felt the coldness of the ground beneath her. She gasped for breath, gagging again as he forced his tongue down her throat. The pain as he rammed into her was unbearable, and it was then that she thought she would never see the light of day again. After he'd finished with her, he dragged her further into the park where she started pleading with him for her life. But he just laughed in her face, telling her that she was now soiled goods, and nobody would want to know her now. Not even him, throwing her underpants at her as he walked off lighting up a cigarette.

How Chrissie had got home that night she'll never know. But luckily, her parents were in bed when she had finally made it home, so she'd been able to go to the bathroom, where she scrubbed herself until her skin was red sore.

Three months later she found out that she was pregnant, and it was then that she had to tell her parents that she had been raped. The police were then involved, and the history of Stewart came to light. He had raped two other women before meeting Rosie (as she was known then), and he was jailed for five years, serving only two and a half of them. That's justice for you!

"Well," Simon said, seeing the sadness in her eyes. "Are you going to tell me what's going on in that head of yours?"

Chrissie swallowed a mouthful of coffee, shaking her head at him as she snapped out of the reviere she'd gone into.

"Oh for God's sake, Simon, stop being so melodramatic. I'm feeling tip-top and ready for anything that comes my way. Now come on," she said, getting up and helping him out of the chair. "It's time that you got back down to your restaurant and opened up for lunch. And I've got to get on with my work," she tutted, shoving him out of the door.

"Mmm, not much wrong with you, bossy pants," he said. Tossing his head in the air. "Still bossing people around as normal, I see." Then tossed his eyes into the air as she poked her tongue out at him, asking her before descending down the back stairs what had happened this morning to the lady in room 213.

"God, it doesn't take long for gossip to fly around the hotel does it? She tutted, picking up her clipboard as she closed the office door behind her.

The fire drill had gone off well. All the girls came down off the floors, assembling in the hotel car park. All of them that was, except for Janie the junior housekeeper, who arrived five minutes after everyone else. The poor girl had come running out to the assembly point looking very harassed and red faced. She had been in the toilet when the alarms had gone off, and was halfway through doing her business, so she couldn't just jump up and pull her draws up and start to run. When she had told Chrissie this, after she had given her a bollocking for not being out there with the rest of the girls at the assembly point, Chrissie had to turn her head away and hold her breath so she didn't burst out laughing in front of her. The vision of poor Janie sat there on the toilet, panicking at what to do was just too much for Chrissie's imagination.

Rushing home, Chrissie wanted to catch up with Daisy before going out again to meet Jake that evening. She was staying in to revise for her exam, that she would be taking in a few days' time. She was in her last year at college studying law, but still had not decided what she was going to do when she came out. Most probably she would take a 'year out,' as they called it these days before going on to university, working and travelling around Europe to widen her horizons. But that was now, it could all change when the time came for her to make her mind up.

They ate the lasagne that Chrissie had brought home from work, compliments from Keith, the head chef, as they caught up on everything that had gone on over the last week. Daisy had been bogged down with swatting up on the her forthcoming exams with Jasmine, telling her mother that she had hated every moment of it, and she couldn't wait for it all to be over so she could get back to the real world, and start living again. Chrissie had smiled at her. "Typical teenager," she thought. Always thought the grass was greener on the other side. But then again, she didn't have room to talk. Her daughter was as strong headed as she had been at that age. But she didn't tell her that. Instead, she told her to enjoy her years at uni. She had the rest of her life to catch up with the 'real world'. Then smiled inwardly, as Daisy completely ignored her, changing the subject. Reminding her mother that it was her father's wedding in a few weeks' time, and was she still going with her, seeing as the invitation had been for the both of them to attend!

"Touché! One in the eye for me," Chrissie sighed. She really didn't want to go to the wedding. But from the look on Daisy's face, she knew that she would get a lot of agro from her. So she said yes. Of course she would be going.

After taking a shower, Chrissie slipped into a black dress that was one of her favorites. It was comfortable after eating a meal, and much more comfortable than wearing a pair of trousers with a belt, which would show off the dreaded rolls of fat that were appearing around her waistline. "It's all in your imagination," Natasha would say whenever she complained about it to her. "You've a body of a twenty year old."

"Mmm, I don't think so." Chrissie tutted to herself, smoothing down the skirt of her dress as she looked at herself in the mirror. Then chided herself for being so vain. "For Christ sake, Chrissie," she muttered, slipping her feet into a pair of black slingback shoes. "You're only meeting up with Jake to catch up on things from work. It's not as though you're on a damn date or anything!" Twisting her blonde hair back into a bun, she took one more look at herself as she sprayed on some Paris perfume, before going back downstairs to see Daisy, who had her head stuck in a book when Chrissie went through into the dining room area. Her textbooks were spread out all over the table, and she didn't look up as Chrissie told her that she would not be late back, and to make sure that she kept all of the doors locked.

Daisy raised her head up from the book she was reading, and told her mother that she wasn't a baby any longer. But, yes, she would make sure that the doors were locked. Then she looked her up and down, admiring the simple black dress she was wearing, asking her who was the lucky man was tonight. Chrissie playfully cuffed her ear, reminding her once again to keep the doors locked. Then hastily made a retreat before Daisy could ask her anymore questions of who she was meeting.

Jake had arrived early at the cocktail bar where they were meeting up, and was checking the time on his watch when Chrissie came through the door. He watched her from afar as she looked around for him, drinking in her long slender neck, complimented by the little black dress she was wearing that fitted her like a glove. Running his eyes down over her, he lingered on the long slender legs that seemed to go on forever. My God, what he wouldn't do to see them in the flesh, then shook his head for thinking it. They were just work colleagues, nothing else, even though he wished they were. As she searched around the room for him with her sparkling blue eyes, he waved across to her, once again reminding himself that this was just a platonic meeting between them both. They were not on a date, even though he was wishing that they were! They were just meeting to catch up on what was happing over the next few days in the hotel. And nothing else! He got up, pulling out a chair for her to sit down on.

"You look great," he smiled. "What can I get you to drink? The cocktails are great here, or do you want to stick to wine?"

Chrissie watched as he walked up to the bar after asking for a glass of wine. At least she knew what she was drinking with that. If she had a cocktail she wouldn't know what had gone into it. She admired the navy silk shirt that he was wearing, that was hung down outside of the waistband of his light blue jeans, fitting neatly into his pert bottom. And loved the way his wavy dark hair tipped the collar of his shirt, shining under the light at the bar.

She looked away, blushing, as he turned and caught her looking at him. "Damn. Now he'll think I'm lusting after him," she cursed, smiling at him as he walked across the room with her glass of wine. His arm brushed against hers as she took the wine

74

from him, and pushed a packet of nuts towards her as he sat down, telling her to help herself, as he again reminded himself that this was just a working date... Mmm!

They sat enjoying their drinks, as Jake told Chrissie that Mrs Jacks' sister had come down from Bath to visit her in hospital, and that she was going back to Bath with her, and would be staying for a while until things could be sorted out. He also told her that Mr Grey had not been amused that he hadn't been informed about the incident. Chrissie gave Jake one of her looks when she wasn't happy with something, feeling the hairs bristle on the back of her neck. Jake smiled, taking her empty glass from her to get it refilled as he finished off saying that he had told Mr Grey that he wasn't around when it had happened, and that she had handled the situation like a true professional.

Chrissie glared at him. "Don't be so condescending, Jake," she said coolly

"I'm not," he laughed, knowing that she was ready to blow. "I just told him the truth," he said, getting up to go over and get another drink for her from the bar.

"Bloody cheek of the man," she cursed under her breath. "The only time you ever heard from God almighty, (meaning, Mr Grey,) was when something went wrong. Never when things were right." She took a long sip of the ice cool wine that Jake had brought back for her, calming herself down.

"God, you look sexy when you're mad."

Chrissie almost choked on her wine. "Jake," she gasped, shocked at his boldness. "I'm old enough to be your mother, behave yourself," she laughed, trying to cover up her embarrassment.

"You know I've always held a torch for you, Chrissie. You're very funny. And very fiery too!" he laughed. And so beautiful."

"No more drink for you," she tutted, moving his glass of beer away from him. "I told you not to have that cocktail after having a beer," she said. Waving her finger at him, her face now crimson. He laughed, catching hold of her hand. "Too old my foot," he said, brushing his soft warm lips across the tips of her fingers. "What's in seven years, anyhow?"

A shudder went down her spine. It had been a very long time since somebody had stirred her feelings. But Jake was her manager, and having an emotional relationship with somebody you worked with did not go down too well in her book. So she made a quick retreat, saying she had to get back to Daisy, who would be waiting up for her. But Jake insisted on walking her back to her car, and as she was about to thank him for the evening, he gently cupped her face in his hands and brushed his warm lips across hers, making it quite clear that he wasn't going to give up on her.

Chrissie was in heaven all the way home, her mouth still tingling from the touch of Jake's soft lips on hers. My God, where did she go from here? She didn't want to get tied up with anyone. She was happy with her life as it was. Coming and going when she pleased. Pleasing herself whether she cooked at six o'clock or seven o'clock. Sure, she had Daisy to think of, but she was easy-going like herself. And true, she did get lonely sometimes in the evenings when Daisy was out, but she filled her time up working around in the garden that she loved. Talking to the plants and to the birds, anything that moved really. Except for slugs, she hated slugs with a passion. Often she was out in the garden at night with a torch and salt pot, looking for them under her plant pots. Daisy would yell out at her for being so cruel. "But what about all of my plants they bloody eat?" she would yell back at her. Daisy would then put her hands up in the air, tutting at her as she went back into the cottage, yelling back to her mother that she was going to get the men with white coats in to take her away.

Okay, so perhaps she was a little eccentric, but who cared. Not Chrissie. And if she really wanted company, she always had her soulmate Natasha on the other end of the telephone. Who also thought she was cruel hunting the slugs down… But even then. After doing all the things that she loved. And having the freedom to come and go. She did miss the companionship of a man. Admitting to herself that she was still tingling from the attention that she'd got from Jake tonight!

CHAPTER SIX

It was a bright sunny Wednesday morning, and Chrissie was up with the larks. All week at work they had been running around like lunatics. Taking two steps forward, and one step back. But getting there in the end. Tomorrow they had a very important visitor staying over at the hotel. Who just happened to be the Prime Minister. The whole of her entourage would be taking over the ninth floor. So that meant that all of the hotel staff would have to go through a police check, which also meant, it was certain that some of the staff would be 'jumping ship,' as the saying goes. It took all sorts of human beings to run a large hotel, and it was the 'norm' that you would end up hiring some people that would have (unbeknown to anyone that hired them), a criminal record, and would not want the limelight shining on them, let alone a police check done!   But Chrissie was almost certain that she was okay with the staff she had working for her at this moment in time. She was a stickler for chasing up references before she took anyone on, mainly because it was always her staff that would be in the firing line if anything was to go missing from any of the bedrooms. But saying that the system wasn't foolproof, and there was always somebody that would slip through her fingers now and again. Luckily for the police, the hotel was full of the Conservative Party leading up to her arrival, so at least it made it easier for them to do a police check on them!

The first thing that Chrissie had to do this morning was to make sure that she got hold of the laundry company who supplied the hotel with linen, and to speak with Ian, who was the top boss. She'd had many a run-in with him over the years. Especially when the linen had not been up to standard for a four-star hotel, pulling no punches when telling him that she would not take his crap linen. But he'd always turned up trumps, even delivering the laundry himself when she had been short delivered over a weekend.

The first person to greet her across the foyer as she walked towards reception was Jake.

"Morning Chrissie," he beamed.

The evening they had spent together last Friday was still foremost in his mind, and if they had been anywhere else, he would have gone over to her and planted a kiss on her cheek. But work came first. Especially when they had a VIP guest arriving tomorrow. And he had a restaurant manager who was flipping his lid.

"The laundry has arrived and Simon is flipping out over the state of the tablecloths. Apparently, they are disgusting, and every other one has stains on them," He said, coming up for air. "And, oh yes. They have forgotten to deliver the blue slip covers."

"For God's sake. Stop panicking, and give me chance to get in for Christ sake," Chrissie tutted, raising her eyes to the ceiling as she grabbed hold of the keys that Shelly was handing over to her. "And tell Simon to stop panicking. I'll sort it."

"And good morning to you, Chrissie. Hope your day goes well," Shelly said, glaring across at Jake. "For God's sake, give her time to get in before you start," she said out loud as Jake followed Chrissie towards the lift. But he was to slow to catch up with her as the lift doors closed on him. Taking in a deep breath,

Chrissie leaned back on the handrail. "Struth, give me bloody strength," she cursed under her breath.

The first thing she did after clicking the kettle on was to phone the laundry. Why people panicked over things that could be rectified she'd never know. All she wanted now was for Simon to burst through the door... And guess who was on cue...

"Bloody hell, Chrissie, have you seen the state of these bloody cloths?"

"Ssssh," she put her finger across her mouth, a sign telling him to zip it. "I'm on the phone to the laundry now," she growled. The cold flash from her ice cold eyes stopped him in his tracks, also stopping Daphne, who was on her way over from the linen room to moan on about the state of the bed linen. But feeling the vibes, she didn't bother, and turned back towards the linen room, tossing her eyes up at Simon.

The daily meeting wasn't any calmer either. Mr Grey was working himself up to having a heart attack. "Head chef, have you ordered the beef? What about staff? Have you got enough staff now half of them have bloody legged it before the police check? Luke, (who's head porter,) have you had the red carpet cleaned? Housekeeper, have you told your staff to stay off the ninth floor? Only yourself and your deputy are allowed up there. Reception, do your staff know how to greet our VIP guest? Restaurant manager, do you have enough waiting staff?"

For God's sake, give them all strength. How the hell did he think they survived running their bloody departments for the rest of the bloody year???!!!

By midday, things had calmed down a little. The linen had been sorted. Ian himself had filled up a laundry van with fresh linen for Chrissie after she had threatened to change laundries. He couldn't afford to lose the yearly income that came in from the hotel. And what with her bending his ear (to put it mildly), this morning, he thought it best to personally deliver it himself.

The red carpet had been freshly steamed cleaned, and was ready to go down across the foyer and steps, leading out to where the Prime Minister's car would draw up. Chrissie had warned all her girls to be on time in the morning. Uniforms to be looking spick and span, and nobody would be excused for being sick unless they were dying.

Jake had caught up with Chrissie through the morning, asking her if she would join him for lunch to go over tomorrow's programme. He wanted to make sure that she had everything in order upstairs, and to let her know where she would be standing in the foyer when the PM arrived. It would be more that his job's worth if there were any slip-ups. He told Chrissie that herself and Dawn would line up in the foyer with the rest of the management, and would shake hands with the Prime Minister. At this point, Chrissie got up and shook his hand, almost falling over. "Like this?" she teased. Jake completely ignored her, going on to say that the PM would slowly make her way up the red carpet, and eventually make her way over to the lift, where one of her private detectives would be waiting for her. Her hair dresser and make-up artist, et cetera, would already be up on the ninth floor waiting there for her. Chrissie had never seen so much security for one person. There were men up on the hotel roof, with the ninth floor lift being manned by a security officer at all times. Even Chrissie herself would have to show a special badge that she'd been given to wear while the PM was staying up on the ninth floor before even she would be allowed to get out of the lift! When they had finished their working lunch, Chrissie took hold of Jake's arm, and told him to calm down. She could see that he was really uptight about this visit, and needed to cool down a bit before he burst a blood vessel "It's not the Queen that's visiting Jake!" she smiled… "Well... Maybe!" she added, as he rushed off to see Mr Grey who was beckoning for him across the foyer to come to his office.

After lunch, Chrissie finished off checking the whole of the ninth floor with Dawn before it was sealed off for the arrival of the PM tomorrow. Then, feeling really exhausted with the buzz of it all, went back down to her office where she was going to make herself a well earned coffee. But just as she'd reached the office, a familiar voice called out to her. She stopped and looked along the corridor, putting her glasses on from off the top her head, as she squinted her eyes up to see who it was.

"Curly Whirl," she yelled out in surprise as he beamed down the corridor at her. "Where the hell have you come from? I thought you had fallen off the edge of the world."

He stood aside as she opened up the office door, giving him a hug as she ushered him into the office.

"You look really good. How are you?"

Again he beamed at her as he sat down on the old tattered chair with its wobbly leg. "See you've still got the death trap," he laughed. Nervously tapping his fingers on the arm of chair, he stopped abruptly, as he remembered that it was Chrissie's pet hate when somebody started tapping against something with their fingers. It always grated on her nerves.

Curly Whirl, or Carl Johnson, his real name, worked for Chrissie as a chamber boy for well over a year, until he had left to go into rehab. Chrissie had fought tooth and nail to get past the 'so called' red tape to get him into somewhere for his own safety before he really did some harm to himself. And in the end, it was through a friend of a friend who worked for social services who had managed to cut through the red tape, and got him into a psychiatric ward at a local rehab clinic after he had almost killed himself through drink and drugs She had taken Curly Whirl on her staff roll, thinking he wouldn't have a cat in hell's chance of lasting the month out if he didn't fit in with the girls.

But she needn't have worried. The girls loved him, especially when he helped them with their loaded trolleys, and turned heavy mattresses for them when they had to spring clean a room. He was in with the clan! And after a month of being there, he started to go out with someone called James, who worked in the restaurant. But then, all too soon, crack's started to appear in the wallpaper, and Curly Whirl started to come in late of a morning with giant hangovers. At first Chrissie thought that it was a one-off. But when it started to be every other morning that he rolled in late, Chrissie started getting agitated with him. Giving him hell, threatening him even with his job. But he would win her around by putting his back into his work, and somehow would always finish the same time as the girls who went off duty at three o'clock. Unless, that is, he'd forgotten to put milk or sugars into the rooms, or worse still, forgot to put towels in. But even then he would be away by 3:30 at the latest, and this had always puzzled Chrissie. That is, until Dawn had told her that some of the girls would rally around for him if he was behind in his work, and it was only when Curly could not hold a mug in his hand without spilling the contents of it all over the place, and started to borrow money off anyone who would give it to him to spend on drink, and God knows what else, that Chrissie decided she would have to put her foot down. She told him that he would have to seek some help, or else he was going to lose his job. She also told him that she would rota him off on a couple weeks' holiday. That way, he wouldn't lose any money. But it would all be down to him from then on. The poor lad had broken down in front of her, making Chrissie feel terrible for being so mean. But somebody had to put their foot down with him before he did some harm to himself. He told Chrissie that he had no family to speak of to turn to, and knew that he needed help desperately. He told her that he'd been sleeping rough on park benches, and the shiner that he had come into work with that morning was from a mugging from off a gang of boys that had set into him. Poor lad. He really desperately needed help from somebody! But here he was now. Large as life, and looking good. He told Chrissie that he'd been out of rehab for six months now, and had been dry for well over a year. He had gone back up to the north to live for awhile, but couldn't settle there, so had decided to come back down to the south. Where he bumped into Keith in the village, and he'd offered him a job as a kitchen porter, telling him that he would try and get him a room in the staff house if he proved to him that he could work himself up to help prepare the veg, for veg chef. He was over the moon about that, because at the moment he was renting a room above the baker's shop in the village, having to travel eight miles into work each day. Chrissie was so thrilled to see him back, and gave him another hug. It was good to see him back on his feet again.

By the time Chrissie got home that night she was feeling more than shattered. Parking up the car, she walked slowly up to the cottage, struggling to get the keys out of her pocket so she could open up the door, as Marmalade came trotting up behind, greeting her, as he purred in and out of her legs. Opening up the door, the quietness of the cottage hit her ears. There was no sound of Daisy with her music blaring out, or chatting to Jasmine on the phone. Hanging her coat in the closet, she bent down and picked up the post. There were only two letters today, and both of them looked like bills, with a folded piece of paper tucked in between them. "Strange," Chrissie thought, as she sauntered through into the kitchen, placing the post down onto the kitchen table, before going over to the fridge and retrieving the half bottle of Chardonnay she had left from last night, almost losing her footing as she tripped over Marmalade, who was meowing for attention. He was starving and wanted something to eat.

"All right, Marmalade, give me chance to get in," she said, lifting him out of the way with the end of her toe. "And if you're a good boy, I think that I've got some chicken for you in the fridge," she said, patting him on the back as she sat down at the kitchen table. She reached over for a glass from off the Welsh dresser, pouring herself out a large glass of wine, taking a couple of sips from it before opening up the post. Both of them being bills. One was the water rates that were sky high. But the plants had to be watered when the water butt ran out, and the other was a reminder for the television license, and that could wait. She threw them both on to the table, muttering to herself as she got up to feed Marmalade, who was driving her round the bend with his insistent meowing. "Keep on working, Chrissie!" she sighed.

Glancing at the cuckoo clock that was hung above the Welsh dresser, she jumped up when she saw it had gone 6:30. No wonder her stomach was rumbling, she hadn't eaten since her lunch with Jake, and that had only been ham sandwiches. She filled her glass with the rest of the wine, putting the bills in the letter rack, along with the piece of folded paper. She would look at that later. "Probably only someone advertising something," she thought. Right now she was starving, and Daisy would be in any minute now looking for her dinner. She was going to do a quick stir-fry, adding the rest of the chicken that was leftover from yesterday to it.

After catching up with Daisy on what she had been doing that day, then telling her all about the forthcoming visit of the Prime Minister, and of all the extra work that had to be done, she excused herself and retired to bed early. She was really feeling shattered. Daisy told her to get a good night's sleep. It wasn't every day that you got the Prime Minister of England staying at your hotel, and she really wasn't getting any younger either for all of this excitement. Chrissie clipped her ear, giving her a hug before leaving her to clear the kitchen up as she retired up the stairs to bed.

The night had been a long one, tossing and turning. Had she done this? Had she done that? And by six o'clock she was up, and was in work by seven. The PM was due to arrive at eleven o'clock that morning, so she wanted to be ahead of things. Just in case! Jake was not long after her, with Mr Grey arriving shortly after him. Chrissie and Jake looked up at the clock in reception with a smirk on their faces as he called Jake into the office. Mr Grey was never in his office until nine o'clock.

Jake and Simon joined her for a coffee in the restaurant, going over things for the last time before the day really kicked off. When Chrissie got up to leave, Jake followed her out catching hold of her arm.

"Chrissie, wait a minute, are you free tonight? Let's go out somewhere and celebrate today once it's all over and the PM is tucked safely up in bed," he laughed, catching hold of the lift door as she was about to disappear inside of it. "Simon, Keith, and Shelly will be joining us, and probably a few of the others as well. It will do us all good to relax down for awhile, what do think?" Chrissie wasn't that hot on going out with staff when the day was over. She was a boring fart really. But the beaming smile that Jake was wearing, she couldn't say no. So she said yes, she'd join them, pressing the lift button before she could change her mind.

WOW. What an experience to meet the Prime Minster. They had all lined up to greet her as she came through the door. Each and every one of them smiling like Cheshire cats. She was shorter than Chrissie had imagined, but looking very smart, dressed in a navy blue suit, with a knee-length skirt, wearing comfortable brogue shoes. She shook everyone's hand as she passed them by, stopping to talk to some, smiling at others. The hotel was abuzz with reporters when she arrived, flashing cameras everywhere. Chrissie had never seen such a wide grin on Mr Greys face as the Prime Minister stopped to talk to him. His cheeks were flushed, and he looked like a young boy who had just been given a lollypop. Chrissie could see her girls on the stairs, hanging over the banister to get a better look at the Prime Minister. They had all been warned to not make a sound as they took a sneaky look at her. But the PM must have felt their presence, and as she turned towards to the lift, she raised her head and smiled up at them, waving as she disappeared through the lift doors. They all let out a sigh of relief as they watched the numbers on the lift dial until it had reached the ninth floor. Then they all dispersed to get on with their day's work that was still waiting for them, as Jake followed a smiling Mr Grey into his office.

When the working day was over, they all congregated in the pub a few doors down from the hotel. All of them were exhausted, but somehow they found the energy for a quick drink down the pub, or for Chrissie it was going to be a quick drink, she couldn't stop yawning. Keith went over to her, where she was sat at a table staring out of the window, and asked if she had seen Curly Whirl yet? She said that she had, and was pleased to see him looking so well. "But you make sure you keep him on the straight and narrow," she teased, shaking her finger at him, knowing that Keith went to the pub for a quick drink most nights after finishing work.

Jake came over with a tray of drinks with the beer slopping over the rim of the pint glasses for the men. "First round on me," he laughed, handing Chrissie a glass of wine before going around to the others. "Enjoy it all of you. And thanks for all of your hard work today," he said, sitting down by Chrissie, winking at her. As she took a sip of her wine, she could feel her cheeks colour up, as she felt the warmth of his hand gently slide across on to her knee, giving it a gentle squeeze, sending a tingle down her spine.

When she reached home three hours later, she was feeling really relaxed as she let herself in quietly through the door, slipping her shoes off so she wouldn't wake Daisy with them clicking on the tiled kitchen floor. She wanted a coffee before going up to bed, her adrenaline was still pumping from the visit of the PM today. She had really enjoyed buzz of it all. Not that she didn't enjoy most days working at the hotel, for every day there was something different going on. And at times, it was bloody hard work, but in the hotel trade you either loved it, or hated it. There was never any in between. But today had been a special day. And as Daisy had said, 'It wasn't every day that you had the Prime Minister of England staying at your hotel.' Sipping on the strong black coffee she'd made for herself, her face flushed at the thought of Jake tonight. He had sat beside her all evening, playing with her hand under the table, and she hadn't stopped him either. It had felt good. Then he had walked her to her car where he kissed her goodnight lightly on the lips. He didn't want to push things with her. What he felt for her was pure and simple love. But how Chrissie felt about him, she didn't know, only that he made her glow whenever he was near her.

Still sipping her coffee, she remembered the slip of paper that was tucked in between her bills, and pulled it out of the letter rack to read it. As she slowly digested what had been typed down on the piece of paper, her blood ran cold as her hand flew up to her mouth.

"My God," she cried out, dropping it onto the floor, as her hands started shaking, and she swallowed hard to stop herself from throwing up.

"YOU ARE"

(B) AD

(I) LL-BRED

(T) RASH

(C) RETIN

(H) AS-BEEN

Her face drained of blood, as she got up steadying herself against the kitchen table. Her head was swimming around and around at the thought of him being out there somewhere. Stalking her. She had to take in deep breaths to stop herself from passing out. "He has been to my home," she sobbed, her eyes darting around the kitchen, expecting any moment now for somebody to jump out on her. She knew who had left that message through her door. It just had to be Stewart... Nobody else had ever called her a BITCH but for him.

Her heart hammering against her ribcage, she darted around the cottage checking all the doors were bolted and the windows were closed. He could be out there now, watching her. My God, what should she do? She could feel her life was about to fall apart around her, and she just couldn't bear that. What about Daisy who knew nothing of her past, and Natasha, her dear friend? What would she think? If she went to the police all of it would come out. The rape, the baby. Oh God, she wouldn't be able to stand it. Chrissie went over to the Welsh dresser and pulled out a packet of cigarettes. She hadn't smoke since giving it up over two years ago after being diagnosed with asthma. But if there was ever a time for her to start smoking again, it was now. Searching around in the draw for some matches, she lit up a cigarette, taking a long drag on it, inhaling the smoke back into her lungs, and straight away her head started to spin as the nicotine hit the back of her throat, and within seconds, she was coughing and spluttering, gasping for breath, with stars floating in front of her eyes. She threw the cigarette into the sink, searching around in her handbag for her inhaler. "Bad move, Chrissie. Not good for your asthma," she wheezed, dropping into the chair.

The sound of Chrissie coughing and spluttering had woken Daisy up, and as she gingerly made her way down the stairs, she peered around the kitchen door that had been left slightly ajar, hoping that she wasn't about to come across an intruder. Her eyes darting around the kitchen, she came across her mother bent over in the chair, sucking on her inhaler. She rushed over to her thinking that she was having a asthma attack.

"Mum. Are you alright?"

CHAPTER SEVEN

Chrissie had crawled out of bed and took a warm shower before venturing down the stairs to get herself a strong black coffee. Her head was still reeling from last night. She hadn't slept a wink after reading the abusive letter that had been put through her door. What was she going to do about it? Should she go to the police? And then what? She really couldn't face up to being interrogated by them while all of her sordid past came out. She would have to tell them all about the rape, and at this moment in time that was the last thing she wanted to do. She had Daisy to think of, who new nothing of her past life, nobody did, not even her ex-husband Freddie. But somebody had been to her cottage and posted through the letter box an abusive message, not even put into a sealed envelope. What if Daisy had picked it up! Thank God she was the one who had found it and not Daisy. Was the message a warning to her that he was still out there? Watching her? Just bidding his time before he showed his face? But why after all this time? What could she possibly have that he would want from her? So many questions filled her head that it was almost at bursting point. Thank God that she had managed to convince Daisy, after calming her down, that she had come home feeling a bit tipsy from having a drink with her work colleagues after work. She told her that they were all on a high after meeting the PM. And the day had gone without a hitch, so they had all decided to go down to the pub to celebrate, and it was only after she'd got back home that she decided that she fancied having a cigarette. Daisy had been furious with her, telling her off for being so stupid as she screwed up the packet, throwing it into the bin, calling her stupid for lighting up a cigarette. (Hey, who was the mother here!?) Then Daisy had seen state of her mother's eyes. Why were they so bloodshot? Had she been crying? Chrissie again managed to fob her off by saying that she had laughed so much that night that she had cried with laughter. She thought that Daisy had half swallowed the story, but her daughter wasn't stupid, and Chrissie hated lying to her. Once you started to do that, it had a habit of turning around and biting you in the ass. She had already lied to her when she'd picked the piece of paper up from off the kitchen floor. Daisy wanted to know what was on it, and Chrissie had told her that it was a reminder for her to leave the money out for the milkman tomorrow. It was Friday, and he needed to be paid. Daisy had raised her eyebrow at her, but didn't say anything. So, after tossing and turning all night, Chrissie had made her mind up that she would see Jake today about having a few days' off. It was her weekend off anyway, so it would only be a few days in the week that she would need off to sort things out before it all blew up in her face. She would phone Natasha as soon as she got in to work today, knowing that she would be the one who would give her sound advice on what to do with this mess that she found herself in before she ended up having a nervous breakdown.

After going around the cottage twice to make sure that it was all locked up, she drove to work checking in her rear-view mirror more than she normally did, looking to see if anyone was following her. That note had so rankled her, she was becoming paranoid. When she stopped at the first set of traffic lights on the way to work, a man parked in a car beside her waiting for the lights to change smiled at her, and her heart almost stopped beating. What if it was him and he was following her? Then chastised herself for being so bloody stupid. If it was him, she would recognize him straight away. She would never forget his face.

She rushed through the hotel foyer. Thankfully, she didn't have to go over to reception this morning. Dawn was on the early shift today, thank God. She started at seven, and left at three with the girls. So she would be doing the rooming list for the girls when they arrived, giving Chrissie time to phone Natasha before they all piled through the door. She waved across at Daphne, then looked surprised to see Curly Whirl coming out of the linen room with his arms full of linen.

"What are you doing up here?" she asked going towards him.

"Morning, Chrissie," he said, colouring up as she eyed balled him. "Keith sent me up for some kitchen clothes, and Simon asked me to bring him down some tablecloths while I was up here.

"Mmm, Daphne, make sure that you make a note of what Curly Whirl is taking," she said, winking at her. "You know Simon, he'll be up for more linen swearing blind that he's had none today," she laughed, knowing him only too well. He had a habit of hiding a stack of linen in his office calling it his 'emergency supply'. Only trouble was, when it came for the monthly linen stocktake, Chrissie would be pulling her hair out at the end of it looking around for linen that had supposedly gone astray, only to find a pile of it in Simon's office! Tracey, who came from the laundry to do the stocktake, was used to looking into all the crevasses for linen that would be tucked away in the most ridiculous places, even after Chrissie had warned them that there would be a stocktake being done that day, and if there was any shortage of linen at the end of it, of which the laundry would charge them for, it would be their necks on the line and not hers. But thankfully so far, she had always managed to wangle her way out of paying any of the charges that were asked for!

93

Chrissie phoned Natasha, asking her what she was doing that evening, and did she want to come over for a meal. If she didn't speak to somebody soon, she was in she was going to explode. Natasha picked up the vibes that were coming from Chrissie, and cursed herself for not being able to go over for a meal, but she had called out the vet this morning because Rosie had been unwell through the night, and he'd told her that she had a touch of cat flu, but she should be okay in a few days time, leaving her with a course of tablets to mix in with her food at feed time. So Natasha being Natasha didn't want to leave her until she was on the mend, so she managed to talk Chrissie into going over to have a meal with her, and to stay the night so that they could catch up on things over one or two bottles of wine. Chrissie was okay with that. Daisy was away for the weekend in London with Jasmine, and she'd not been looking forward to spending the night on her own. So she'd go home first and feed Marmalade before making her way over to Natasha's and burdening her with her problems.

Chrissie made her way up to the ninth floor after the P.M. had departed. She wanted to check all the doors and windows had been closed in the rooms that had been used, because the ninth floor would not be put back on for letting until tomorrow. Most of the furniture had been moved around to make room for all the extra items that the entourage brought along for the PM so it was going to take some time to straighten it all out again. Thank God, most of the hotel had departed with her, and there were not so many bookings for the weekend, so it would give her girls breathing space to clean the departure rooms today without breaking a leg. They were all working like Trojans as it was, and Chrissie doubted whether they would get through all of their departures today. Some of them had 12 to 13 rooms to service, which was no mean feat. But at the end of the month, she did know that they would be getting a big fat tip…. Courtesy of the Conservative Party. So that had put a smile on their faces.

It was gone two o'clock before she caught up with Jake who was having a late lunch break like herself in the snack bar. She wasn't feeling that hungry, but she got herself a cheese sandwich with a coffee before going over to sit with him. He patted at the seat next to him for her to sit down, but she chose to sit opposite him.

"Hi Chrissie, how's your morning been?"

"Not bad, we're getting there," she said, biting into her cheese sandwich. "At least most of the rooms had vacated by eleven. Wanting to get home for the weekend I guess."

"What's up?" He could see by the look on her face that something was bothering her. "All of your staff turned in this morning?" He sat waiting for her to explode at him like she normally did when he asked her a question like that. For some reason, she always thought he was interfering with her day to day running of the floors. But that couldn't have been further from the truth. All he'd wanted to know was that she had enough staff to see her through the day, and nothing else.

She nodded her head, swallowing a mouthful of coffee, then came straight out with what she wanted. A few days off from work, something personal had come up, and she needed the time to sort it out.

His face clouded over. "How much time?"

"Look, Jake. I'm owed time, and I need time off. Right," she snapped, crossing her legs over as she sat glaring at him.

"Whoa, steady on. I'm only asking how much time do you need off. It's not a problem!"

"Sorry."

He could see that she was upset about something, but didn't want to pry. "Look, Chrissie, if you need time off that's fine by me. Will Dawn and Janie be able to cover for you?"

"I'll see to it. But I'm off anyway this weekend, so it will only be for a couple of days in the week."

"Take the week off, Chrissie, you're owed it."

He squeezed her hand, and she got up to leave before she started to blubber. She could feel the tears building up in her eyes, muttering she would sort it out with Dawn and Janie to cover while she was off.

"Wait a minute," Jake said, seeing that she was upset about something. "Can we meet up tomorrow? I finish work at seven. We could go out for a meal somewhere." He caught hold of her hand and squeezed it again affectionately.

Chrissie so wanted to say yes. She would love to meet up for a meal with him somewhere. And to forget everything that was going on in her life right now. But first she had to clear this mess up before she could move on. So she declined, saying that if his offer was still open when she got back to work, she would love to have a meal with him.

Before leaving to go to Natasha's, Chrissie wandered around her beloved garden. She needed to put things into perspective. How dare that bastard sneak back into her life after all these years. Hadn't he done enough to her. It was a horrendous to think that he could be hanging around out there somewhere, waiting to pounce on her. But why? What could she possibly have that he would want from her? She let out a deep sigh. Tomorrow she was going to contact the police. She couldn't let this go on any longer. What if he was to approach Daisy again! But what did she have to go on. A piece of paper with some abuse typed on it. It could have been typed by anyone and hand posted through the door. Perhaps it was somebody from work with a grievance against her. But then again, she was sure that she would know if she had upset someone to that extent at work that they would want to verbally threaten her. No, deep down she knew it was him that was lurking around out there somewhere.

Waiting for her. She let out another sigh as she bent over to de-head her roses, they had given her so much pleasure this year with the wonderful display of colours of red, peach, mauve, pink, white. And still the bushes were producing buds for her. Usually she had roses blooming until the first frost appeared, because of the garden being sheltered. As she made her way back up to the cottage, she looked under the pots for the dreaded slugs that were the bane of her life, making a fuss of Marmalade before leaving him.

"I'll be back in the morning," she said to him, filling the cat tray with clean litter after making sure that he had enough water and food to keep him happy until she returned. "Look after the place for me," she said, closing the door on her way out, happy knowing that he could get in and out through the cat flap if he wanted to.

Fifteen minutes later she had arrived at Natasha's. Lugging her night bag over her shoulder, with usual bottle of wine tucked under her arm. The first to greet her was Scamp, running up to her yapping out his greetings as he jumped around her legs. Natasha swung open the door, greeting her with a kiss on each cheek, as she relieved her of the wine. Once inside of the house, Natasha told her to take her bag up to her usual room that was at the back of the house, overlooking her long garden. She also yelled up the stairs after her that she was welcome to take a shower if she needed one. Not that she thought that she needed one, but there was a strange smell that had just followed her through the door. Chrissie laughed, blowing a raspberry down at her, calling her a 'cheeky bugger' over her shoulder. She was back down the stairs five minutes later, sitting in Natasha's cosy lounge, sipping on the cool glass of wine that had been poured out for her.

"Okay. What's up?" Natasha was not the one to hang around when she knew that there was something bothering her friend. She wanted to know what was going on before the evening went any further.

Chrissie stared ahead of her. Where did she start? And did she really want to? Was she ready to unfold her secret past? She was a very private person, and there were things that she didn't want unlocked from that small box she'd tucked them away in the recess of her mind. But she knew that she had to tell somebody before her mind exploded. So taking in a deep breath, she began to tell the tale, starting with the rape. Natasha was so shocked that she almost choked on her wine as Chrissie went on to tell her about the child she had conceived through the rape, and of giving her away. Natasha shook her head, she felt numb from the neck down. My God, she had known Chrissie for all of these years, and had had no idea of the hell that she had been through in her teens. Clearing her throat, she asked Chrissie if she knew where her daughter was now, then wished she hadn't as she saw the pain in her face. She got up and refilled their glasses with wine, swallowing hers back with almost one gulp as Chrissie continued to tell her of how she had moved down here to Thatcham to start a knew life, taking on her mother's maiden name of Rosie Grimes. Natasha's mouth fell open. She couldn't believe what she was hearing. She was dumbfounded. After all these years of knowing Chrissie, she really thought she knew her inside out. But she didn't. My God, you never really knew a person, no matter how long you'd known them. There were things that even Chrissie didn't know about Natasha. Like why she wasn't interested in men! Everyone had their secrets. But my God, she had locked away all of the suffering that she had gone through for all of these years. It was a miracle that she was still sane. Natasha got up and went over to her, wrapping her arms tightly around her, giving her a hug as the tears ran freely down both their faces. There was a few moments of silence between them before Natasha got up and got them both a tot of brandy.

It was needed, and after drinking it back in one gulp, Chrissie said to her as she smiled weakly, "We're a right pair, aren't we?"

No more was said on the matter until they had settled down after eating the meal that Natasha had cooked of grilled pork chops and noodles, out in the conservatory on a tray, wash down with another bottle of wine. It was Natasha that brought it up again, asking Chrissie what had brought it to the surface after all these years. Chrissie then told her about the note that had been slipped through her door. She took it out of her handbag and handed it over for her to read, while she quickly told her about the brief meeting that Daisy had had with a complete stranger a couple of weeks ago. 'Accidentally' bumping into her when she was going to draw money out at the hole in the wall, apologising to her, then asked if she knew of anyone named Rosie Grimes living around in the area.

"My God, Chrissie, you have to go to the police," Natasha said after reading what was printed on the paper.

"I know. But what can they do? I've no proof of who it's from."

"Chrissie, you have to phone the police and asked them to come out to the cottage. There's a bloody psycho running around out there. And he's after you."

Natasha could have bitten her tongue off for saying that. She could see the state that Chrissie was in already, without her being melodramatic about it.

"I know," Chrissie said, burying her head in her hands. "But how do I tell Daisy all of this? How do I tell her that she's got a sister out there somewhere?"

After a long evening of discussing what to do about the predicament that Chrissie was in, they finally made it up to bed at three in the morning, with Natasha pushing a giggling Chrissie up the stairs from the rear. They had both drunk too much, and the pair of them were giggling like a couple of teenagers as they helped each other along to their bedrooms, with Natasha pushing Chrissie onto her bed. After the tears she had shed that evening, it was good to see her wind down a little, even if it was through consuming too much alcohol.

After having a breakfast of bacon and eggs and a large mug of black coffee, Chrissie finally left after promising Natasha that she would phone the police and try and get this mess sorted out. Natasha waved her off, putting her hand up to her ear, pointing to it to remind Chrissie to phone the police when she got home. Chrissie tutted as she gave her the thumbs up, waving to her as she drove out of the driveway into the small lane that would take her up onto the road home. What was she like!

On the drive home, Chrissie really had to concentrate on the roads. Her head was still thumping from the lack of sleep last night, as she tried to switch off from what she had to face the next day. As she parked up in the driveway, Marmalade came running down the drive to greet her. She picked him up, and nuzzled her nose into his ears, mumbling a good morning to him.

"And good morning to you, my dear."

Chrissie nearly jumped out of her skin, dropping Marmalade on to the ground as she looked around to see where the voice was coming from. "God, you frightened me to death," she said, laughing with relief as she caught sight of her neighbour, Mr Roberts, plodding up the driveway towards her.

"Sorry, dear, if I made you jump. I came round to tell you." He had to stopped to get his breath. Poor old boy. "There was a hell of a noise coming from your cottage last night. So I thought I had better come round to see if you were alright."

Chrissie tensed up, walking up towards the cottage as she got her key out to go in. "What sort of noise?" she asked, as he struggled up the drive behind her.

"It sounded like somebody was banging on the door. I looked out of my window, but it was pitch dark and I couldn't see a thing. Must have been in the early hours of the morning I would have thought, because I had been sound asleep." He had to hold on to the door frame until he caught his breath.

Chrissie unlocked the door, and gingerly went inside. The old boy followed her in, wheezing behind her. Chrissie opened up all the doors to the rooms downstairs, before going up to the bedrooms to check there. She thought for a moment that Daisy might have come back early from London, because she had already phoned Chrissie to say that she would be home tonight instead of Sunday because it was too expensive to stay on any longer than one night in a bed and breakfast for a 'poor' student at college After thoroughly looking around, and finding nothing untoward had happened, she thanked Mr Rodgers, letting him out of the door.

"Sorry if I worried you, love," he said as Chrissie helped him over the doorstep. "Must have been a fox or one of the farmers pigs that got loose," he chuckled, as Chrissie watched him go down the drive, smiling to herself as she turned to go back in. But as she went to close the door behind her, something caught her eye, and as she looked down towards the cat flap, she gasped aloud. It wasn't there. All she could see was a gaping hole in the door. Gingerly, she went back outside looking around her, thinking that perhaps Marmalade had been on the run from something, and had crashed into the cat flap, breaking it as he went through. But if that had happened, then the cat flap itsself would be lying around on the doorstep. A shiver went through her as she went back inside, slamming the door behind her. 'He's been here again, I just know it," she groaned, slumping down on to the chair in the hallway as she picked up the telephone to contact the police.

CHAPTER EIGHT

As Chrissie waited for the police to arrive, she phoned Natasha to let her know about the hole in her door. At first Natasha thought she was winding her up, but then she knew by the tone of her voice that she wasn't.

"Christ, Chrissie, what next, Do you want me to come over? Have you phoned the police?"

"Yes, I have phoned the police. And no please don't come over. I'm fine. I will phone you as soon as the police have been."

"Make sure you do. I will be worrying."

"Yes, yes, Tash. Don't worry. I'm alright. The police will be here soon, and I'll phone you later." Chrissie put the phone down. She had lied about being alright. She would do anything to have Natasha there with her, she was shaking like a leaf. But this was something that she had to do herself. So she sat and waited for the police to arrive.

They arrived an hour later. Two of them. One quite stockily built, and the other tall and lean, looking around the cat flap before following Chrissie into the kitchen. They asked her if she had touched anything on the door, and she said no, she'd only opened it up to come in. Their eyes took everything in as she asked if they wanted a mug of tea. Both of them had said yes together, making her smile. Then it was down to business. Had she heard anything last night? She told them that she had stayed over at her girlfriend's, but old Mr Roberts from next door had heard a noise in the early hours of the morning. Tom, who seemed to be the one in charge, started writing in his notebook, saying that they would go round and see him after leaving her. Chrissie then got up to get the note out of her handbag, and handed it over to Tom, saying that she had found it with her post on Thursday. He took it from her and read it through, raising his eyebrows as he handed it over to his mate Jimmy, who had just come back into the room after taking another look at the door. Then Tom asked Chrissie did she have any idea of who it could be? She glared across at him biting down hard on her tongue. For Christ sake. You would think that they would have checked their damn files before coming out to see her. Taking in a deep breath before she exploded, she told them that she had already been down to the police station to report the abusive phone calls that she'd been receiving. Tom raised his eyebrows at her before asking her if she was still getting the phone calls. "Not for the last few weeks," Chrissie told him. But let him know that she thought that it was Stewart that had made the phone calls. She swallowed hard to contain the tears that were threatening to spill. She was not going to waste any tears over this evil man that was trying to worm his way in back into her life. She also told them about the incident of somebody bumping into Daisy the other night, asking her if she knew of anyone by the name of Rosie Grimes. Tom cleared the frog in his throat before he went on to explain to her that at this moment there was nothing they could do, except to tell her to be more vigilant than she normally was when she was out. And to warn Daisy also to keep her guard up. The vibes that he felt coming from Chrissie made him flinch. They were not what you would call friendly. But he went on to say that until there was more proof of this Stewart pestering her, physically or mentally. There was nothing more they could at this stage. But he did say that he would take the note that was posted through her door with him, and a officer would be round to take fingerprints off the door, so not to board it up until he had been. Chrissie frowned, asking if he would be back before it was dark. Tom nodded his head, saying that when he got back to the station he would make enquiries to try and find out where Stewart was at this moment in time, and an officer would be sent straight out to do the fingerprinting on the door. But in the meantime, if he was to approach her, or she saw him hanging around the cottage. To phone the station straight away, and somebody would be sent out immediately. Feeling a bit happier in herself knowing she had someone to contact if anything else was to happen, she said goodbye to them both as she watched them go round to Mr Roberts, hoping they wouldn't frighten the life out of him, giving him a heart attack as they asked him questions about last night.

Daisy arrived home from London, just in time to catch her mother before she went to bed. She was shattered after having a late night out last night after going to a nightclub with Jasmine, which had been very daring for them seeing as a great night out for them was going to a disco in the village. They didn't get back to their bed and breakfast place until two in the morning, and what with the travelling, she felt she could sleep for a week. But they had a great time, and she had managed to find a wedding outfit for her father's wedding. She had walked, what seemed to them, halfway around London to find the dress that she wanted. Poor Jasmine's feet were throbbing by the time Daisy had found a grey jersey woollen dress, fitting into her curves like a glove, and she had been lucky to match it up with a pink jacket, but had been unable to get any shoes to match, so she would have to go into the village in the week. She had seen a pair of grey stiletto-heeled shoes that she'd got her eye on, but hadn't had enough money on her to pay for them. But now she had just got paid from work, where she worked park-time as a filing clerk, plus tea girl in a solicitor's office. She would be able to afford them without having to ask her mother for the money.

First thing she noticed when she went to open up the door was the black polythene bag tacked over the cat flap. She would have to ask her mother what had happened. Had Marmalade taken a running jump through it, and got stuck halfway through? She could just visualize her mother chiseling away at the door to free him! Chrissie was sat at the kitchen table reading the Daily Mirror when Daisy went through to her. She had spent a quiet evening on her own, trying to sort things out in her mind. After phoning Natasha to fill her in on what happened after seeing the police today, she was going to go into the village to do some last minute shopping, but she hadn't been in the mood for it. So she decided, after pulling out a joint of pork from the freezer for tomorrow's lunch, she would go out into the garden and mow the lawn instead, deadheading her flowers as she chatted away to the birds that were eating off the bird table. But as hard as she tried to forget the last few hours, her head was still full of how she was going to break it to Daisy about the sister she knew nothing about. To tell her of how she had been raped at the age of 17, and given her baby away. She couldn't even think about it without feeling ashamed. Ashamed for giving her baby away. Ashamed for not even knowing her name….. Ashamed that she didn't even give her name. All of it was going to come out. Coming down to Thatcham. Changing her name to her mother's name, who was now no longer here. Chrissie's mother and father had died in an accident, long before Daisy had been old enough to remember them. Chrissie smiled at Daisy as she came through into the kitchen, asking her how the visit had gone to London. Daisy told her that she had managed to get the outfit, but still had the shoes to get. She thought that her mother looked tired, she had been worried about her over the last couple of months. She hadn't been her usual bubbly self. Working too hard, that's what it was. Well----that's what Daisy thought, but she was just about to find out the truth of it.

Chrissie made her favourite hot chocolate drink as Daisy showed her the dress and jacket that she had brought for her father's wedding. The wedding was only a week away now, and she was very excited about it, especially as her mother was coming. Chrissie asked her to try it on. She wanted to see what it looked like, and as she paraded in front of her, Chrissie's eyes glistened. She looked exquisite in it. A lady, Chrissie thought, smiling across at her as Daisy walked up and down the kitchen floor.

"What happened to the cat flap?" Daisy asked, as she sat down drinking her hot chocolate.

"God knows. It must have worked itself loose somehow. Probably came away when Marmalade charged through it," she laughed. Chrissie had made her mind up that she wasn't going to spoil things now. It could wait. Daisy had just got back from having a good time in London with Jasmine. Tomorrow was soon enough to burst the bubble.

"Come on, Daisy, we're going to be late," Chrissie shouted up the stairs to her as she waited by the open door for her to appear. They were going to church this morning. Chrissie often went to the morning service in the village when she was off on a Sunday. Sometimes Daisy would go with her, sometimes not. But today she decided she would go with her mother. They hadn't spent much time together just lately, what with Chrissie being at work, and Daisy swatting up on her exam work. The days had flown by. Chrissie liked to catch up with the local people to find out what was going on. It was always good to know what events were coming up when you lived in a small community, and of course to catch up on all of the gossip! Chrissie was just about to shout up again for Daisy, when she stepped out of her way as she came crashing down the stairs, straight through the door, and out to the Mini, where she then struggled to get her long gangling legs into it. Chrissie smiled as she walked over to the car. She was lanky like her father, having his large brown eyes, not blue like her own, and his dark wavy hair that she constantly moaned on about every time she tried to straighten it. Chrissie would have given an arm and leg to have had wavy hair like hers, everytime she had to sit with her curling tongs to get a wave in hers. And it still went straight within hours. You couldn't win really, could you!

After the morning service was over, Chrissie stayed behind for a coffee along with the vicar and some of the other parishioners, as Daisy went out to wait for her in the fresh air. Attending church with her mother was one thing. But to stay behind to catch up on all of the gossip was entirely another thing! As she sat outside in the sun, she suddenly remember that she had spotted a red Jaguar car parked on the other side of the road as they had turned into the car park this morning. And the man sitting behind the wheel looked just like the man that had bumped into her a few weeks ago. "I really must remember to tell Mother," she thought, gazing out over the graveyard.

Chrissie found Christian, who was the vicar of Saint John's, refreshing. He had very modern views on certain topics that were discussed, but she also had a soft spot for him. She thought he was cute. In his forties she would have thought, but he could've been older. Maybe wearing his hair tied back in a ponytail made him look younger. But what tickled her most about him was seeing the tip of his trainers that he wore under his cassock. Wicked. He looked almost human. Plus the services he held were simplified by preaching them to his congregation in plain simple English, not all that gobbledygook that most people found hard to understand... Well she did anyway. Chrissie had never been overly religious, but she did try to live by the Ten Commandments.

Asking Daisy if she wanted a glass of wine with their late lunch, Chrissie sat down as she handed over her wine glass to her, smiling at the surprised look on her face. It wasn't often that Chrissie offered wine to her on Sunday lunchtime. Daisy asked her if they were celebrating anything, and Chrissie laughed, saying no, she just thought it would be nice for them to have a glass of wine with their late lunch. But really, the reason she had got the wine out was to put them both in a mellow mood. She wasn't looking forward to what she had to say to her after lunch, and she was hoping the wine would help with the shock of it all. Usually Daisy wouldn't drink wine at a lunchtime, it always left her feeling tired. But seeing as it was a Sunday, and she wasn't going anywhere, why not. Chrissie had cooked the loin of pork to where it melted in your mouth, it tasted delicious. Professional chefs would have called her a moron for cooking it so long, but Chrissie couldn't stand any meat that was pink or had blood running out of it.

She always remembered Freddie taking her out for a meal when they had first met. He had taken her to a fish restaurant, where he had ordered a meal for two of fresh lobster, served with different condiments. It was a very posh restaurant that he had taken her to, and she was looking forward to having a tasty meal. But what Chrissie didn't know was that the chef would come to the table and show them the lobster that they would be eating. Still alive and kicking. He showed it first to Freddie, who was smacking his lips together with pleasure at the thought of eating it. Then to Chrissie, who had to stifle a scream, almost falling off her chair as she looked up at the chef in horror. He had laughed, saying he was sorry if it offended her, but this was how this particular dish was cooked. You just dropped the lobster into the boiling water while it was still alive. Disgusting, Chrissie thought, as he went on to say that it was just as it read on the menu. 'Fresh Lobster'. So it went without saying that Freddie found himself eating all of the lobster, while Chrissie

108

filled herself up with the rice and condiments. And it also goes without saying, she has never asked for fresh lobster since. Daisy saw her mother smiling to herself and asked what she was smiling at as she finished the last of her roast potatoes off her plate.

"Oh nothing, just memories," Chrissie smiled, getting up as she collected the plates, taking then over to the draining board. "Which reminds me, I have something to tell you later. We'll just clear up the kitchen then retire into the lounge, if that's okay with you?"

Daisy frowned, nodding her head as she tried to think of what she'd done wrong now.

Chrissie settled down on the settee, putting her full glass of wine down onto the side table next to her, as Daisy settled herself down opposite her, sucking on one of the plums that Chrissie had picked yesterday from off a very old Victoria plum tree that grew at the end of the garden.

"Christ where do I start," Chrissie thought. Clearing her throat, she looked across at Daisy who was frowning at her. This wasn't like her mother. If she had something to say, she would say it. She wasn't a one to beat around the bush on anything.

"Daisy, I have something to tell you that's going to be very hard for me to say."

Daisy raised her eyes at this. What the hell had her mother got to say to her that could be so bad? Had somebody died? Was she getting married? She did go out the other night dressed up to the nines. Or was she going to tell her that she was pregnant? Please, God, no, anything but that. Let it be that she's going to get married again. That would be great. Another wedding to go to, and her mum would make a beautiful bride, and would have somebody to share her life with.

"What I have to tell you Daisy will probably change our lives forever. But I want you to listen until I have told you everything, then we can talk. Okay?"

Chrissie smiled at her as the tears started to sting the back of her throat. But she had to take control of her emotions until she had told her daughter everything about her past life. Daisy didn't say anything, but she was starting to get worried. This wasn't like her mother to be so serious about something. After Chrissie had finished telling her the story of how she had been raped at the age of 17, and of giving birth to a daughter who she'd conceived through being raped, who she had never seen because of giving her up at birth, then of how she had moved away from everything she had known, taking on her mother's name to start a new life, she watched the blood drain from Daisy's face.

Daisy felt numb, swallowing hard not to be sick. Her head was spinning as she sat stiffly back in the chair, pulling on the ends of the tassels that hung over the sides. She was numb from the neck down. But her brain was doing overtime. Her mother had been raped. And she had a sister who she knew nothing about. She was finding it incredibly hard to take it all in. Half of her wanted to get up and hug her mother who had suffered so much when she was young. But the other half of her wouldn't let her as she felt a surge of rage rising up in her. She clenched her hands into fist, biting hard down on her tongue so she didn't say anything that she would regret. But she had remembered that her mother had had the guts to pick herself up, and start her life over again. That could not have been easy. Locking away all of the pain that she must have been suffering, just to face another day. But then the anger took over... How could she have kept all of this from her? And oh my God, did her father know? Had she told her father about her past life? She looked across at Chrissie, whose eyes were so full of pain that she almost felt sorry for her. But the anger wouldn't go away. She really felt that she had never known her true mother. Daisy got up saying nothing to her, only

110

to say that she was going to bed. She needed time on her own to digest all of what her mother had just told her. She had a sister out there somewhere, who knew nothing about her. Or of her biological mother. Chrissie didn't try to stop her. What more could she say to her? "I'm sorry, Daisy, for deceiving you for all of these years! Please don't turn your back on me now... I need you!"

The sun was scurrying in and out of the clouds when Daisy woke the next morning. She came down to breakfast, and managed to make small talk with her mother. But she didn't mention anything about last night, only about what she would be doing that day. But that was only after Chrissie had started up the conversation, asking her if she had slept well, and did she want coffee or tea with her breakfast that morning. The atmosphere was strained between them at the table. Daisy asked her what she was going to do with her week off, which Chrissie found unnerving. Her daughter was being very distant with her. She was acting more like a robot, with no warm feelings towards her mother. But Chrissie said nothing to her, she obviously needed time to get her head around things. It wasn't every day that you were told by your mother that she had been raped when she was young, and that you also have a sister out there somewhere. Chrissie didn't even know how she would have handled it if the shoe was on the other foot. But she did have the week off from work, so perhaps they could spend some prime time together as mother and daughter. Talk things over with her, try and put it all into perspective. Chrissie herself was going into town to try and get a pair of shoes for the wedding. She already had a plum dress in the wardrobe that she thought was okay to wear for Freddie's wedding, so she just needed a pair of black shoes to go with it. Natasha was coming over for the day on Wednesday, so hopefully it would be a warm autumn day, and they could both relax out in the garden. If not they would go into the village for lunch. Whatever they felt like doing at the time.

It was two days later before Daisy said anymore about the conversation she'd had with her mother on the Sunday night. Chrissie had tried bringing it up a couple of times, but Daisy had just brushed it off, saying that it was all in the past now.

Chrissie was speaking to Jake on the phone, he had phoned to see how she was. When he had last seen her she had been down in the dumps and he wanted to know if the time off was doing her good. He told her that everything was okay at work, but he was missing her being there. A couple of the girls were trying it on with Dawn. "Usual thing when the boss is off," he'd laughed down the phone at her. Then asked her if she was free on Friday night to go out for a quiet drink. She thought for a moment, did she really want to get involved again? Then turned around and saw Daisy sat there with a long face, and said yes, she would love to meet up with him. She really needed cheering up. Coming off the phone, she felt brighter than she had done for awhile now, and was pleased she had said yes to Jake.

Daisy had thought hard on whether or not she was going to speak to her mother about what she had on her mind. In truth, she would rather leave it, pretend that the conversation that she had with her mother the other night didn't happen. But as she saw her walking through the hallway towards her, she decided there and then that she would sit down and talk to her. Chrissie followed her into the dining area, sitting down opposite her on the rocking chair that looked out onto the garden. Her favourite place. Daisy had worked out what she was going to say to her mother, and had to say it now before she lost her nerve.

Clearing her throat, and avoiding Chrissie's eyes, she said very calmly. "I want to try and trace my sister, Mum."

Chrissie's hands clenched together so tight, that her knuckles went white. This was just what she'd been dreading. Her daughter wanting to find her sister.

"Will you help me? I'll understand if it's too painful for you. But that's what I want to do, Mum."

If Chrissie's heart beat any faster, it was going to burst right through her ribs. She didn't want Daisy looking for her sister. She didn't want the child that she had conceived through a vile rape coming into her life. Daisy had no right to ask that of her mother. Chrissie got up and opened up the doors into the garden, staring out, her mind was in a turmoil. She could feel Daisy's eyes boring into the back of her, waiting for an answer. God, when was all of this ever going to go away? Then, after a long pause, Chrissie turned towards her daughter, stemming the tears that were fighting to flow. She went over to her and took hold of her hand, squeezing it tightly, swallowing back the tears as she forced a smile on her face.

"I think, Daisy, that we have to wait for her to contact us, and that's only if she ever wants to. She is probably very happy living with her family, or even married by now with children of her own." Chrissie was looking into Daisy's eyes, and she could see that she was struggling with this. The next moment she suddenly jumped up and went out into the kitchen, leaving her mother behind feeling emotionally drained. Chrissie stepped out into the garden, looking up into the clear sky. The stars were out in force tonight, not a cloud in sight. She breathed in the chilled air. As much as she had not wanted to, she had often thought of that small baby that she had given away. Especially when her birthdays came around. Wondering what she looked like. But as her life had moved on, the memory of it all began to fade, and it had got easier for Chrissie to push it into the background. But she had never forgotten her, and she never would. And if her child did come searching for her, she would try very hard to let her into her life.

It seemed an age before Daisy came back into the room. She stood watching her mother for awhile out in the garden, her cheeks stained with tears.

"You're probably right, Mum," she finally said, brushing her own tears aside as she went out to her. "But I want you to promise me something."

Chrissie turned around smiling weakly at her, letting out a sigh of relief as Daisy put her arm around her shoulder.

"You must promise me that if she ever does get in touch with you... You will tell me!"

Chrissie was so drained of emotions that she only just about had the strength to drag herself up the stairs. That bastard was still out there. All the abusive phone calls were from him, she just knew it. A voice from the past had finally come back to haunt her. She flopped down onto the bed, biting hard down on her lip as bitter tears escaped from her eyes. "If ever I come across him again, I will kill him with my own bare hands," she whispered into her pillow.

After a restless night, Chrissie was up with the larks, and had cooked herself and Daisy a breakfast of bacon and eggs. Daisy had an early start at uni today, and Natasha was coming around to see her, so she was feeling in a much brighter mood this morning. She turned around and smiled at Daisy as she came into the kitchen, she didn't even have to call her down this morning. She had smelt the cooking of bacon wafting up the stairs, and was out of bed and down like a shot as Chrissie served it up on the plates. Last night had seemed to have cleared the air a little, but things were still a bit tense between them, however, Chrissie hoped this would soon pass, and they could get back to where they were before she had told her about her about her sordid past. As Daisy went to go out the back door to collect her bike from the shed, she told her mother that she would be home a bit later today, as she was going back to Jasmine's house for awhile after uni. She was cycling to uni today, meeting Jasmine on the way. They had decided last night when they were talking on the phone, that they would ride instead of taking the bus. Daisy had said that she needed to do some exercise as she was putting on weight around her waistband, joking that it was the handlebars on a bike she wanted to hold on to, not the ones around her waist.

After Daisy had left, Chrissie cleared away the breakfast things, and tidied up around the cottage before Natasha arrived. She tutted as she heard Marmalade outside of the front door, meowing to be let in. She really was going to have to get another cat flap put on so he could get in and out by himself. But she just hadn't found the time to get around to doing it. As she opened up the door to him, Marmalade flew straight in between her legs, and over to his feeding bowl in the kitchen. "Hmm, and good morning to you," Chrissie said, looking around outside at the dahlia's that were growing along the side of the driveway. They were almost out in flower, and would be a wonderful splash of colour when out in full bloom. As she was just about to close the door, something from out the corner of her eye caught her. Over by her Mini, there was a plastic bag stood against the wheel. She thought that was strange, seeing as it wasn't there last night when she went to lock the car. Going over to pick it up, she looked inside of the bag, gasping as she jumped back, turning around in a full circle to see if she could see anyone. Inside of the bag was the cat flap that had been ripped off her door. After making sure there was no one watching her, she rushed back indoors, taking the bag inside with her, locking the door and pulling the bolt across. She couldn't believe her eyes as she looked in the bag again, but there was no mistaking it. It was her old cat flap. Her hands were shaking as she dropped the bag onto the floor, walking slowly through into the kitchen. She made herself a strong mug of coffee to help calm herself down before phoning the police. She had been unable to talk to Tom because he was off duty that day. But when she gave them her name and address, they brought up her file on to their computer screen, and knew straight away the details of her case. Chrissie told them about the cat flap that she had just found in a plastic bag, leaning against the wheel of her Mini in the driveway. They told her that they would send someone round for it, and not to touch it as it would be examined for fingerprints when they got it back to the station.

Unbeknown to Chrissie, she had had a late night visitor prowling around her cottage last night. Stewart was enjoying himself, putting the fear of God into her. He would make her pay for keeping his daughter from him, and especially for letting another man think she was his daughter. He knew all about the wedding next week, and that Chrissie and Daisy would be there. You didn't stay in a small village without picking up on all the gossip from where you drank at a local watering hole. He had placed the cat flap by her precious Mini just to let her know that he was still out there…. Biding his time. "Bringing the police in, Bitch, will not help you," he'd sneered… "Soon, very soon. You and I are going to meet up."

CHAPTER NINE

"For God's sake, Chrissie, come and help me," Natasha yelled out from the garden.

Chrissie looked around her. She was deadheading her daisies that had been flowering since April, and were now beginning to look a bit sad. But if she smartened them up a bit, they would carry on flowering for her until the first frost arrived. Well, that was her physiology of it anyhow. All that plants needed was a little bit of love and attention to keep them going. Just the same as us humans.

Again Nats yelled out for her. "For Christ sake, Chrissie, come over here and help me now."

Tutting, Chrissie put her secateurs down, and wandered off down the garden towards the sound of the cursing that was coming from one of the bushes. As she approached the bush, she took one look at her friend, who was bent over under the rose bush, swearing like a trooper, and burst out laughing.

"What bloody kept you?" she cursed again, hanging onto Scamp who was struggling to get away. Nats had brought Scamp over with her today as a treat for him. He loved coming over to Chrissie's because she always spoiled him with tidbits that he wasn't allowed at home.

"What the hell have you done now?" Chrissie asked, clapping her hands together at the sight of her backside jutting out of the bush. When she didn't get up, Chrissie went over to her thinking that she had put her back out.

"Your bloody rose bush has attacked me. Get me out," She screamed, hanging onto Scamp with all of her life.

"Well that will teach you for going under it," Chrissie said, still laughing as she eased away the thorny branch that was attached to her back. "And why the hell did you dive into it in the first place?" She helped her out still sniggering as she took Scamp from her grasp. "Poor doggy," she said, kissing his head as he jumped down from out of her arms, scampering back up to the cottage as fast as he could, where it was safe away from these two mad human beings.

Natasha was still pulling out the thorns from her jumper as they sipped on a glasses of wine to get over the excitement of her being stuck in the rose bush.

"If he goes under another bloody bush chasing after Marmalade, he can stay there. Stupid mutt," she moaned on, as she tried threading back through a snag on the sleeve of her jumper. Chrissie felt so much better for the laughter, and thanked god she had a friend that was so much fun to be with when they were together. As they sat there relaxing, Natasha thought it was a good time to say what was on her mind. She had hardly slept last night worrying about Chrissie and Daisy being on their own, while that maniac was out there prowling around somewhere.

"You know, Chrissie, I'm really worried at the thought of you and Daisy being here on your own, while that maniac is still out there somewhere." She paused to take another sip of her wine, then shushed Chrissie with her finger going up to her lips. "No. Let me finish. Come and stay with me for awhile. You can get to work just as easy from my place, and Daisy can get to uni.

As you say, she only has a few more weeks there and she's finished hasn't she?" Chrissie opened up her mouth to answer her, but Natasha wasn't finished with her yet.

"And besides, it would be great to have you both for awhile, I talk so much to the animals, that I've almost forgotten how to hold a conversation with human beings," she laughed, punching her playfully on the arm "But joking aside, Chrissie, you can bring Marmalade along with you, too. I am worried something dreadful will happen. Especially now you have told me about this latest episode."

Chrissie got up and went over to her, giving her a hug. "What would I do without you," she said, pouring herself some more wine, then refilling Natasha's as she held her glass out to her. "For a start, Nats, nobody is going to drive me out of my home. And least of all that bastard." Then she told her that she had had a long talk with Daisy the other night. Telling her about her past life. About the sister that she had never met. About Daisy having a talk to her about the sister she has never met. Natasha took in a deep breath. She knew that could not have been easy for either of them. Then Chrissie told her that things had changed between them since then, and sadly, things were not the same. But they were gradually getting there.

"Of course you'll both get there, darling. As you say, it's going to take time. Daisy is a great girl. She'll come around soon," Natasha said, wrapping her arms around Chrissie. "It's just that I thought you would be both safer away from the cottage for awhile. But I know what you mean. I wouldn't be driven out of my home either. But just be careful. And you phone me whatever time of the day or night it is if you are in trouble. And you know the offer of staying with me will still stand."

Over the next couple of days Chrissie had done just what she wanted to. She had really enjoyed having time to herself. Going shopping in Thatcham, where she bought herself a new outfit to wear when she went out with Jake. He had called her again insisting that he picked her up from the cottage, and he wouldn't take no for an answer. He was taking her to a place out of town, so it would be silly to take two cars, and anyhow, it was on the way to where they were going. So she had given in, sending caution to the wind, saying she would be ready by seven o'clock.

She wore the pair of jeans and a pink cashmere jumper with a cowl neck that she had brought from a boutique in Thatcham, and was just struggling to get into a pair of black boots when Daisy came into the bedroom, asking her where she was going tonight. She told her she didn't know, but Jake was picking her up, and they were going for a drink somewhere. "That's nice," she said, and had meant it. It was about time that her mother had a social life outside of her work, instead of just coming home and spending her time in the garden hunting slugs down and talking to the flowers. Chrissie had gone over and given her a hug. They were gradually getting back to where they were. Thank God. Daisy said that Jasmine was coming over for the night and might stay, if that was okay? Which of course it was, Chrissie was pleased that she would have Jasmine here with her while she was out.

Jake arrived at the door ten minutes early, ringing the doorbell and wondering why there was a black piece of polythene tacked over a hole in the door, but didn't think anymore of it as the door was opened up, and Daisy, who was smiling at him, asked him to come in, showing him through into the lounge. Chrissie was still upstairs finishing off her make-up, and hadn't heard him arrive. But Daisy was the perfect hostess, offering him a drink, which he declined, saying he was the chauffeur for the night, which had really impressed Daisy. Looking around the lounge as he sat waiting for Chrissie to appear, he smiled at all the china dolls she had around the room, with teddy bears of all sizes scattered here and there. Chrissie had never come across to him as being a 'girly' sort of person. But the room looked warm and cosy, with the walls painted in a light green emulsion, and a large canvas picture hung over the fireplace that had a red poppy painted in oils on it, set in a middle of a field somewhere. "Very tastily done," he'd thought, as Daisy excused herself, saying that her mother wouldn't be long. Jake smiled at her, she didn't look anything like her mother, he thought, except for her long slender legs and her smile. While he waited for Chrissie to come down, he got up and took a look around the cottage. She had a lovely countrified kitchen, with a wooden table stood in the middle of it and four matching chairs that had cushions with cats embroidered on them. Stood against one of the walls was a large welsh dresser, filled up with plates and cups and saucers that were hung on hooks. And on the smaller of the walls, there was a cuckoo clock. He went through into the open dining area that overlooked the garden. He peered out of the patio doors, and was amazed at the sight he saw. There were roses growing everywhere, and were still flowering even though it was nearly at the end of September. And in the middle of the lawn stood a weeping willow with a bed of colourful plants around it. Further on down the garden he could see a couple of trees, but couldn't make out what they were in the half-light. "She works hard in her garden," he thought, turning around to go back into the lounge.

"Sorry to have kept you waiting," Chrissie said, as she appeared in the doorway smiling. She could see that she had caught him on the hop as he looked sheepishly across at her. Daisy had said she had left him in the lounge, so he had gotten up to have a bit of a nose around. But she didn't let on, and apologised to him for not being ready.

"I was early," he said, going over to her and kissing her on the cheek.

She stepped back blushing, she wasn't expecting him to do that. But it felt good all the same. Jake smiled as he ran his eyes down over her, thinking how sexy she looked.

"You look nice," he said, as Chrissie took his arm to go, still blushing.

She shouted up the stairs to Daisy that she wouldn't be that late back. Jake had smiled at that comment, knowing that was for his ears as well. As he helped her into the Jeep he was driving that evening, they didn't see the shadow that was lurking behind the edge.

"It's time for me to make a move, bitch," Stewart cursed as he watched them disappear out of the driveway. "Have fun with your man tonight, Rosie love. Because very soon…"

****

"Nothing changes, does it?" Chrissie laughed as her bleep went off just as she'd got in to work after having her week off.

"Welcome back to the madhouse," Shelly laughed. "We missed you, and I think that could be Janie bleeping you. She's got an awkward customer. Came in yesterday, and was not happy that she didn't have her usual room. But she didn't book until a couple of days ago, so the room she normally had was already booked out. So best of luck."

Luke waved across the foyer to her, raising his eyes to the ceiling. "She had my night porter up and down for the best part of the evening," he said going over to her. "She's being a right pain in the ass," he laughed. Then he remembered that she had just come back from being off for a week. "Hope you enjoyed your holiday," he laughed, answering his bleep that was going.

"What holiday!" Chrissie tutted. "Two minutes back here and I've forgotten that I've been off," she grinned, getting into the lift.

122

Chrissie had looked forward to getting back to work. The week that she'd had off had just flown by, but at least she had been able to catch up on all the things that she'd not had time to do when she'd been working. But now it was time to get back to work and earn some more pennies to live on.

Jake had waved to her as she got into the lift, her cheeks flushed remembering the evening they had spent together. It had been heaven. He had treated her like a lady, taking her to a very old pub in the country. She had caught up with all of the news from work, and had fell about laughing when Jake had told her that Curly Whirl had gone back to being a chamber man for a day. Dawn apparently had phoned down to him, telling him that two of the girls had phoned in sick, and that she had over half of the hotel departing that day, with most of the rooms being re-booked. So Curly Whirl had come to the rescue, so to speak, and gone up on to the floors to help. But the only problem was, he had put his linen trolley into the guest lift instead of the staff lift. Which was a no-go area for staff with trolleys! He said that he had waited for over five minutes for it to come so he could get his trolley in to get up on to the floors. But when it didn't arrive, he went through to the front of the hotel, and got into the guest lift, thinking that he could get up on to his floor before anyone saw him. But it was just his bad luck that one of the wheels got stuck in the ridge of the door. Chrissie's eyes widened as Jake carried on telling her that all hell let loose, as an hour past by as they waited for the maintenance man to come from the lift company to release the wheel that had got jammed. Mr Grey had almost a nervous breakdown, asking when she was due back at work. Poor Curly Whirl really had the mickey taken out of him. But the girls rallied around once again to his rescue, by helping him out with the rooms that he was way behind with after the hour's delay. The rest of the evening they had made small talk, and Chrissie said no to another glass of wine that Jake had offered to get for her. She was feeling the effect from all the wine that she had already drank, her head was feeling light, and she was giggling a lot, a sure sign that she was on her way to being merry. But when the hiccups started with the last glass of wine, she knew she had consumed enough wine for that evening, and needed to go home. Jake had been the perfect gentleman, helping her on with her jacket, and guiding her out to the Jeep. He was smiling to himself as she hiccuped, giggling to herself. He hadn't seen Chrissie this inebriated before, and she was fun to be with. But he had noticed that she had been very quiet on the journey to where they were going, noticing that her eyes were peeled to the window as they went out onto the main road. It was as though she was looking for someone. When they got to the Old Inn, he was going to mention it to her, but as the evening went on, he had forgotten all about it.

When he had walked her up to the door, she had turned and said that she'd had a wonderful… hiccup… evening, and had kissed him on his cheek. Jake could see that she wasn't going to invite him in. It was almost midnight, and he didn't want to push it. Also Daisy would probably be listening out for her mother to get in. But he did take her in his arms, and kissed her firmly on the lips, that took her breath away. "I want us to do this again, Chrissie," he said, kissing her again before she could say anything. Then making sure that she was safely through the door, he left, smiling to himself as he went back to the Jeep, still hearing those hiccups in his ear.

How Chrissie had slept that night she'll never know, probably passed out on the bed! But the next morning she was still tingling from his kiss and knew that she wanted more.

She went to her office before going up to see Janie on the seventh floor. She needed to know the name of the guest and the room number she was in. As she went to bleep her, she saw Simon coming out of the linen room with his arms bursting with linen. She banged on the window making him jump, as she pointed to the linen that he was struggling to carry in his arms.

"Oh God. The witch is back," he said, tossing his eyes up at Daphne. "And she's caught me red-handed," he grinned, going over to the office as Chrissie noted down the room 606, and the name of the guest, who was a Mrs Jacobs. She told Janie that she would be up in five minutes. "I've just got something to sort out first," she said, frowning across at Simon.

"Hello, darling." Simon walked across to her, planting a kiss on her cheek before she could start nagging him for taking too much table linen. "Did you enjoy your time off? I missed you, darling."

"I bet you did," she said, pushing him away playfully. "How much linen have you got there?" Then looked across at Daphne, winking at her. "Morning, Daphne. Have you taken note of what he's taking?" she asked, winking again.

"Oh for God's sake, Chrissie, give yourself a chance to get back in before you start worrying about the poxy linen," Simon tutted, striding away from her. "I'll see you later, after you've had your coffee," he said, tossing his eyes up again at Daphne as he went down the back stairs to his office, chuckling under his breath. If Chrissie saw what he had stored in his cupboard for emergencies, he'd be in deep trouble.

As Chrissie got out of the lift on the six floor, she saw Maria, one of her chambermaids, who had been with her for a few years now. She was Spanish by birth, but had come over to England when she was just six years old, and had always classed herself as being English, even though her parents had returned to their homeland years ago. Chrissie said good morning to her, asking her how she was. Maria smiled, saying that she'd missed her, asking her if she had enjoyed her week off. Chrissie raised her eyes to the ceiling.

125

"What week off?" she tutted. "It seems as though I've not been away." Maria laughed, saying it was good to see her back as she took a clean sheet from her trolley, then going back into the room she was servicing, humming to herself. Maria was a happy soul most of the time. But if you happened to cross her on a bad day, she could cut you dead with one look. As Chrissie had found out many times. Making her way along to room 606 to see Mrs Jacobs, she smiled remembering when Maria and the other chambermaids were bringing their room keys back to the office before going off duty. Dawn was hanging them up on the hooks in the office, when Maria had sneezed loudly, making everyone jump, followed by her top dentures flying across the office floor. At first there was a ghastly silence, when everyone just looked at each other. Then, as Maria bent down to retrieve them from off the office floor, she went into a fit of giggles, where everyone ended up with a stitch in their sides from laughing so much. It was the closest that Chrissie had ever been from losing control of her bladder, as she laughed along with them, crossing her legs. She waved to Janie who was coming along the corridor to meet her. She told her about Mrs Jacobs not being happy with her room, and was now demanding to be moved. Chrissie asked exactly what was she complaining about, and Janie told her that she had been a pain in the ass since she'd arrived yesterday.

Chrissie asked her again. "Exactly what doesn't she like about the room?"

Janie clicked her tongue in annoyance. "She has said that the room is filthy."

'FILTHY,' Chrissie repeated. Louder than she had intended to do. But that was one word you did not use to a housekeeper if you wanted to stay alive.

Chrissie knocked on the bedroom door. Her hairs were already bristling on the back of her neck as Mrs Jacobs let her into the room. The first thing that she caught sight of was the bed. It had been stripped back to the mattress, plus all of the drawers had been pulled out, and before she could say a word, Mrs Jacobs was at her. Ranting on like a lunatic about the state the mattress was in. In the left-hand corner was a small stain, that Chrissie had to screw her eyes up to see. Then she pointed out a thin layering of dust on the skirting board behind the bed. Chrissie pulled her glasses down from the top of her head so she could see it. It was so minute! What a sad person she must be to have nothing to worry about in her life than to pick holes out of a hotel bedroom. It was a wonder that she hadn't put her back out pulling the bed away from the wall. Then to top it all, she pointed out a small hair lodged in the back of a drawer!

"So. What are you going to do about it?" she asked Chrissie, after coming up for air. Chrissie noticed that Mr Jacobs was standing out on the balcony, smoking a cigarette. He didn't seem to want to get involved while his wife was letting off steam.

Chrissie gave Mrs Jacobs a friendly smile, while all she wanted to do right now was to tell her to piss off home. But she couldn't do that. It would be more that her job's worth. She could just see Mr Grey now. Giving her her marching orders, as he reminded her that, "The customer is always right." Yeah right! So she calmed herself down, and told Mrs Jacobs that she would send Maria in straight away to thoroughly clean her room. But oh no. She wasn't having any of it, demanding that she wanted to be moved to another room straight away, and to make sure that it was up to a four-star standard. As advertised. Chrissie knew from the start that's what this was all about. She was just nit-picking because she wasn't in the room that she usually stayed in. So biting her tongue, Chrissie was just about to give in to her, and go down to see Shelly in reception to see if they could get her moved to another room, when Mrs Jacobs used that fatal word.

"And the room is FILTHY," she spat out.

Now Chrissie's feathers were ruffled. "The room is not filthy," she said as calmly as she could, holding her arms down stiffly by her side before she belted her one. "I will get Maria along to attend to the things you have pointed out to me. But I'm sorry, the hotel is full, and there is not a room to move you into."

Mrs Jacobs had gone so purple in the face as Chrissie was saying this to her, that she thought she was going to burst a vein in her forehead, as it swelled up beating against her temple. Chrissie left before she could say any more. But as she closed the door behind her, she overheard Mr Jacobs telling her to shut the fuck up.

When she got back down into reception, she found Jake speaking to Shelly, asking if Mrs Jacobs could be moved to another room. From the time it had taken her to get back down to reception, Mrs Jacobs had phoned down to speak to a manager.

"Guess who's just rang down asking to be moved?" Shelly said to Chrissie, raising her eyes to the ceiling.

"I wipe my hands of it all," Chrissie said, barging out of reception and over to the lift. "I have more important things to do than to run around on a neurotic woman."

The rest of the day went by with no more hiccups, and Chrissie managed to get some lunch with Jake and Shelly. They didn't move Mrs Jacobs in the end. Shelly told Chrissie that she wouldn't have dared move her after her outburst in reception this morning. "My outburst," Chrissie said, looking outraged as Jake kept his head down, he wasn't getting involved. But he did have a grin plastered across his face. Shelly finished her lunch, and went back to work, leaving Jake and Chrissie to finish off their coffees. She knew that there was something going on between them, and gave Chrissie a knowing look as she got up, winking at her. Chrissie scowled back at her, kicking her foot as she got up. It was a warning for her not to embarrass her.

"I really enjoyed the other night," Jake said, moving in close to her. "Can we do it again soon? Like this weekend?"

"I have the wedding to go to on Saturday."

Jakes face fell. Damn, he'd forgotten all about the wedding.

"But I'm not staying on for the evening reception," she added, smiling across at him as she got up to leave.

"Good, so shall I pick you up at seven?"

"To go where?"

"Oh, I don't know, where would you like to go? Out for a meal?"

Chrissie thought for a moment. She would be eating in the afternoon at the reception, so she wasn't going to be that hungry later on. "Shall we stay in?" She smiled. "I'll do a light meal, and we could relax after with some good music and chilled wine."

His face lit up, then laughed at her as she reminded him that it was just food and drink they were having between good friends! "Whatever," he said, squeezing her hand.

CHAPTER TEN

They both made a scramble for the bathroom this morning, with Chrissie just beating her daughter to the post, laughing as she told her that she needed to go first, because it was going to take her longer to get ready filling in all of her wrinkles. Daisy hadn't argued with that, poking her tongue out as she sauntered back to her bedroom. It was Freddie's wedding today, and there was a nip in the air this morning, but at least it wasn't raining. They were both keeping their fingers crossed that the sun would come out from behind the clouds in time for the wedding. They had to be at the church for two o'clock, and it was now eleven o'clock, so they had plenty of time to go before Patsie, who was an old friend of Chrissie and Freddie's, picked them up. She had offered to take them seeing as she would be passing by where they lived. So it wouldn't be out of her way to swing into the lane down to the cottage. She was also staying on for the evening reception, and had offered to bring Daisy home, which was good because she would have had to have taken a taxi, the same as Chrissie was going to after the speeches were over. But when Jake had heard of this, he had insisted on picking her up. As they were spending the evening together, it worked out well, plus it would save Chrissie the taxi fare of getting home from Brownlie, where the wedding was being held in the next village down from hers.

Daisy came into her mother's bedroom, doing a twirl for her. "What do you think? The dress doesn't look too tight does it?" she asked, smoothing it down over her knees.

Chrissie looked at her daughter who was twirling around the room, looking absolutely gorgeous. Where had her little girl gone, with the dark brown ringlets, and dimples in her cheeks that melted Freddie's heart every time she smiled at him? She could always twist him around her little finger when she wanted something from him. "You look delightful," Chrissie beamed. "And your jacket and those stiletto-heeled shoes finish it off. Let's hope there are some handsome bachelors at your dad's wedding," she teased.

"Mother, don't you dare try matchmaking me off with anybody."

Chrissie got up and did a twirl for Daisy. "What do you think?"

Daisy took in how attractive her mother still was. She had her long blonde hair flicked back into a bun at the back of her head, with tendrils of curls around her face, accentuating her large blue eyes. She had an hourglass figure, and long shapely legs, that looked great in the black wedged shoes she was wearing.

"Well?" she said, waiting for Daisy to say something. "Do you think the dress is too plain? I can dress it up with a black silk scarf that I have."

"Mother, you look really good for your age," Daisy laughed. "Now come on, Patsie will be here soon."

"Well thanks very much," she tutted, turning to look at herself in the mirror. She put her face up close, sighing as she tried pulling the skin back from around her face to see how she'd look without the creases around her mouth. "Mmm, a facelift is needed soon," she sighed, shutting the bedroom door behind her as she heard Daisy calling for her to come down.

Patsie was dead on time, making a fuss of seeing Daisy again. She hadn't seen her for awhile now, and she couldn't get over how she had shot up. She told her that she looked just like her father. But was beautiful just like her mother, smiling up at Chrissie as she came down the stairs. She said hello, kissing her on the cheek, saying how great it was to see her again after all of this time. They all managed to get into the old Morris Minor that was Patsie's pride and joy, and they laughed at Daisy struggling to get into the back of the car. They arrived at the church ten minutes early, but there were a few people already there. Some of them Chrissie knew from the old days, but Freddie and herself had both moved on since they had separated, and both had a different set of friends now. Daisy also knew a few of her father's friends, meeting them when she had visited his place. She got on well with Jackie, his wife-to-be, and thought that they were well matched. Chrissie also liked her. She was good for him. He had calmed down a lot. Jackie seemed to have a calming effect on him. Perhaps he was keeping his stick of rock tucked well into his trousers now he was getting older! Chrissie had also calmed down with age, she wasn't so fiery these days. Not that her daughter thought that. Eccentric was what she called her. But Chrissie was okay with that. It was amazing what you could get away with when people thought you were a bit odd!

They took a pew about three rows back in the church. It was already quite full, and Daisy and Chrissie nodded their heads at the people they knew, smiling as they settled into their seats. Freddie was already waiting with Harold, his best man, turning and smiling at them both as they'd walked down the aisle, blowing Daisy a kiss. He looked very handsome in his dark green suit, with a red carnation pinned to his lapel, matched with a snowy white silk shirt and a handkerchief that was tucked in his top pocket. "Not something I would have chosen for him,"

Chrissie thought, as Daisy said how smart her father looked. Which of course Chrissie replied yes to. Jackie arrived ten minutes late. It was the first time for her to walk down the aisle with the church organ echoing around the church playing 'Here Comes The Bride'. And she looked stunning, wearing a beautiful ivory dress that clung into her slim waistline, with the skirt gradually flaring out down on to the tip of her ivory silk shoes. She was holding a bouquet of red roses that trailed down over the skirt. Walking behind her came the two bridesmaids dressed in lime green. Again they both looked stunning, carrying a posy of red and ivory carnations, with green silk flowered tiara's in their hair. Freddie had asked Daisy if she had wanted to be one of the bridesmaids. But for some reason she didn't want to, even though Chrissie had tried to talk her into it. But at the end of the day, it was down to her.

Back at the reception that was being held in the village hall, all of the tables were set up with crisp white tablecloths, with a single red carnation held in a rose stem vase placed in the middle of all the tables. Chrissie and Daisy searched around for their nameplates to see where they were sitting. They were sharing the table with old friends which Chrissie was relieved about, and it was non stop chatter as they ate their food of melon wrapped in parma ham for starters, followed on by wellington beef, served with fresh broccoli and carrots, and new potatoes, finished off by a fresh fruit salad. The wine was plentiful, as one bottle was emptied, another one was placed on the table. So it was a good job that Chrissie was eating as well as drinking. At least the food would hopefully balance the intake of the wine she was drinking and she wouldn't end up with hiccups all afternoon.

The speeches had taken longer that Chrissie had expected them to be, and by the time she had said goodbye to everybody, and checked that Daisy still had a lift home with Patsie, and by the time she got out of the hall and looked at her watch, it was gone seven o'clock already, and it was just starting to get dusk.

She searched around in her handbag looking for her mobile to switch back on, and saw that she had a message from Jake. She was hoping that he was still able to pick her up. But when she listened to the message, he was telling her that he had been delayed at work, something to do with the night porter not turning up, so he would have stay on at work until he could sort it out. He said he felt terrible for letting her down, and God help the bloody night porter when he did eventually turn up. But as soon as he could get away, he would drive to the cottage to see her. Chrissie was disappointed, but she knew all about working in the hotel. It wasn't a nine to five job. If something went wrong then you had to stay behind and sort it before you went off duty. She looked up the local taxi number from her phone book, and asked if she could be taken to Rose-Moor lane as soon as possible. As she waited for the taxi to arrive, she sat on the bench outside of the hall, listening to the music that was just starting up. It was a beautiful evening even though it was just starting to get chilly. When the taxi turned up, she told him where to go, asking him to drop her at the top of the lane. She wanted to get some fresh air and stretch her legs, so she'd walk slowly down to the cottage. She had been inside all day, and the fresh air would be good for her.

Paying the taxi driver, she said goodnight to him, and took in a breath of fresh air, feeling better already as her head started to clear of all the wine she had drunk at the reception. As she got halfway down the lane, she stopped to look at the black-faced sheep that were still grazing on the grass before settling down for the night. She could just see their woolly white coats under the quarter moon that had raised its head into the sky. It was so peaceful around there that you could of heard a pin drop. She was so lucky to be living where she was, and hoped that she would always be able to rent the lovely cottage she lived in forever. As she walked around the slight bend that was almost on her driveway, she stopped abruptly as she heard footsteps coming from behind her. She swung around, expecting to see a neighbour from one of the other cottages taking an evening stroll. But there was no one there. Shaking her head, she carried on walking, putting a spurt in her step. She wanted to get indoors and kick her shoes off, and have time to relax with a coffee before Jake arrived. But just as she went to turn into her driveway, a hand went over her mouth from behind her, dragging her into the field opposite the cottages. As she was flung down on to the ground with such force, it took her breath away. She started to struggle, kicking out her feet, but it was of no use. The person who was knelt down beside her was much stronger than she was.

"Hello, Rosie,"

Chrissie's eyes widened. Her attacker could see the fear in them, as he smiled evilly at her. There was only one person who would call her by that name! And she would know that voice from the past anywhere. "Stewart," she managed to mumble behind his rough hand.

"I'm going to take my hand slowly away," he said, pulling her up on to her feet so she was standing face to face with him. "But if you scream out…… I'll kill you," he snarled, shaking her so hard by the shoulders that she could hear her teeth rattle He could see her whole body shaking as he stepped in closer to her. Asking her if she'd enjoyed the wedding. When he saw the surprised look on her face, he smirked, stepping in closer again, until his nose was almost touching hers. She flinched back away from him as she smelt the drink on his breath.

"Oh my God, he's been watching me," She shuddered, trying hard to pull herself together. She must not show him that she was afraid. He would only feed off it.

"So you've finally showed your face," she said, sounding much braver than she felt. "Got bored with the phone calls and sneaking around, have you?" Chrissie didn't know where she was

135

getting all this bravery from. But she knew that if she was to weaken now, he would pounce on her, and she needed to know what he wanted from her.

"What do you want from me, Stewart? What could I possibly have that you would want?" She didn't see the hand come up that landed hard across her face, knocking her backwards against a tree that saved her from falling.

"You bitch. Don't play with me," he sneered. "You know what I want," he spat out at her between gritted teeth. Prodding her with his finger.

Chrissie wished to God right now that she hadn't drunk so much wine. She was really racking her brains trying to think of what he wanted from her after all these years. Surely he knew that she would go straight to the police, and he would then be arrested and thrown back into jail. But he would know already that she had reported him to the police if he had been watching her all of this time.

"Well?" he said, clenching his teeth together, rolling his hand up into a fist.

"For Christ sake, Stewart, I don't know what you want from me," she said as loud as she could. Praying that somebody would hear her from one of the cottages.

He slapped his hand over her mouth again, and she could taste the blood as her lip split open from the force of it.

"I want to see my daughter, BITCH."

Chrissie started to shake from head to tail now. She was scared. And if it wasn't for the tree behind her, she would have collapsed to the ground. He was asking to see the daughter that she had given away. "Please, please wake me up from this nightmare," she pleaded silently to herself, shivering as he moved in closer again. God, if only Jake would come along now.

136

"I'm going to give you two minutes to tell me about my daughter, and if you haven't filled me in by then, I'm going to beat your brains out, bitch."

She could see by the glaze in his eyes that he had lost it. She was going to have to tell him that she had never seen his daughter because she had given her up for adoption at birth. Swallowing hard as he again took his hand away from her mouth, wiping off the blood from his hand down the front of her dress, lingering his hand on her bust as he leered at her through the glazed eyes. She thought for a moment that her legs were going to give way from under her. She was so frightened that he was going rape her again.

"I d-don't know where your d- daughter is," she stuttered as the tears started to flow from her eyes.

"YOU LIAR," he growled, looking around to make sure that the coast was still clear. He didn't want to be caught roughing her up. He wasn't not going back into prison for this whore.

"I have already met her," he said, watching the alarm spread over Chrissie face. But she still didn't connect that it was Daisy that he had met.

"When did you meet her?" she managed to ask calmly, trying to calm the explosive atmosphere that was built-up between them.

He looked at her swollen lip, thinking that even in this state she was still a looker. He brushed his finger down over her face, tracing around it her lip. She felt sick, pressing herself further back into the tree.

"Don't kid yourself, love. I wouldn't touch you with a barge pole," He sneered, looking her up and down as his steel cold eyes bore into her. He saw a flicker of relief pass over her face. So he leaned into her, lifting her chin up roughly as he banged her head back against the tree trunk. "But I will kill you if you don't tell me all about Daisy."

Her head spun as she tried to control the sheer panic that was running through her veins. "Oh my God… He thinks that Daisy is his daughter." He squeezed his fingers tighter around her chin, pushing her head up so high, that she thought her neck would snap. He then shook her head so hard, that she thought she could feel her brain move inside of it.

"DAISY IS NOT YOUR DAUGHTER," she managed to yell out in sheer terror, as he loosened his grip around her chin so she could speak.

He clapped his hand back over her mouth, and started to violently shake her again, and Chrissie knew that if she didn't get away from him now he was going to kill her. Again his fist came up and he smashed it down into her face, but she somehow managed to turn her head as the blow missed her nose by a fraction of an inch. He had really lost it now. Calling her everything under the sun, but still managing to keep his voice menacingly low so he wouldn't attract any attention if somebody was to walk by. He was threatening her with her life if she didn't tell him the truth. And he said he was going to drag her back to the cottage where they would wait for Daisy to come home from the wedding. Chrissie knew then that she had to somehow calm things down between them. He had obviously been following them today to know that they had been to the wedding. But she was still feeling dazed from that last punch. Her eye was swelling up, and it was almost closed. Then for some reason, Stewart released his grip from around her chin for a few seconds, and somehow, Chrissie mustered up all the strength that she could find to bring her knee up so hard into his groin, that she thought she had lost it up his scrotum as Stewart roared out in pain. He was in so much pain, that liquid started to spew out from his mouth on to the grass, as he rolled over and over. Chrissie ran towards the lane, falling over and then dragging herself up again. Not daring to look back to see if he was coming after her. She used every drop of strength that she had left in her to scream out for help before she finally blacked out, falling face down into a ditch.

It was old Mr Roberts who had found Chrissie lying in the ditch. He was in his kitchen just making a hot drink for himself, when he had heard somebody screaming from outside. He stopped what he was doing, and listened again, but didn't hear anything. So he thought that he would go outside to investigate what was going on. He looked all around the front of his cottage, before walking down the end of his driveway where he looked out along the lane. And that's when he saw Chrissie lying face down in the ditch. Thank God he had had the sense to go and fetch Maggie, who lived in the next cottage down from him for some help. As soon as she had seen Chrissie lying there, she had phoned for an ambulance and the police. She really thought that she was dead. But by the time that the ambulance had got to her, Chrissie was just coming around, and the first face she saw looking down at her was Colin, the same paramedic who had attended to Mrs Leven after her fall in the hotel. For a moment she wondered what he was doing there. Then she remembered, as she went to move. Groaning out in pain as it shot through her body, suddenly realising that she was lying on the cold ground with a blanket thrown over her.

"Hello Chrissie. How are you feeling?" he smiled down at her, gently pushing her back down as she tried to sit up. "Whoa there. Steady sweetheart. Just stay where you are until I've taken a look at those injuries," he said, gently running his hands down over her looking for any breakages.

"I'm not going to hospital," she managed to say, as things were slowly coming back to her of what had happened."

"Alright, Chrissie, just stay still until I've seen what injuries you've received. Then we'll get you moved to somewhere more comfortable."

"Not the hospital," she repeated, before letting out a groan as he moved her jaw to see if it was broken.

"I would be happier if you would just let me get you to the hospital to be checked over for any breakages," Colin was seriously worried about her. But he kept the smile on his face.

She didn't have the strength to argue. But she did ask Colin if he had been caught, meaning Stewart. Colin looked across at Sergeant Noble, who was the policeman that Chrissie knew as Tom. He had dealt with the broken cat flap when Chrissie had reported it missing, and he had also made a visit to the cottage with Carl, who was the other constable with him, checking to see what damage had been done to the door. He was now bent down beside her, wanting to know if the person who had attacked her this evening was the same person who had been pestering her all of these months. She managed to nod her head, asking, in between catching her breath as the pain ripped through her jaw, if they had caught him. Tom had said no, but he had men out there now searching around the fields for him.

"Trust me, love," he said, gently squeezing her hand. "We'll catch him!"

Natasha answered her phone not recognising the number that came up, asking briskly who it was as she shooed Bubbles out of the lounge on the end of her shoe. The little bugger was chewing on one of her house plants again, leaving chewed up leaves all over the floor. Natasha almost drop to the floor when Colin had told her that Chrissie was in hospital, and that she had been attacked. He asked her if she could she get hold of Daisy to let her know where her mother was. Natasha slammed down the phone, gathering all the animals up to the back of the house. Closing the doors to the lounge and dining room, checking that all of the bedroom doors were closed, leaving them some food and water, then running out of the house to fetch Daisy from the wedding reception, where the poor girl was oblivious to what had happened to her mother.

As Chrissie laid back while the nursing team took a look at her injuries, she knew that she would never rest until they had caught Stewart. He was still out there somewhere, deranged and dangerous. Still thinking that Daisy was his daughter. My God, what was she going to do?

CHAPTER ELEVEN

It's over three weeks ago now since Chrissie was attacked by Stewart, and there still had been no sightings of him. She was now back at home after staying for just one night in the hospital, and a few nights with Natasha. She had badgered the poor doctor who was making his rounds around the wards to go home. But really, he would have preferred that she stayed in for another day. But Chrissie really wanted to leave. She just hated hospitals, even the smell of them made her feel ill. So after nagging the poor doctor, which hadn't been easy through swollen lips that were still very painful, he had relented. But only after she had promised to stay with Natasha for a few days until she got her strength back. Thank God there were no bones broken in her face, but she suffered a lot of pain as the bruising came out. Her face had been black and blue for awhile, but now it was fading into yellow patches around her eyes and chin. So after arguing with Natasha and Jake over whether or not she would go back to work next week, she won, even though they were not talking to her right now. (But they both still phoned her every day to see how she was!) She was going back to work, and that was that. She would cover up the remaining bruises with her make-up.

Chrissie had finally ended up staying with Natasha for a week after coming out of hospital. She was much weaker than she thought she'd be, so was really grateful for her friends support. Natasha had told her she would have to take it easy.

"You're just getting over from one hell of a beating, and it's going to take some time for you to heal. Let alone run." she said, waving her finger at her. So Chrissie promised her that she would take it easy. But she wanted Natasha to go back to work. She was quite capable of getting around the house in her own time. And she would be well protected with all of the animals around her. Natasha looked at Scamp, who would run a mile if you said "Boo" to him, and then at Bubbles, Rosie and Marmalade! Two cats and a rabbit..... Well, maybe... So after Chrissie had managed to reassure her that she would be okay, Natasha gave in and went back to the veterinary practice, where she worked in the reception area looking after the pet owners that brought their sick animals in for treatment. They loved her friendly attitude towards them, always having a smile on her face whatever time of the day it was as she sorted out their next appointments for their beloved pets. She made sure before leaving the house in the mornings that Chrissie understood her instructions that Bubbles, Scamp and Rosie were not allowed in the lounge, especially Bubbles because he would nibble on all of her house plants in there. Daisy had stayed at Natasha's with Chrissie for a couple of nights, but then went and stayed with Jasmine, checking with her mother first that she would be okay. It would be easier for her to travel to uni, plus she wanted to put some normality back into her life.

Natasha's house had been full of flowers. Freddie and Jackie had sent her a beautiful bouquet of flowers before going off on their honeymoon, with a message from them that they would come round and see her when they got back. Daisy had told her father about the attack on Chrissie. But how much she had told him, Chrissie didn't know. Some of the flowers were sent by people that Chrissie hardly knew, only mingling with them when she'd stayed behind after the Sunday church service, and they'd had coffee together as they caught up on all of the gossip. (People really surprised her at times.) Even Christian, the vicar from Saint John's, had called round to see her when she was staying at Natasha's. Making her a cup of tea, insisting that she sat down while he made it as she tried to hobble around the kitchen. (She still thought that he was cute.) Mr Grey and the staff had sent a beautiful basket of flowers to her, and Dawn had phoned her saying how sorry she was for what had happened to her, and that she wasn't to worry about work. She would keep the ship running for her until she got back. And even dear Simon had made her laugh after phoning her when she'd got back home. Joking with her to get her ass back as soon as possible, because Dawn was worse than she was with dishing out the linen. Counting out the exact cloths and napkins that he would need for that day, And not one over. "She's bloody worse that you are," he cursed, as she held on to her jaw laughing, telling him to stop making her laugh as it hurt too much. But now it was time to stop feeling sorry for herself. She had to get herself back out there, into the real world. And by going back to work, she would do just that. Vowing to herself that that bastard was not going to ruin her life all over again as he'd done all those years ago. The police had warned her to be more vigilant until they had caught him, saying that they didn't think that he would come back to the cottage. But then added that with someone who was in that state of mind, you would still need to be aware. They had installed an emergency button on her phone so she could just press it if ever she felt threatened, or saw him lurking around the cottage. Putting her straight through to a officer instead of hanging on for somebody to connect her through. Also, if he tried to phone her they would be able to trace the number straight away. But Chrissie knew that until they had caught him, she would have to be on her guard. She knew that Stewart still thought that Daisy was his daughter. He had no idea that Chrissie had given his daughter away at birth.

Daisy, thank God had gone away for a while. Uni had broken up, so she had gone to stay with Jasmine's Aunty Lilly, who lived in Cornwall. She was going to stay for a couple of weeks. Her boss at the solicitors' office told her to take a couple of weeks off after hearing about her mother's ordeal, saying that they would pay her two weeks holiday pay. Daisy had let out a sigh of relief when she heard that. It meant that she could stay with Jasmine's aunty, and have enough money to live on without having to ask her mother for any. Not that Chrissie let her go without putting some money into her bank account. "For emergencies" she told her when she'd found out. It had taken some convincing from Chrissie that she would be quite safe in the cottage without her, even though she was going to miss her like mad. But Jake and Natasha would be in and out, and she would be returning to work with her bruises camouflaged by make-up.

As Chrissie checked the salmon that was steaming on the cooker, the phone rang. She tutted, hurrying out into the hallway to pick up the phone. It was probably Daisy checking that she was okay, and to ask what she had been doing all day. As she picked the phone up she glanced at the time on her watch. Jake would be here any time now, so it would have to be a brief call. She would phone Daisy tomorrow to catch up on everything. When she heard the voice on the other end, she was taken aback. She couldn't quite make out who it was she half recognised the voice, but couldn't put a face to it.

"Who is this?" she asked nervously.

The line went quiet for a few seconds, and Chrissie could feel the fear building up inside of her. She was just about to press the emergency button when somebody spoke.

"Hi Chrissie. It's me, Colin."

"Colin," she repeated, as her heart started to beat again.

"Sorry if I startled you," he said, now feeling a right idiot for not answering her straight away. "But when you answered the phone, it didn't sound like you, and I thought that I'd got the wrong phone number," he laughed. Feeling the tension coming from her down the phone line. "I just thought that I'd phone to see how you are...How are you?"

A smile crept across Chrissie's face as the feeling of relief ran through her. For a moment there she thought that it was one of those phone calls. God she really had to try and take more control of herself. Just because somebody doesn't speak straight away over the phone, it didn't mean that it was Stewart on the other end of it.

"No, no," she laughed, "I didn't recognise your voice either. What a surprise. It's lovely to hear from you."

They spoke on the phone for a time, Colin asking how she was, and how were the bruises on her face now. She said that her face looked like a plucked chicken. And he had laughed, saying that he bet she still looked beautiful. Then Chrissie said that she would have to go because she was expecting somebody to arrive any minute now. Colin then asked her if she would like to meet up for a drink at sometime, and because Chrissie didn't really have time to think about it, she said yes, that would be nice, shaking her head as she came off the phone. She said that she would meet him after work one night in the hotel bar if he was okay with that. She wasn't up to going out anywhere at the moment, and seeing as she was starting work next week, they could meet up one night after she'd finished work. She cursed herself for saying she would meet him as she went through into the kitchen to switch on the greens. She was seeing Jake now, but it was still platonic between them, even though she knew that he would like more. But he wasn't pressing her, and she wasn't ready for any sexual relationships yet. Anyway, Colin was a very attractive man. She remembered seeing his friendly face looking down at her as she came round, finding herself lying down in the ditch. His words comforting her as she lay there in agony. He had visited her at Natasha's, bringing her a large bunch of flowers. Natasha had teased her for days after that. ("He really fancies you, and what a looker. Did you notice his pert bum? And as for his cute ponytail...") Chrissie had to tell her to shut up in the end. She didn't need any man in her life right now, thank you.

Halfway through her glass of wine the doorbell rang. She got up and went to let Jake in, almost tripping over Marmalade as he made a dash through the door into the warm hallway, purring around Jake's legs. Jake kissed Chrissie on the cheek before bending down to stroke Marmalade after handing over a bottle of Chardonnay and a huge bunch of pink Lilies to her that she had smelt even before opening up the door. Marmalade, soon bored of being stroked, went off into the kitchen to find his supper, as Jake followed in behind him, sniffing in the air at the smell of the cooking.

"Mmm, that smells good," he said, standing close behind Chrissie as she struggled to open up the Chardonnay. Smiling, he took it from her, giving her another peck on the cheek. "I'll do that for you," he said, his hand brushing against hers. Chrissie felt a warm glow go through her as she went over to the cooker to check the greens were not being overboiled. There was nothing worse than overboiled broccoli. She showed him through to the dining room, settling him down on the rocking chair with a glass of wine, switching on the outside light so he could look out into the garden while she went back through to the kitchen to serve up the meal. Chrissie could not stand anyone hovering over her when she was serving up food. (Just in case she dropped something, and had to quickly wash it under the tap.)

Jake relaxed with the glass of wine as he looked out on to the garden, thinking of the night that he had turned up at Chrissie's with the police swarming all over the place. It was 9:30

before he had finally got to the cottage to see her. He had just missed the ambulance that took her off to the hospital, although he remembered seeing one passing him at speed along the road just before he got there. When he had driven into the lane, all he saw were police swarming all over the place. They were searching in the fields with bright torches, and out along the lane. At the end of Chrissie's driveway, there were a few people huddled around in a crowd watching the police looking for whatever they were searching for. And even as he drove into Chrissie's driveway and all the faces turned towards him, he had no idea that it had anything to do with her. But he did think at the time it was strange that she wasn't out with the rest of them having a nose. Parking up his Jeep, he was greeted by a six foot policeman, asking him what he was doing there. To say that he went into shock after finding out what had happened to her was an understatement. He had headed straight off to the hospital, where he found Daisy and Natasha waiting in a small room that was just off from the ward where Chrissie was being treated. After hugging both of them, Natasha filled him in on what had happened. Then as they both told him of why it had happened, it sent him into shock once again as he heard about her past life. They sat looking at each other as they sipped on ghastly cups of coffee that Jake had got from the machine that was out in the hallway. Costing £1.20 for a plastic mugful. And the only thing you could say about it was, it was wet and warm… Just! Jake had sat quietly taking in everything that they told him about Stewart, and of who he was. About the obscene phone calls he had made. Even of him going to the cottage and ripping out the cat flap. He couldn't believe his ears. But then he did remember seeing the cat flap missing when he had gone to pick her up to take her out for a drink, but had forgotten to say anything about it to her. "My God," he thought. He had known Chrissie all these years and had had no idea of what she had suffered over the past few months, or of the horror she had been through all those years ago. She had said nothing to anyone, only confiding in Natasha when she had been so desperate for some help. (What was the saying? You could know somebody all of your life, but you never really knew them.) And that could be said for most people. Poor Jake, he had forgotten how many times he had said sorry to Chrissie for not being there to pick her up from the wedding. Cursing himself for letting work get in the way. But as Chrissie had pointed out to him, there was always going to be a time when she would be on her own. And Stewart would have waited for that time to pounce. "So stop banging your head against the wall," she told him, "because in a blink of an eye life could be over for all of us." Well, he couldn't argue with that could he, and had promised her that he wouldn't mention it to her again. But it didn't stop him from having nightmares about it.

They had a great evening together. Chrissie served up the hot steaming food, followed by biscuits and cheese. It was a simple dinner, and they had enjoyed reminiscing over things that had happened at the hotel when they had been on duty together. Chrissie remembered on one occasion when Simon had called her up on to the fourth floor, saying that one of his staff had found somebody dead in their bed when they had taken up their breakfast order. At first Chrissie thought that he was having her on. It was 8:30 in the morning, and she had only just come on duty. So she had told him to find a large black bin liner, because the body would have to be taken out in it. And to use the service lift so the guests wouldn't see. Outside of the back door there would be a hearse waiting to take the body to funeral parlour. Then added..... Oh. But first call a doctor to check that the person is dead. Then she had put the phone down and clicked the switch down on her kettle for a coffee. It was only when Daphne had come into the office seconds later, asking if she had heard from Simon as he'd found somebody dead in a room, that she'd jumped up and raced past her, taking the stairs two at a time up on to the floor, where she found Simon in the room 413 looking across at Jake who was on the phone phoning for a doctor. She wouldn't be able to repeat what Simon had called her as he rolled his well manicured hand up into a fist, shaking it in the air. And it was months before she lived it down for not believing Simon about the dead body in the room. He had told everybody never to call Chrissie if they found somebody dead in a room, because the poor bugger would be decomposed before she got to it.

They had both laughed a lot tonight, and Chrissie felt very comfortable having Jake there with her. But it was now gone midnight, and he was on duty in the morning. So Chrissie suggested that when they had finished their coffee he should really hit the road to get home. Really, she didn't want him to go. But she knew that he had to. So perhaps it was a good job that he didn't know what she was thinking right now, because then he would never leave to go home. They said goodnight at the front door as Jake took her into his arms, kissing her lightly on the lips. He looked deeply into her big blue eyes and saw the passion in them and pulled her closer into him, kissing her again as he ran the tip of his tongue around the edge of her mouth before planting his lips firmly over hers, only letting go of her when they both had to come up for some air. Jake then nibbled on her ear before asking her if she really wanted him to go, and it took all of her inner strength to push him out of the door before she gave in to him, and invited him up to her bed. She waved goodbye as he climbed in the Jeep, telling him to drive safely as she hugged her arms tightly around herself, trying to keep the warmth of him with her until she got into bed.

She sauntered into the kitchen now wide awake, needing another coffee before going up to bed. So she made one for herself, lacing it with brandy, and took it through into the dining area sitting herself down on the rocking chair as she looked out into the garden. As the light of the room shone out into the darkness of the night, she could see the willow tree dancing around in the cool breeze, as the heads of the colourful flowers looked out at you from under the swaying branches. Marmalade jumped up on to her lap, purring as she stroked his fur, telling him how handsome he was. But then her hand froze from stroking his back, as the hairs on the back of her neck stood up. She couldn't move with the fear that was running through her. Marmalade jumped down off her, scurrying out into the kitchen as he felt the fear coming from her. She knew she had to get up to the phone and press the emergency button, but her legs wouldn't move as she felt the panic pumping through her veins. But somehow she tore herself out of the chair, spilling coffee all down her as the shadow she had seen from under the willow tree was coming closer to the door. She screamed, then broke into hysterical laughter as she saw that the shadow wasn't 'HIM' that was prowling around in her garden. But a fox that ran off at a such a speed when he had heard her scream that his feet skidded from under him, almost making him lose his balance as he darted towards the hole in the hedge that he had come through. It took Chrissie some time to calm herself down, making herself another cup of coffee laced with more brandy. She sat in the kitchen counting the days off to when Daisy would be back home with her. Up until now, she had been alright at night on her own. She had drawn all the curtains when it had got dark, and made sure that all of the doors had been securely locked and bolted. Having the emergency button on the phone had also made her feel secure. But after having this fright tonight, Chrissie knew that until Stewart had been caught, she would never be free of him in her life. He would always be out there somewhere. Haunting her.

CHAPTER TWELVE

Daisy loved Christmas with all the bright lights that shone in the windows of the houses and cottages as she travelled home from work. And she couldn't wait for the new year. She was taking a year out to travel around Australia along with Jasmine. They were going to find work as they travelled around, but had both saved enough money to cover them for a few months before they had to start worrying about looking for work. Jasmine had an Uncle Brad living in Sydney, and for the first month he and his wife Trudy had offered to put them up in their attic room until they had the chance to look around and decide what they were going to do. Every minute of their days were now taken up with planning their journey, in between working at their part-time jobs to get more money in for the adventure of their lifetimes. The only thing that worried Daisy was leaving her mother behind. They still had not caught Chrissie's attacker, and although she knew that her mother was getting on with her life, she still knew that it worried her mother that he was still out there somewhere. The only thing that she was pleased about was that she had a very dear friend in Natasha, who would die for her. And two very good friends in Jake and Colin, or more than a friend with one of them! But which one she didn't know. Her mother was encouraging her to go. "Go and spread your wings, Daisy. Don't be like me and just dream about it. Go and get out there, girl. There's a big wide world waiting for you." It was also Daisy's twentieth birthday next Saturday, and Chrissie had organised a small gathering of friends to get together in one of the function rooms in the hotel. It would be a good way to celebrate her birthday and also to say goodbye to some of her friends. Her father could also be there to see her before she left for her adventure. At first Daisy had kicked against it, saying she wanted to go out with her friends. But Chrissie had finally talked her around, saying that she could invite all of her friends, and that she would also hire a DJ for the evening. (Gary, who was hired for all of the hotel functions. It would be cheaper, and he was also very good.) So Daisy eventually gave in, and was now looking forward to the night.

Chrissie had returned back to work on the Monday as she'd planned to a few weeks ago now. She had gone in later in the morning, letting Dawn open up and get the girls started for the day. She had promised herself that she was going to break herself back into work slowly. She had been off for a time now, and would need to get back into the system again. Shelly had given her such a welcome back, going over and giving her a huge big hug as she kissed her on both cheeks. "God we've missed you," she'd beamed, running her eyes over Chrissie's face. "And you look good," she winked. Even Mr Grey had come across to her, putting his arm around her shoulder welcoming her back. When she had finally got up to her office, there was a banner that had been draped across the door with 'WELCOME BACK CHRISSIE' on it. She felt so choked up with emotion, that she had to go into the office before anyone saw her tears. She'd calmed herself down with a coffee, and it felt good to be back in the folds of her second family. It was Simon and Curly Whirl who had put the smile back on her face. She could see from the office window Curly Whirl coming out of the linen room with a handful of kitchen cloths. Which was okay, nothing wrong with that. It was the normal procedure each day to replenish with oven cloths and tea towels for the kitchen. But as he looked up and saw Chrissie looking out of her office window, he waved across to her, looking surprised to see her face at the window. He dropped some of the linen on to the floor as he said something over his shoulder to somebody behind him who was following him out of the linen room. He was warning Simon that Chrissie was back, and he knew that she would say something about the amount of linen that Simon had in his arms.

"Morning, Simon."

"Chrissie. Darling," he heaped the bundle of linen into Curly Whirl's arms and swept her up twirling her around. "Its great to have you back, you old battleaxe," he teased, hugging her into him. "How are you?"

She looked across at Curly Whirl who was struggling not to drop the linen stacked high in his arms on to the floor. "Mmm, I can see that," she kissed him on the cheek with her eyes still on Curly Whirl who was beaming behind the linen.

"And yes. I do need all of it before you ask," Simon tutted, tossing his eyes into the air as he unloaded the linen from Curly Whirl's arms. "See you for lunch, we'll catch up then," he said over his shoulder as Curly Whirl followed him after telling Chrissie that it was great to see her back, leaving her there with her mouth agape, looking like a goldfish coming up for air.

The hotel looked very inviting with all the Christmas decorations up, and with the Christmas trees standing over nine feet tall in the foyer and restaurant, with sparkling and flashing lights all over them. It had taken Chrissie and Darren from maintenance a week to get them all up. It was no small feat to decorate a large hotel like the Rose Mount, and there had been plenty of cursing going on as they were going up. Especially when 'do gooders' came along, giving you so-called advise as to where things should be placed and hung, then gone off whistling and left you to it. Chrissie will mention no names. But a lot of hot air was coming from the restaurant area!! It was also the season for being merry, with lots of office parties being held.

And if Chrissie had her way she would ban the lot of them. She hated the morning after. Her poor cleaning lady who covered all of the public areas had to mop up the sick from off the floors, and urine from where the so-called merrymakers had missed the pan and had peed all over the floor, or sometimes something far worse! She would leave that to your imagination... Then there were the rooms. Three in a bed. Four in a bed. Nothing went on of course! When asked what they were all doing in the one room it was because they hadn't been able to make it back to their own room! Yeah, and pigs can fly... Then there were the fights that the poor night porters, Andy and Luke, had to split up on the floors when couples were going back to their rooms. One accusing the other of flirting with the man sat next to her at the table. Or the wife accusing the man of dancing too close to one of his employees. It was times like these that you had to remember that you worked in a four-star hotel, and not the dosshouse round the corner. But aside from that, generally, Christmas was a great time in the hotel trade. The guests that stayed over for the Christmas and New Year period were mostly families, but with a few single people of a certain age that enjoyed joining in the fun. Usually they were divorcees, or had lost their nearest and dearest and had no family to share the festive season with, and wanted to be around people. Families that stayed in the penthouse and the suite's, usually had Chrissie and her housekeeping staff put up trees and decorate them with fairy lights and anything else they could find in the box where all the decorations were kept. When they arrived on Christmas Eve the parents would be loaded with presents, handing them over to the porters to take up to their rooms, with the children jumping up and down with excitement. The atmosphere was explosive. But what they didn't see, thank God, was the staff backstage, running around like lunatics. Keith pulling his hair out as he checked that all of the food that was delivered for over the Christmas season was fresh and was all there. It was a nightmare for him. To check that you had enough food for over the

Christmas period for a family of four was bad enough. But to cater for over five hundred people. That was quite a feat. Then there was the staff to prepare it all. Bloody nightmare. It was the same for Simon and Chrissie, only difference was, Chrissie had to make sure that she had enough laundry in to cover the rooms, restaurant and kitchen over Christmas and Boxing Day. It was the only two days that the laundry ever closed in the year. So if you were to run out….. She needed to go on Valium….. Only joking, but the pressure on all of them was tremendous. Christmas Eve all management had to be at work to meet up at seven o'clock in the Palace Lounge that was up on the first floor, that ran along the side of the restaurant. There they greeted all of the guests with a huge big smile, offering them a glass of red or white wine from off the tray that they were holding. Then after serving them drinks, they would mingle in with the guest's and make small talk. Fortunately, most of the guests were in the festive mood, drinking back at least two glasses of wine that had been offered to them. But, you always had one that wasn't happy with something or the other. Mr King, who was on his own staying in room 112, had gone to the bathroom to freshen up after the long journey down from London. After relieving his bladder, he went to wash his hands. But when he saw a Father Christmas wrapped in red tin foil, he had opened it up taking a bite out of it. After coughing and spitting it out like a rabid dog with foam around his mouth, he realised that it wasn't a chocolate Father Christmas, but a bar of soap shaped like Father Christmas! Chrissie really had to muster up every bit of self-control to stifle the laughter that was bubbling up through her. When she'd asked him why he hadn't seen that the Father Christmas was white and not brown like chocolate, with a sweet perfume aroma to it, he replied that at the time he hadn't had his glasses on! She had to excuse herself before she split her sides and embarrassed herself. When she had told Simon about it, he had roared with laughter. Thanking her for brightening up his manic day, as he passed it around to his staff who were standing like soldiers waiting to wait on their tables when the merry guests finally got into the restaurant to eat a succulent meal. And they had all found it just as funny as he had as they chuckled to themselves. After the evening came to an end, Simon, Keith and whoever was on late in reception, along with the late night manager, would go to the pub before going home to wind down. They had another full day tomorrow of the festive season. So they needed to make merry before it all began again. At least Chrissie would be home by 9:30. Once the guests were in the restaurant, and she had checked that her evening housekeeper had completed her rounds of the turn downs, then checked that the leisure centre had been securely locked up for the night, she would go home. But she'd be back in for Christmas morning with the rest of them to open up, keeping her fingers crossed that all the staff turned in. Then Dawn would take over from two o'clock. They had done this every year. Swopping over duties so at least one of them would be home by two o'clock on Christmas Day. The chambermaids hardly had to touch the rooms as the guests wished them a Happy Christmas, asking for some clean towels along with teas and coffees. Well…. Most were okay. But you always got the one or two that would still want a full service, and if that was the case and the girl couldn't get into a room, then either Chrissie or Dawn would see to their needs, making sure that the girls got away by one to get home in time to have their Christmas dinner with their families. Leaving with a bottle of wine under one arm, and a box of chocolates under the other. It was a gift from management, given to them for all the hard work that they had put in to get the hotel up and running for the festive season.

Everyone was going over to Natasha's this year for Christmas lunch. She had offered to hold it over at her place for them all. She thought that Chrissie deserved to come home and put her feet up when she had finished at the hotel. But besides that, she thought that both Chrissie and Daisy were due for a treat after all the turmoil they had gone through over the past few months. Natasha knew that Chrissie was still very uptight about Stewart still being out there somewhere, always being on her guard. Rarely fully relaxing down. But she was trying hard to get on with her life. Natasha couldn't make out whether or not she was seeing Jake seriously, or whether it was Colin that she was more interested in. But she had noticed that she had a sparkle in her eye just lately. As for Natasha, she had been seeing Angie for a few months now, and she was wondering how she was going to break it to Chrissie. Although they had been best friends for all of these years, Chrissie didn't know about Natasha's tendencies toward the same sex. (It was called being a Lesbian.) Of course Natasha had been out with the opposite sex, and had enjoyed her relationships with men. But in the end, women had outshined them. Angie was becoming a special person in her life, and it was about time that she came clean with Chrissie. Although she loved Chrissie, it was as a friend. Not as a lover. And besides, Chrissie would run a mile if she made a play for her. She was straight as a die. But what her reaction would be to find out that her best friend was a lesbian? Well…. That did worry Natasha. It would break her heart if she was to lose Chrissie as a friend. So she was going to invite Angie over for Christmas dinner, and say that she was a work colleague. See what Chrissie thought of her, then find the right time to tell her!

Chrissie eventually met up with Colin after he had phoned her reminding her that she had promised him a drink for saving her life. She had laughed at this, saying that she would meet up with him for a drink when she had finished work that night. He was as handsome as she had remembered him, and tonight he had his black hair loose instead of tied back in a ponytail. It hung just below the collar of his pale blue shirt, looking very sexy. Chrissie didn't know what it was, but she did have a thing about men with long hair. Maybe it was the Gipsy in her trying to break out. She had really enjoyed his company, and some of the tales that he had told her about his working days were hilarious. They were not all sad as you would imagine them to be working as a paramedic. Like the drunk they were called out to treat on a Saturday night after coming out from a nightclub. There had been a fight, and he had been knocked out, hitting his head on the pavement. Colin and Paul, the other paramedic who he was on shift with, arrived at the scene with the police trying to calm things down. They took one look at the man who was lying on the pavement, and they decided that it was a hospital job. He had been unconscious for awhile, but nobody knew for how long, and although he was now coming around, Colin thought it best that he was given the once-over at the hospital. They had managed to get him into the ambulance after a struggle, and after finding out that his name was Billy, they tried to calm him down as he tried to escape from the ambulance. He didn't want to go to the hospital. He thought that they could just treat the cut on his head, and then he could go home. But he had tried jumping up from the pavement and had fallen back down flat on his ass. So after eventually getting him into the ambulance after a struggle, he became so irritable that it would have been a danger for them to drive off with him in this state, so Colin decided to give him a sedative to calm him down. But just as he got the needle into his arm, Billy knocked Colin of his balance, pushing Paul out of the way, then he jumped down off the ambulance into the road almost losing his footing, as he swayed off down the road with a needle stuck out of his arm. Luckily, a policeman saw what happened, and had him back in the ambulance in no time. But not without the help of Colin and Paul, who had to make sure that the needle didn't break in his arm in the struggle. The strength that was coming from Billy was unbelievable. But after things had died down, they strapped him to the stretcher for his own safety, and he was delivered to the hospital safe and sound. Blood test were then taken, and there were traces of drugs found in his bloodstream... So it wasn't just the alcohol that was running through his system! And as Chrissie was laughing at the sight of seeing someone running down the road with a needle hanging out of their arm. It wasn't funny really. It was just a waste of the taxpayers' money. They were in a deep conversation when Jake and Keith arrived in the pub for a drink, so Chrissie didn't see them go over to the bar and order a drink. Jake had decided at the last minute to go for a drink with Keith after missing Chrissie going off duty tonight. He was going to ask her what she was doing after work. He didn't see Chrissie until Keith had pointed her out, and his face fell when he saw who she was with. They were both leaning into each other, and he had to fight down the feeling of jealousy that rose up in him. He had never felt this way about anyone before. He drank back the Guinness he was drinking in four gulps, and ordered another one just as Chrissie spotted him sitting at the bar with Keith. She waved across at them, as a feeling of guilt ran through her. Why she didn't know. She was just having a innocent drink with Colin, and enjoying his company. But it was the look on Jake's face. He was definitely not amused to see who she was with. Jake was a close friend…. Okay, maybe more than a close friend. But she wasn't tied to the hip with him. Keith had got up and went over to say hello after spotting her sitting there, offering them both a drink. But Chrissie declined, getting up as Keith got into a conversation with Colin. She went over to Jake who had not made the move to come over to their table.

"Hello, Jake," she said, smiling sweetly at him.

"Hi," he said coolly, barely turning his head to look at her.

"I didn't expect to see you in here tonight." Then wondered why the hell she had just said that. Why shouldn't he be in there tonight.

"And I didn't expect to see you either," he said, turning and looking her straight in the eye.

Chrissie stood for a while as the silence wrapped around them. For some reason he was upset with her. Then the penny dropped. It was because she was with Colin. Oh for God's sake, she wasn't ready for this. She was tied to nobody. She was a free agent. "Well, fuck you," she thought as Jake made no effort to make any small talk between them.

"Goodnight," she said coolly, going back over to Colin who was laughing at something that Keith had said. She told Colin that she was feeling tired, and she was going to make her way home, but for him to stay there, she could see that he was enjoying Keith's company. But he insisted on seeing her back to her car, saying goodnight to Keith as he followed her out the door. As they left the building, Jake clenched his jaws together, using all of his willpower not to get up and follow them out. Colin walked her to her car, asking if he could see her again, and Chrissie hesitated, she really did not know what she wanted. Part of her was feeling guilty for leaving Jake sat at the bar. She really did like him, and she had been seeing him for awhile now. But she also liked Colin. Then he kissed her goodnight fully on the lips, sending a tingle down her spine, and she gave in to her feelings and agreed to see him on the Friday, making a hasty retreat into her car, wondering why the hell she had just done that. Colin's kiss had touched her somewhere in her soul but something was missing. Her head was not spinning around after his kiss. And the tingle that ran down her spine was not the same as it was when Jake held her in his arms. Oh God. Was she really falling in love?

The next day at work, things were cool between Chrissie and Jake. He had hardly spoken to her, and when they had come out of the meeting that morning, he had gone straight back down to his office, where usually he stopped to say hello. Well she wasn't in the mood for childish games, so went back to her own office to get on with the day's work. The first thing she had to do was to check that there were four Christmas trees in the store cupboard. Christmas was only a couple of weeks off now, and guests had been in touch with reception asking for trees to be put into their rooms. One was for a family of five staying in the penthouse suite, so she would ask Janie to check that they had enough in stock. Janie had come on leaps and bounds as a junior housekeeper, and Chrissie could see that she would have to give her more responsibility to keep her interested in her job, but as for promoting her up, there was nowhere to go as a housekeeper. Chrissie had her full staff load of a deputy, junior and evening Housekeepers. Also it was Daisy's party this Saturday, so it was going to be a busy week, chasing around making sure that everything would be okay on the night. She had ordered pink and white tablecloths to come in for all of the tables to be set up in. The tables would be placed around the small dance area, and a buffet would be brought through by Curly Whirl and another member of the kitchen staff. Keith would make sure that the food was fresh for her, and it wouldn't cost her an arm and leg for it because of the discount that Mr Grey had given to her. It was at times like these that it was good to know people that were in the trade of catering. The birthday cake that Chrissie had ordered with Keith would have pink and white icing on it to match the table theme, and she had checked that Gary would be there at seven to start the disco off. She wanted music all through the evening, playing 'quiet' music when the food was being eaten which would be at nine, and 'Happy Birthday' played when the cake was brought through. But first she had to get through this week which would be busy as usual with the Christmas office parties, and the clearing up after the night before, and that was without the day to day running of a very busy housekeeping department. She would have to make sure that enough pool towels were ordered in for the leisure centre. There would be lots of children wanting to swim. The only time it would be closed over Christmas was on Christmas Day, for the rest of the season it would be open from ten until 7:30, which were the normal opening hours of the leisure centre. When Chrissie got down from off the floors, she went to her office to make herself a coffee. Where the time had gone this morning, she didn't know.

162

It had just flown by. Dawn was still up on the floors working with Janie. Sorting out which rooms were having the Christmas trees in, so when the time came for them to go in, they could just get them out of the store cupboard and put them straight into the rooms along with the fairy lights. Chrissie was just feeding some rooms into the computer that were ready for letting that day when Jake came into the office, closing the door behind him

"Look, Chrissie," he said before she could say anything. "I'm sorry for being rude last night. I don't know what came over me. Hard day at work, I guess," he grinned sheepishly, knowing full well why he had been off with her. He had been just plain jealous seeing her with Colin. But they worked together and he couldn't bring his personal feelings into work, even though it was hard not to.

"That's okay. Let's forget it, shall we," she said coolly. Then regretted instantly sounding so cold. She liked this man who stood in front of her and had the guts to apologise to her. There were not many around like that these days. In fact, she more than liked him. But she wasn't ready for any commitment at the moment. "Shall we pretend that it never happened," she said in a softer tone. Then offered to make him a coffee as they caught up on what still had to be done for the Christmas season. But she knew now that she wouldn't be meeting up with Colin on Friday. She would have too much to lose.

CHAPTER THIRTEEN

"Scat, scat all of you. Get out of my way," Natasha yelled as she scooted all of the animals out of the door while she got on with cooking the turkey for today's Christmas dinner. Where the hell the time had gone, God only knows. Granted she had been on the phone for over an hour, wishing Angie a Happy Christmas, and trying to calm her nerves down as she told Natasha perhaps this wasn't the time to meet Chrissie and her family. But after Natasha calmed her down, she told her that if the time was not right to tell Chrissie about her she would know, and would leave it for another time to let her know that she and Angie were lovers. There would be four of them for the actual festive lunch, Jake would be joining them later in the evening to celebrate the rest of the day with them.

Chrissie was now fully committed to Jake. She had phoned Colin up, apologising to him that she would not be meeting him on Friday night, and at first he had tried talking her into keeping the date. He told her how much he had enjoyed spending the evening with her, and wanted to see her again. But in the end he accepted that Chrissie was seeing somebody else, as she told him about Jake, so he bowed out gracefully saying that if ever she changed her mind….

Chrissie had asked Jake around to her place after he had invited her to go out for a drink with him on the Wednesday night. "Why sit in a pub when we can snuggle up at home," she'd thought to herself after he had said that would be great, and he would bring a bottle of wine with him. They sat and nibbled nuts and crisps, as they drank the two bottles of wine that Jake had brought with him. Daisy had left them to it, saying that she would not be home that night. Jasmine and a load of her other friends were meeting up for a get together before they both went to Australia in the new year. So Jake and Chrissie really had a relaxing time, catching up on their families' histories. Jake told her about his parents who were elderly, and lived in Bath. He was an only child like herself and had gone into the hotel business when he was just eighteen, working his way up to management through the departments, starting with the kitchen. "It was the only way to learn, going through each department so you knew what every member of your staff was going through when they had had a tough day." Chrissie agreed with him, saying too many youngsters were coming into the hotel business straight from college. Which was good. But they still had to learn to be hands on. Hotels were not where you spent your time tucked up into a office giving out orders to your staff. You had to be out there on the floor, putting in some elbow grease when needed. (What was the saying? You were not just given respect. You had to get out there and earn it!) When they had both caught up on everything, Chrissie offered Jake a nightcap. It was just after midnight and Jake would have to make a move soon as he was on duty at 8:30 the following morning. So he said yes, he would just have a small one then he would hit the road. Chrissie yawned stretching herself, she was also on duty tomorrow. She went out to the Welsh dresser in the kitchen and got out a bottle of brandy from the cupboard underneath it and poured them out small brandies into glasses. Coming back into the room, she looked across at Jake who was looking at a photo of herself and Daisy. And before she could stop herself, from out of the blue she asked him if he would like to stay the night. Both of them had consumed quiet a bit of drink, and she didn't think he should be driving home. (Well that's what she told herself.) She saw the sparkle in his eye and added quickly, "In the spare room of course!" "But of course," he smiled. After finishing their brandies, Jake followed on behind her as she switched all the lights off as they went up the stairs. She showed him where the bathroom was, giving him a set of clean towels from the airing cupboard. Then showed him along to his room before saying goodnight as she kissed him on the cheek. The next thing she knew she was in his arms in a tight embrace with Jake sensually nibbling on her lips before pressing his firmly onto hers. Stars spun around her head as she tried to push him away. But the urge of her wanting to make love to him was too much. They fell back on to the double bed where Jake seductively stripped her of all her clothes, leaving her lying naked on the bed as she watched him undressing himself. He ran his eyes down over her sensual body, smiling as he smoothed down her fair hairs with his warm seductive tongue that were standing erect all over her body. She gasped, groaning at the tingling sensation that ran through her body as he sucked on her erect pink nipples, wrapping her long slender legs around him, waiting for him to devour her. He was sensational. As their bodies locked together she thought that she was going to die of desire as he gently entered into her, climaxing in minutes. She hadn't made love for so long now that she just couldn't hold back. In the end Jake had taken her to heaven three times before they fell exhausted into one another's arms, locking themselves together as they slept the rest of the night through. Before leaving for work the next morning they shared a shower, making again passionate love, then set off to work separately. All day Chrissie had been in a world of her own. She was still tingling from the long night of lovemaking, and she felt just great. Simon had asked her if she was in love or something after asking her for a particular tablecloth that was used for the top table of a wedding table that was being held in the hotel on Saturday. Three times he had asked her if she could drop it down to him when she was around the restaurant area. But in the end he had to go up himself to get it, asking her who the lucky guy was as he felt the love vibes oozing out from her. She blushed, ignoring the question, punching him playfully on the arm as she hummed to herself, walking away with a swagger in her shapely hips. "When am I going to meet him?" Simon yelled out after her, laughing as he collected the tablecloth from Daphne. "Now that's what you call being in love," he winked, leaving Daphne smiling as he made his way back down to the restaurant.

It was over two weeks now that Chrissie and Jake had become lovers, and she felt a totally different person. She had at long last been able to close the pages on the old chapter of her life, and was now starting anew. Chrissie had talked over with Jake the chances of Stewart reappearing in her life. But as Sergeant Tom Noble had told Chrissie, he was probably long gone by now. But, she would still have to be aware that he was still out there somewhere! They had searched high and low for him with no result. But the file was still open, and would stay open until they got him. Also she had discussed with Jake the possibility of the daughter she had given up for adoption. She may try and find her. But as Jake had said, "There could be ifs and buts all through their lives, and there just wasn't enough time on this earth to put it all on hold. So whatever was to happen in the future, they would face it together." So they had decided that Jake would stay over more often when Daisy had left in the new year. Chrissie was still not ready for him to move in permanently, but she knew that in time she would be spending the rest of her life with him. But until then, they sneaked in a few love-ins when Daisy had stayed over at Jasmine's.

Natasha had been over the moon when she found out that Jake and Chrissie were an item. "About time too," she had said over the phone. "So I'll start saving for the wedding, shall I?"

The smell of the Christmas lunch that was wafting across the drive from Natasha's house when Chrissie and Daisy drew up outside with a carload of presents was divine. Chrissie had managed to get away from work half an hour earlier, leaving Dawn behind to hold the reins. All of her staff had turned in for work this morning, and had been away by 12:30. The guests had been great, with not many of them wanting anything done in their rooms except for clean towels and teas and coffees. The atmosphere had been great with everyone being in the festive mood, wishing everyone a Happy Christmas as they went around doing their thing. Chrissie had left Jake at work. He was on duty until eight that evening, but he was hoping to get away earlier. Natasha greeted them at the door, helping them in with all of the pressies that were tucked under their arms.

"Oh my God, Chrissie, what have we got here? Have you brought for all the neighbours," she laughed, as Daisy fell over Scamp who was jumping up and down for her attention as she bent down to pick up Bubbles. Rosie happily purred around Angie's ankles, where she was sat nervously in the lounge waiting to meet the other half of Natasha's 'family'. She had already consumed two glasses of sherry and was on her third feeling very light-headed, wishing that she had stayed at home. But Natasha was adamant that she was to meet Chrissie, she was tired of all this creeping around, and not sharing her happiness with her best friend in that she had at long last found love. Following Natasha through into the lounge, they emptied their arms full of Christmas presents under the Christmas tree that filled the corner of the room with flashing fairy lights and silver angels hung all over it. Turning around, Chrissie spotted Angie sat in the other corner of the room holding Rosie, who was struggling to get down to greet her.

"Oh... Hello. I didn't see you there," Chrissie smiled going over to her with her hand extended as Angie got up out of her seat.

Natasha stopped what she was doing and went over to Angie's rescue before Chrissie could ask who she was. "This is

Angie, a working colleague of mine," she said hastily. A bit too hastily that didn't go amiss with Chrissie. And they were both blushing too. "Drink, anyone?" Natasha asked, leading the way into the kitchen as they all followed her through, except for Daisy who stayed behind in the lounge arranging the presents that they had brought with them around the Christmas tree.

"Mmm," Chrissie sniffed into the air. "Whatever it is that you are cooking, it smells divine," she said, clinking glasses with Angie and Natasha, thinking she hadn't seen anyone drink a glass of sherry for a long while now. "Happy Christmas to you both," she said raising her glass in the air. She saw Natasha and Angie glance at each other as Natasha's eyes softened. "Mmm, something is going on here," Chrissie thought. But right now she just couldn't put her finger on it. But before she could think anymore of it, Daisy had come into the kitchen asking where her glass of wine was. They all worked together getting the Christmas lunch on to the table that Natasha had set up with crackers and hats. Chrissie opened up a couple of bottles of wine, putting them into ice coolers that were stood on the table, while Daisy helped through with the dishes of hot steaming food (with Daisy and Angie) of sprouts, beans, broccoli and a splash of colour with the swede and carrots, as Natasha followed through with the turkey and a joint of ham, surrounded by chipolata sausages wrapped in streaky bacon. Yum. As they settled down at the table, Chrissie was wishing that Jake was there with them to enjoy what would have been their first Christmas meal together. But he was coming over later, so she'd make it up to him then for missing out on what looked like a succulent meal that Natasha had cooked for them all. Through the meal, they all chatted away about this and that as they supped on their wine, remembering Daisy's birthday party at the hotel with fond memories. Keith had put on a great spread of food for her, and Simon had waited on the guests himself, not letting Chrissie do a thing. "It's your daughter's birthday," he'd said. "Just relax down and come off duty!" Freddie had been there with Jackie and given a wonderful speech to his daughter, saying how proud he was of her, and what a joy she had been to her mother and father when she was born. A few tears were shed when he went on to say that they were all going to miss her when she went to Australia, and she was not to forget to come home again. After the cake was cut the tables were cleared and the disco started. Chrissie went out to see Jake who had been on duty, and he handed her a red rose. At first she thought that he had brought it for her until he told her that it was for Daisy. It had been delivered by the florist that they used for the different displays of flowers that were dotted around the hotel. Written on a small card that was attached to the rose was a message. 'Wish I could be there with you! And nothing else. Chrissie had felt very uncomfortable with this. Not having a name given. When she gave it to Daisy and asked who she thought it was from, she said she had no idea. But thanked whoever it was as the rose was really lovely. Chrissie had phoned the florist the next day to try and find out who had sent the rose. But all they could tell her was that it was ordered over the phone, and the person on the other end had asked them to add the message to it. So Chrissie pushed it to the back of her mind thinking that she was probably overreacting to it. But she still didn't feel easy about it, and decided that when the Christmas season was over she would get hold of Sergeant Tom Noble and mention it to him.

Chrissie thought that Angie was a very nice person. She was quiet at first, but once the wine started to flow, she was really chatty, asking Daisy all about her coming trip, and laughing, flashing her beautiful white teeth, at the tales that Chrissie told her of what could happen in the day to day running of a hotel. Natasha had relaxed down, and it didn't go unnoticed by Chrissie of how fond she was of Angie, and found it strange that she hadn't mentioned her to her before. They were obviously very good friends at work. When they finally went back through into

170

the lounge, they opened up their presents, all feeling very excited to see what they had under all of the Christmas wrapping. It was almost six o'clock, and in another hour or so Jake would be joining them. They took their coffees through with them after all deciding that they needed to come off the wine as they still had the evening to go yet. The floor was covered in wrapping paper within minutes, as they all excitedly opened up their presents. Angie had brought Natasha a lovely bright red scarf with matching gloves. Natasha had been thrilled with them, they would keep her warm when she was walking Scamp and Bubbles. She got up and went over to her, thanking her by kissing her gently, but fully, on the lips. It had been a very brief kiss, but again, it did not go unnoticed by Chrissie who felt shocked by seeing it. Natasha and herself were very close as friends. But they had never kissed fully on the lips! Then she tutted at herself for letting her wild imagination run away with her. It was all the wine's fault. Jake arrived just after seven. He had managed to get away a bit earlier, and Chrissie was pleased to see him, taking his coat from him as he gave her a warm kiss on the lips.

"Who was that just leaving as I arrived?" he asked, putting his arm around her waist as they joined the rest of them in the lounge.

"Nobody's left," she said, frowning up at him. "We're still all here," she laughed, counting each one of them sat around the fire.

Natasha got up and gave him a kiss on the cheek, wishing him a Happy Christmas as she introduced Angie to him as her friend from work. "Nobody has left from here. Why? Did you see someone come out of the door?" She poured him a glass of wine out as she moved over to sit with Angie on the settee, giving up her chair for Jake to sit down on.

"No. Nobody came out of the door. I just saw the back end of someone who I thought was coming out of your gate. But it

171

must have been next door's gate." He smiled, raising his glass in the air. "Cheers," he said before taking a sip of it.

They had a cold supper with the leftover turkey and ham. Eating it with assorted cheeses and pickles that Natasha had laid up on the dining room table. She had taken ten minutes looking around in the kitchen for the Dundee cake that she had made a couple of months ago for Christmas, but couldn't find it. So she went into the lounge and asked Chrissie and Angie if they had moved it, but they also had not seen it, so the hunt for the missing cake started. They looked in the fridge and in the cooker, even in the waste bin. Natasha would never put it past herself to do something stupid like that after all the wine she had consumed that day. Then Daisy spotted Scamp and Bubbles lying flat out on the floor by the back door with Rosie licking her lips. She went over to them and saw traces of currants spread out all around them. Looking closer, she lifted the edge of the tablecloth on the kitchen table, and there on the floor underneath it was the leftover Dundee cake. Natasha at first started cursing at all three of them until Daisy started laughing.

"They are really going to suffer for the next few days," she said, bending down to very sick-looking Bubbles and Scamp. "And I think you will be changing their litter trays more than once a day," she laughed as Chrissie came through into the kitchen to see what all the ruckus was about.

They had had a great evening playing games, their favourite being charades. Chrissie was hopeless at it, and what made it even worse was she couldn't spell! So when they had got tired of trying to guess what she was miming, they asked her for a clue. And she told them that it began with a C when all along it had began with a D… Duh! They were not happy, but they all teased her about it in the Christmas spirit they were in. Natasha brought the brandy out, and they all had a small glass with some mince pies. She was trying to find the courage to tell Chrissie about

Angie, but she was failing dismally. There just hadn't been the right time to tell her today. Not with Jake and Daisy being there. So she decided that they would have one of their evenings together in the new year where they always caught up on everything. And she would tell her then. As midnight approached Chrissie got up to leave. She had work in the morning, and so had Jake. And Daisy had been yawning for the last half an hour and was more than ready to go. She was driving her mother home as she'd had more to drink than herself, and Jake was going to drive home to his place. But Daisy had stepped in saying she would drive him home to their place where he could stay the night in the spare room. At first Jake said that he would be okay to drive home, but after Natasha and Chrissie nagged him about drink driving, he gave in saying he would do as he was his told and pick his car up in the morning. Natasha saw them out along with Angie. Daisy had offered to give Angie a lift home to, but Natasha had said that she was staying the night, which again did not go amiss with Chrissie as both of their cheeks flushed. There was something going on between them, but what she didn't know she was going to find out. She would phone her in a couple of days' time and meet up with her. Maybe Angie was going through some turmoil in life, and she was just helping her out. But again it was strange to see her arm around Angie's waist as they waved them off!

The next day at work, Chrissie found a note on her desk addressed to her. In it it said, "I hope you enjoyed your Christmas with our daughter." She felt the bile rise in the back of her throat as she started to tremble. My God. It was starting all over again. As the note dropped to the floor she staggered along to the toilets, where she just made it before throwing up the contents of her stomach. He was still out there. Watching her every move...

173

CHAPTER FOURTEEN

Tom was out like a flash when Jake had phoned him from the hotel after he'd dashed up the stairs to see Chrissie in her office. He told Sergeant Noble of the note that Chrissie had found, and Tom said that he would be straight there. Grabbing hold of Carl, he told him to go down and get the car parked outside of the station ready to go while he went into his boss to fill him in on what had just happened, telling him that he was now off to see Chrissie. She had looked deathly white when Jake got to her office where she was trying to steady her hands so she could drink the mug of coffee that Dawn had made for her. Jake asked Dawn to carry on with the checking of rooms, and to keep the girls away from the office until he had sorted things out, thanking her for calling him up after finding Chrissie in the office crying. He locked the office door, phoning down to reception asking them to put any calls that came through for him straight through to housekeeping. After calming Chrissie down, he asked her what on earth was the matter? She handed him the note that had been put on her desk by Dawn. Dawn had come in that morning and as she had passed by reception, Shelly had called her over to take a note up that had been left on the reception desk for Chrissie. As Jake read the message, he let out a sigh. He put his arm around her shoulders, holding her close to him as he tried to stop her from shaking so much.

"Chrissie, sweetheart. I know what you're thinking," he said, kissing her cheek. "But this could be anyone."

Swallowing hard, she stifled a sob. "No, Jake. It's him. I know it is. I've been on my guard since Daisy's birthday and the rose arrived for her with no name on it."

Jake raised his eyebrows at her. He could understand her anxiety, but any one of her friends could have send that rose to Daisy.

"Then you said that you thought you had seen somebody leave Natasha's on Christmas Day when you arrived in the evening. Remember?"

Yes, he did remember. But he had also said that he wasn't sure that the person had come from Natasha's house.

Tom had arrived within the hour and had taken statements from the porter and from the girls in reception. He was taking this very seriously. It had gone quiet since the attack on Chrissie, and even after the massive search that had been done on Stewart, they had come up against a brick wall. He had asked Jake for the video tapes that were running at the time over the front entrance to the hotel, and the car park area. He would take them back to the station where somebody would scrutinise them to see if Stewart could be spotted in any of the areas. He also told Chrissie that they couldn't rule out at this moment in time that it wasn't somebody that Daisy knew who left had the rose for her, or the note was from somebody that she knew. Although it looked highly unlikely. She must stay alert until they had arrested him.

An hour later Chrissie was back on the floors after drinking a tot of brandy that Simon had brought up to her after hearing about her being upset. (You could cordon off the whole of the hotel. And swear everyone to secrecy. But anything that happened out of the norm in the hotel world would still be

175

leaked out.) He gave her a quick hug, promising her that he would get all of his butch pals to look out for this crazy person. "And God help him if they caught hold of him before the police did!" he winked playfully. "Let's just say that he would probably never walk the same again!!" Chrissie could always rely on Simon to put a smile on her face. Even Jake cracked a smile as he ushered him out of the office with his bleep going off. Jake gave her another hug before she went up on to the floors, telling her that he would take good care of her, and whether she liked it or not he was going to move in with her when Daisy had left for Australia. She could kick him out if she wanted to after the bastard had been found.

The Boxing Day activities were in full swing, and once again Chrissie was not going to let this bastard get the better of her. She had phoned and checked that Daisy was okay, she was spending the day shopping with friends at the bank holiday sales, buying last minute things to take to Australia with her. She would be leaving next Monday, much to Chrissie's relief. At least she would be miles away and out of the danger of this madman who was still on the loose. Tom told her that he would have a police officer keeping an eye on the hotel and an officer would be doing spot checks on the cottage while he was still out there, telling her once again to be on alert until they had caught him. She was pleased that this had happened at work and not at home. At least she'd been able to lose herself in the Boxing Day activities that were going on. She worked on late, letting Dawn go home early. Daisy phoned her asking if she minded if she stayed over at Jasmine's tonight, so Jake said that he wasn't going to leave her on her own and would follow her home in his car when he came off duty at nine. They got home about 9:30, and as they both parked their cars in the drive, Mr Roberts came out from next door, peering over the hedge at them.

"Hello, Chrissie, I've been waiting for you to get home," he said, coughing as the cold wind caught his breath.

"You shouldn't be out here in this cold wind," Chrissie chided him. "Are you alright?"

"Yes, I'm alright, but I was worried about you. The police have been looking around outside of your cottage and up and down the lane. I thought something had happened to you." He wiped his nose, that looked blue with the cold, on the sleeve of his shirt.

Chrissie felt very humble that dear old Mr Roberts had been worrying about her, and invited him in for a tot of brandy. His eyes lit up as he rushed back to lock up the cottage. Jake prodded her in the ribs, shaking his head as they waited for him to lock up.

"I thought we were going to cuddle up on the settee and relax down," he whispered, tutting as he smiled down at Marmalade, who was purring around his legs.

Natasha had phoned Chrissie at work, asking her to spend the evening with her on Thursday if she was free. Jake was working late, and Daisy was so involved with getting ready to leave on Monday that she was only too pleased to go over and spend the evening with her. She had Saturday off from work and she and Daisy were going to spend the day together doing girly things. Then she was going to cook for Natasha and Daisy in the evening, that way Natasha could say her goodbyes to Daisy. Chrissie was really going to miss her when she left. They had grown close again after the small rift between them when Daisy had found out about her mother's past life.

Chrissie arrived early at Natasha's. It was only seven o'clock when she got there and Natasha wasn't expecting her until 7:30. As she drew up in the driveway, she saw her waving off somebody, and it wasn't until the car had passed her on the drive that she saw it was Angie who was driving the car. She waved at Angie as she past her, and Chrissie could see that she was surprised to see her, thinking it strange as she parked up and got out of the car with her usual bottle of wine.

Natasha looked flustered when she went over to greet her. "You're early," she said kissing her on the cheek.

Chrissie thought that was a funny thing for her to say, usually she was being told off for being late, but she let it go, asking if that was Angie that had just driven out. Why she asked her that she didn't know seeing as she already knew that it was her. But for some reason she had a funny feeling that something was going on. Perhaps Natasha was going to take her in as a lodger, and why not indeed. It would be good company for her. But she did secretly wish that she could find a good man as she had, and settle down with him. She would make a good wife for somebody.

"Yes, she just called in on her way home from work."

Again that didn't sound right. She worked with her all day so why would she call in after work. "Now stop it, Chrissie, you're letting your imagination run away with you again." She followed Natasha into the kitchen. "Mmm, it's nice and warm in here, she purred sitting down at the kitchen table, looking around to see what she had new. Natasha had so many bits and bobs that every time she went over there Chrissie would see something that she hadn't seen before. But Natasha always said that it had been there for an age. She just hadn't seen it before amongst the rest of her treasures, as she called them.

"Warmest room in the house tonight, shall we stay out here?" Natasha asked as she handed Chrissie a glass of wine.

Natasha asked Chrissie if she had heard anymore on Stewart. Were they any closer to finding him? Chrissie said that it had gone quiet again after the note being left on Boxing Day. But Sergeant Noble kept reassuring her that they were getting closer to catching him. One of the farmers close by had said they had seen someone living rough in the copse nearby, but when the police had gone to investigate all they had found were the remains of ashes from a fire that had been used. Then they had laughed about Scamp and Bubbles as Natasha told Chrissie how ill they had been the next day after demolishing the Dundee cake. Scamp spent the day going in and out of the cat flap and in the litter tray. And as for Bubbles, there were little 'black currants' deposited all over the place. She had to confine them to the utility room for the day. Rosie had got off with it lightly, and had obviously not eaten so much of it. After getting through one bottle of wine Natasha opened up another one, refilling Chrissie's as she got up to go to the loo. She now had to pluck up the courage to tell Chrissie about Angie. She would be coming home in the next hour, and she had to let her friend know what was going on before then. Chrissie went into the bathroom to wash her hands and noticed that there were two toothbrushes and two flannels that were being used. She frowned, taking a peek into the cabinet on the wall and saw that there were different types of make-up in it which she knew Natasha did not use. Natasha called up the stairs asking if she was alright as she had been a long time. "Coming," she said, feeling guilty now for being so nosy. When she got back down to the kitchen, Natasha was pacing up and down looking worried.

"What's wrong?" Chrissie asked taking a sip of her wine.

"I think that you should take another drink of your wine," Natasha said nervously. "And I want you not to say anything until I have told you something."

Chrissie was now getting very worried. Was she ill? Had she had some bad news? She nodded her head at her taking a gulp of her wine as Natasha gulped a mouthful of hers.

"I'M A LESBIAN," she blurted out, spilling her wine. She couldn't believe that she had said it out loud. But it felt good. Like a huge weight being taken off her shoulders. But then she looked across at Chrissie. She was stood with her mouth wide open... Speechless. She cleared her throat to say something but nothing came out.

"What did you say?" she mouthed, gulping down the wine and handing her glass over for another one.

After the glasses had been refilled, they both plonked down into the chairs, and they were silent for what seemed a lifetime until Chrissie found her voice after getting over the shock of hearing that her best friend was a lesbian. And she'd had no idea.

"Whoa. That beats everything that I've heard this year."

Natasha bristled. She didn't want to fall out with her friend. But she was in love just as Chrissie was in love with Jake. Only difference was, Angie was a woman!

When Chrissie had got home that night, she was still reeling from the shock of hearing about Angie being Natasha's lover. She had sobered up fast after Natasha had told her that she had been seeing her for over six months now. Six months and Chrissie had never cottoned on that she was seeing anyone. Let alone a woman. She told her what a dark horse she was. And yes she was a bit pissed off that Natasha hadn't told her before now. But they parted as best friends with Chrissie saying that she would see her Saturday night at her place for Daisy's farewell supper.

Angie drove Natasha over to Chrissie's with some wine in the back of the car, and a going away present for Daisy. She was dropping Natasha off and would pick her up later when she phoned to say that she was ready to leave. On Thursday it had been quite a bombshell that Natasha had dropped on Chrissie. When she heard of their relationship, at first she had felt sick at the thought of her friend making love to a woman. But after they had talked it through, and Chrissie was still reeling from the shock. She told Natasha, "Whatever makes you happy. But it's going to take me time to get used to it.' Natasha had gone over to her and given her a bear hug, then broke away when she felt Chrissie stiffen. "Don't worry darling. It's not you that I fancy," she laughed. "I just love you purely as a friend."

Angie had returned home and came shyly in. She didn't quite know what to say, so Chrissie had got up and said, "Welcome to the family," kissing her lightly on the cheek. But with no hugs. It was going to take some time to get use to her friend living with another woman. Why? She didn't know. It wasn't as if she hadn't come up against different relationships before. She worked with gays and loved them all. But they were not going out with her best friend. They decided that they wouldn't tell Daisy at this time. She was going away so it wouldn't matter whether she knew or not. Chrissie would bring it up in conversation some other time.

Daisy was so excited about going away on Monday, and had talked non-stop about it at the table as they ate their meal of homemade lasagne. She had had a couple glasses of wine and her cheeks were pink with excitement. But she didn't see the sadness in her mother's eyes as she chatted away of what she hoped to achieve once she got to Australia. Chrissie thought then that things would never be the same. She would go away being her young daughter and come back as a young woman. Natasha had brought her a beautiful silver pen with her initials on it. "So you will know if somebody 'accidentally' picks it up," she said, kissing her on both cheeks. Jake phoned to speak to Chrissie, he always phoned her if he was on a late shift, just to see that she was okay, but more so tonight because he wasn't staying over with her. They decided that because Chrissie was cooking the meal for Daisy and Natasha, he would go home instead and see her tomorrow. She had talked him into going to church with her in the morning for the Sunday service. Why he had said yes he'll never know. He wasn't a churchgoing man. But as Chrissie pointed out to him, neither was she a church goingwoman. But

181

now and again it cost her nothing to catch up with God and say a few words to him. Whether he listened or not was another thing, but at least she felt she felt good after going. Angie picked Natasha up just after midnight. Chrissie told her that she should stay the night, save Angie coming out at this time of the night. But Angie had insisted on picking her up, she wanted her home. She had already had the scare of her life when she thought she had lost Bubbles. She had searched everywhere for the little minx and had eventually found his 'black currant' droppings, where she followed them through into the lounge where he was sat in a large plant pot munching on one of Natasha's plants. Natasha and Chrissie were waiting for her at the door when she arrived. It was a cold night and there was a slight frost on the ground. Chrissie said that she would have to go out and cover some of her plants that were still blooming so the frost didn't get at them. Natasha had told her to leave it until the morning as she toddled over to the car where Angie had the door open for her. "Then there'll be dead," she called out after her, waving at Angie as she laughed at Natasha as she fell into the car. "See you soon," she shouted out as the car sped off. Daisy had been watching from the window and was chuckling to herself when her mother came back in.

"What?"

"You're both as mad as hatters."

"Don't know what you mean?" Chrissie said going through into the dining room and switching on the outside light.

"Where are you going now?" Daisy sighed, watching her mother go out into the garden. "It's too cold for slugs now," she quipped.

She laughed as her mother poked her tongue out at her. It was after twelve at night and she was out in the garden doing God knows what as she whipped out some plastic sheeting that was tucked behind the privet hedge.

"I'm just covering these plants up or they'll die with the frost."

"God, Mother if it's not the slugs it's the frost. You really are becoming eccentric…. No let me take that back. You are eccentric. I've warned you. They will be here to collect you in their white coats soon," she laughed as Chrissie pushed passed her switching the outside light off before going back through into the kitchen.

"I'm going to bed now," Daisy kissed her mother on the cheek.

"Night night, sweetheart. See you in the morning."

"Oh, Mum by the way. Are Natasha and Angie an item now?"

Before Chrissie could answer Daisy was halfway up the stairs chuckling to herself. "Honestly, what's the big deal. Surely they would know that I would figure that out?"

The church was half full when Chrissie and Jake arrived. And it was bloody freezing. The heating that they had managed to get installed into the church hardly made any difference, it was so old and drafty. A few heads turned when they saw Chrissie arrive with Jake, smiling as they said hello to him as they gave her a knowing look.

"This is the last time that you talk me into coming to church," Jake moaned, shivering under his jacket and scarf. "I could still be wrapped up in bed, or better still, we could still be wrapped up in bed."

She gave him a nudge with her elbow, shushing him to be quiet as the vicar appeared in front of them, beaming out at his congregation.

"I bet he has thermals on!" Jake whispered.

But Chrissie was disappointed. It wasn't the Reverand Christian there this morning but an entire stranger standing there saying how pleased he was to be standing in for the Reverand Christian while he was away for the next two months taking Christianity to the Third World countries. Well that would be good news for Jake because she wouldn't be dragging him along to another Sunday service until the Reverend Christian was back. After all, it was him who she had come to listen to, not some stranger she didn't know. And the vicar who was stood at the altar preaching to them now was using those long hyphenating words that she would need to bring along a dictionary to know what the hell he was on about. But beside that, he didn't have the cute ponytail for a start. And under his cassock he wore black shoes that were highly polished. He was just not in the same category as Christian.

CHAPTER FIFTEEN

Daisy had left on Monday morning after lots of tears had been shed. And Chrissie was now feeling empty as she picked up Marmalade and sauntered off down the garden with him in her arms, as she remembered all the good times she had with Daisy through the years as they gardened together out there. Smiling as she heard her voice in her head, telling her that she was going to get in the folks with the white coats on as she went around at night with the torch searching for slugs. Her baby had flown the nest and she was feeling devastated. It was almost a week ago now that she had left, but she still waited for her to come barging through the door at night. Jasmine's father had taken them to Heathrow Airport, so they had said goodbye at the cottage. Chrissie had tried to stay strong not to break down in front of her. But as soon as she'd got into the car and started waving to her as she looked out of the back window, that's when Chrissie had broken down. She had gone back to work hoping that would help to cheer her up, but she still felt down in the dumps, and even Simon couldn't break her out of the doldrums.

They had spend the Sunday evening packing together. Jake had gone home after they had lunch leaving them to it. They had a lot to catch up on before Daisy left and also Chrissie wanted her all to herself before she went off into the big wide world. They had talked about lots of things, even about Stewart still being out there somewhere on the loose. Daisy worried about her mother with him still not being captured, but Chrissie said that she would be fine. She had Jake to look out for her now. She had told her that he was moving in while she was away and Daisy was thrilled about that. "That makes me feel easier knowing that he will be here with you, Mum. He's a really nice guy." Then as they talked some more, Daisy brought up the sister who she had never seen. She asked her mother if she ever got in touch with her while she was away, would she tell her? Chrissie almost wept. She told Daisy that she didn't think that she would want to get in touch with her. She was probably very happy with her adoptive mother and father and living a fulfilled life. But if she ever did get in touch with her of course she would tell her. But she didn't want to tell Daisy that she didn't know whether or not she would be brave enough to see her if she was ever to search her out. She really had not thought too much on it over the past years. She had locked it away to the back of her mind. And it would stay locked away unless she had to unlock it. It was still too painful to face up to. But then again, if she was being truthful, she had thought of her briefly over the years, but only unlocking part of her mind as her birthdays came around. And then in latter years, of how it might of have been different if her parents had been more supportive of her wanting to keep her. But then it was unfair to say that. Her parents had sat her down, asking if she would able to close this chapter in her life after giving her child away. Yes had been the answer then. At 17, all she had wanted to do was to wipe out the humiliation of being raped. And she had asked herself time and time again over the months of carrying her in her womb. Could she live with a child that she had conceived through rape?! No, she could not. Not at that time. But like most things in life, if she had that time over again, would she have done the same thing? She had to say yes to just to keep her sanity. Daisy said no more on the subject, she could see the tears welling up in her mother's eyes. But at the same time Daisy had to be honest with herself. She really hoped that she did get in touch with her mother. It would be wonderful to have a sister

186

around. When they had finished packing, Chrissie made them a hot chocolate with lashings of cream squirted on top of it, Daisy's favourite, as Daisy sat reminiscing with her, with Chrissie listening to every word, savouring every moment of it. Thinking of how her daughter had matured. Where had the years gone when she was that gorgeous little bundle running around the cottage getting into everything. Helping her in the garden. Pulling all the flowers out, bringing them into her telling her that she had been weeding the garden for her. It hadn't taken Chrissie long to teach her the difference between a flower and a weed! They finally made it up the stairs at two o'clock, feeling exhausted after packing two large suitcases for Daisy, then catching up on everything before she left. Chrissie hardly got any sleep, tossing and turning, thinking of how she was going to cope with Daisy going away. But she'd finally drifted off into a fitful sleep. And now she was gone, and Chrissie was sat in her office at work, loading her computer up with rooms that were vacant and ready for letting that day, trying to carry on with life as normal. Janie had still not turned in for work, and it was most unusual for her not to phone. She always phoned in even if she was only going to be a few minutes late let alone an hour late. Chrissie had checked with reception to see if a message had been left for her. But nobody had phoned through. When the girls collected their rooming list from Chrissie, she asked them to take extra special care of their cleaning today as she may not get around to checking all of the rooms. Maria, bless her, offered to check some for her, she only had half a section to clean, the hotel was quieter at the moment after the Christmas period, thank God, giving them time to catch up on all the early spring cleaning that needed to be done. It wasn't until almost lunchtime that Jake came up to see her, telling her that the hospital had phoned through to the hotel informing them that Janie was in hospital and she had given them her name.

"Oh my God, is she okay?"

"She took a overdose last night."

Jake sat her down in the chair before she fell down. Chrissie's face had gone deathly white.

"SHE WHAT?"

Drinking a very strong coffee, Jake told her that the nurse had not said much to him, only to say that Janie had asked them to phone her, and could she go in and see her.

"God, I knew that she had not been too happy over the Christmas period, but I had no idea that she was this low."

Jake asked if she wanted him to call Dawn in from her day off as she got off the phone to the hospital. They had told her that Janie was brought in last night after her boyfriend had found her slumped over the bath with a bottle of tablets in her hand. Her boyfriend, whose name was Darrel, was there at the moment with her. So Chrissie asked the nurse to let Janie know that she would be in to see her after she had finished work. She had asked if Janie's parents had been informed, but the nurse told her that Janie had asked them to phone through to herself not her parents. Janie's parents lived in Wales, and Chrissie thought that she was probably feeling embarrassed about it all. It was now gone twelve and she hadn't checked one room, so for the moment she put Janie on to the back boiler. She would leave as soon as Annabelle came in on the evening shift and go straight to the hospital. She checked as many rooms as she could, and Maria had finished off the rest for her. She really was shocked by hearing about Janie, and wanted to find out what had brought this all about. But she didn't have to wait until she got to see her at the hospital to find out what had happened to her. It was common knowledge apparently that Janie was two months pregnant and her boyfriend had said that he wanted to her to get rid of it. Chrissie was amazed of what went on around her without her even knowing! (So once again if you wanted to find out any juicy gossip, then just ask around the hotel hotline.)

Leaving work that evening, Chrissie went into Jake's office letting him know that she was now off to the hospital to see Janie. Before letting her leave, he shut the office door and held her tightly in his arms planting a warm kiss on her lips.

"Make sure that you stay alert when you park up in the hospital car park. It's dark out there now and I wish I was coming with you."

Chrissie cupped his face in her hands, kissing the tip of his nose. "You can't be with me all of the time, Jake," she smiled, waving as she left, asking him to feed Marmalade when he got home, and to make sure that she had a glass of wine waiting for her when she got home from the hospital. Janie was in ward three and as Chrissie walked through the ward she could see her lying there asleep, looking very young and vulnerable. There was no sign of Darrel her boyfriend, so she sat down on the chair next to the bed and waited for her to wake up. It seemed a shame to disturb her, and she was in no hurry to leave. But Janie must have felt the presence of Chrissie being there because as she sat down her eyes flicked opened and she gave her a wonderful smile.

"I'm sorry, Chrissie," she said turning her head away from her.

"You have nothing to say sorry to me about," Chrissie said, taking her hand and squeezing it in hers. "What's this all about?" she said, turning her face around to her.

Janie's shoulders shook with the sobs that were rumbling up through her body. She felt such a fool. Last night she had been feeling really down after Darrel had gone out for the evening with his friends, leaving her in the flat alone even though she had asked him to stay in with her so they could discuss about their future together. He knew how low she was feeling after they had argued once again over the fate of the baby. But he had still left her, saying that they were not old enough to take care of a child,

189

leaving her with no alternative but to get rid of it. She couldn't face the shame of telling her parents that she was pregnant. But she also couldn't face up to losing her baby. So in the end the only thing that was left for her to do was to end her life. But now she was engulfed in shame for what she'd done. What had she been thinking of? Chrissie saw the panic in her face as her hand went to her stomach.

"The baby's alright," Chrissie smiled. She had asked the nurse on the way in how was Janie doing. Chrissie put her hand on hers and squeezed it. "Look, Janie. I know exactly how you feel right now. At this moment in time you don't know which way to turn. Please get in touch with your mum and dad. Ring them. They will help you to come to some decision on this. It's too much for you to handle on your own." She smiled, gently wiping with a tissue the tears that were spilling freely from Janie's brown speckled eyes, brushing her golden hair back away from her face before Chrissie went on to say that she would clear it at work for her to take time off. And if she wanted to she could use up any holidays that she had owing so she wouldn't lose too much money while she was off.

By the time Chrissie got home that night she was feeling exhausted. Seeing Janie lying there looking so alone brought back so many memories to her. She hoped that she would come to the right decision with the help of her parents. And if she decided to give up the baby, that it would be the right decision and would not regret it in years to come. Jake was at the door waiting for her with a huge grin on his face, holding out a glass of wine to her. She kissed him fully on the lips. How lucky she was to have found a gem like him. Working with him. Living with him. Making love to him. She was so lucky.

In the darkness of the night a shadow stood outside of their bedroom window looking up. At the same time a shiver ran down Chrissie's back. BBrr… somebody's just walked over my grave," she murmured snuggling into Jake.

Natasha had not seen Chrissie for a few weeks now, since Daisy's farewell supper to be exact, so she was going over to see her today. They were both off work so they had arranged to meet up today at Chrissie's for lunch and then go into town to have some shopping therapy. Chrissie asked if Angie was joining them, but she was working, and besides Natasha wanted to see her friend alone. Catch up on everything. She wanted to know how Daisy was doing in Australia? And how was life since Jake had moved in. But more importantly, had they caught up with the maniac that was still on the loose yet? Chrissie told her that Daisy was doing fine, loving every moment of it, and she hadn't looked back since Jake had moved in, wishing that he'd done it sooner. She handed Natasha a bacon sandwich that they both decided to have after rummaging around in the fridge to see what there was to eat. Chrissie didn't do the big shop until next week, but there were still plenty of tasty things to eat in the freezer and fridge. Natasha asked her again about Stewart. "Any news on him?" Chrissie shook her head saying no, there had been no sign of him. "But once he has been picked up, life will be just perfect." She beamed. Then she went on to tell her what happened the other day at work. She got a funny phone call from a young woman asking if there was any vacancies for chambermaids. When Chrissie had asked her if she would like to come in and pick up a application form, she had asked her if her name was Chrissie and did she have a daughter named Daisy aged twenty. Chrissie had thought that was a rather strange thing to ask, and had asked her why she wanted to know. The woman then went on to say that she knew Daisy from working at the solicitors' office where she'd worked for a short time as a cleaner, and wondered if Chrissie was her mother because she had told her that her mother worked in a hotel. Chrissie thought that was a strange thing to ask her, but brushed it off, asking her to come

191

in and fill in a application form. But that was over a week ago now and she still hadn't been in. Natasha asked what else the woman would want to know her name for? Chrissie just shrugged her shoulders. "You never know these days do you?" she said changing the subject. But her instincts told her that there was more to it. But what, she didn't know. She would just have to wait for the woman to show up. Chrissie could see that Natasha was more than happy with her life right now. She had a glow about her, her eyes sparkled of someone in love. But Chrissie was still finding it hard to come to terms with her friend being a lesbian. But she had never seen Natasha looking so happy, so she knew that she would get used to it. And in time she would. They went into town by bus, and it took them all around the country lanes, taking them half an hour to get into town instead of ten minutes by car. But they had enjoyed the time together watching the fields whizz by them as they caught glimpses of the cows and sheep grazing in them. When they finally got to the shops, they browsed through two or three before making for the café bar in a small hotel, where they ended up drinking a couple of glasses of wine as they put the world to right before catching the bus back home again. Between them they had bought nothing. But they had had a great afternoon out. Just like the old days.

It was Jake's birthday next Wednesday, he would be 35. So on the Saturday Chrissie had invited some friends of his, plus Simon, Shelly and Keith, along with Natasha and Angie, to join them for a small party in the evening. Chrissie was going to do a small buffet with some drinks, and Keith had got his patisserie to make a small birthday cake for him. Chrissie told Jake that it would be a good idea for all of them to meet under one roof, and also it would be great fun holding a party for him. Angie was nervous of going, telling Natasha that she should go along. She would drop her off and pick her up later, but Natasha had put her foot down, telling her that they were partners now, and she had to get along with her long-standing friend. Angie's back bristled up. She did get along with Chrissie, she just found it hard to see how close they were when they were together. It made her feel like an outsider "Well you will have to get use to it," Natasha had snapped, bringing tears to Angie's eyes. She had run up the stairs and slammed the bedroom door before she burst out crying. She didn't want to break down in front of her. After Natasha had calmed herself down, she had gone up to see her, apologising for losing her temper with her. They kissed and made up, and by the end of the evening they were friends again, as they both came to the same conclusion that they'd just had their first argument 'With many more to come over the years.' They laughed, hugging each other.

The outside lights at the cottage were left on for the guests to arrive, and Chrissie was running around the cottage like a scalded ferret, checking that everything had been done. She checked that the buffet was laid up in the dining area and covered over until it was time to eat. She had made one of her punches where everyone asked for the ingredients. But that was her secret. Once they had tasted the ice-cold punch filled to the top with fruits of the season that had been soaked in brandy all day, the rest of the drinks were ignored until it was all gone. She had made some quiches, along with some ham stuffed with cream cheese and chives. Sausage rolls, stuffed tomatoes, stuffed eggs, you name it and it was there, along with her famous meringues filled with fresh cream, and raspberries that she had frozen in the summer. Jake had to pull her out of the kitchen, telling her that they had enough food to feed them for the rest of the year. He guided her towards the stairs telling her that he had run a bath for her. Helping her off with her clothes, he lifted her into the bath as she let out a sigh, sinking down into the bubbles that were floating on top of the steaming water. After scrubbing her back for her, Jake stripped off his clothes and sank down in between her legs with his back facing her while she scrubbed his back lovingly. After an hour of lovemaking that started in the bathroom, ending up in the bedroom, they both hurriedly got dressed, giggling like two schoolchildren as they just made it down the stairs before the first guest arrived.

"Chrissie, you look great," Simon said, picking her up and swinging her around in the hallway as Curly Whirl made his way in with a flushed face behind him. He hadn't wanted to come along with Simon. Chrissie had not invited him, or any other worker except from management, which was a fair shout. It was Jake's birthday and he only knew Curly as being a worker at the hotel, not socially. But Simon had insisted he come along with him after he had caught him down in the doldrums after his boyfriend had let him down, thinking that Chrissie wouldn't mind once she knew the reason why he had brought him along. "I hope you don't mind but I've brought Curly Whirl along. He was at a loose end so I invited him along with me."

Well she did bloody mind, but she didn't say anything to Simon as he kissed her cheek telling her how nice she smelt. But she made sure that she gave him one of her, 'I'll see you later looks', that he knew only too well by now. Then she welcomed Curly in as the next guest arrived. Natasha arrived with Angie a hour after the party had started, and for awhile Chrissie thought that she wasn't going to turn up. But she apologised for being late, handing her the two bottles of wine that she had brought with her, saying that Bubbles once again had gone missing, but they had finally found him in the spare bedroom sound asleep under the bed, oblivious of all the calling for him. "Angie is still getting used to closing the stair gate behind her," Natasha laughed, giving Chrissie a hug. As she ushered them through into the kitchen she could see that Angie was looking tense as she gave them a glass each of her punch. Then they went on through into the lounge where everybody had congregated, all in a jovial mood as they supped on Chrissie's punch. She introduced Natasha and Angie to everyone as a couple, which felt really strange, almost sticking in the back of her throat as she said it for the first time. But as she went around the room, it became easier, and Angie soon relaxed down after drinking the glass of punch that Chrissie had given her, going back out into the kitchen to refill her glass. Simon soon made himself at home, refilling peoples' glasses as they emptied them, having them in fits of laughter with his dry wit. Chrissie announced at 9:30 that it was time for them to tuck into the food that was waiting for them in the dining room area, and everyone must have been hungry because by the end of the evening there wasn't a morsel left except for a few sausage rolls. The punchbowl had been refilled three times through the evening and as the night was coming to an end, some of the men went on to beer. Jake had put on some Motown music after they had all eaten, pushing the table back against the wall in the dining area where most of them got on to the floor and let their hair down. Through the evening Chrissie had kept an eye on Curly Whirly with the drink, but she had to give it to him, he didn't touch a drop. In fact he had been great, clearing the glasses and supplying clean ones after washing them up in the kitchen. He even cleared the dishes from off the table as the plates were emptied. Jake had introduced her to his friends, including Alan, who Chrissie thought was very macho, crushing her hand when he shook it. But he did say sorry to her when he saw her rubbing it as she smiled at him trying not to show that she was in pain. She found out that he had served in the Marine Commando's for five years before buying himself out to join the police force. He was stationed in Reading and had met Jake when they had been at college together in Winchester, (leaving when they were both eighteen), to go their own way

By one o'clock everyone had left thanking Chrissie and Jake for the great party. It was the first time that Chrissie had held a party at the cottage since Freddie had left, and after tonight she was going to hold more. It had been a great evening. Jake told her to leave everything until tomorrow, they would clear up together after a good night's sleep. "And besides," he said kissing the back of her neck as she stifled a yawn, "I want to thank you for the wonderful evening that you have just given me." Chrissie wasn't about to argue with that as she slipped her hand around his pert bottom as they made it up the stairs undressing each other.

The head belonging to the shadow that was lurking outside under the willow tree looked up as the bedroom light went on, smirking as it slinked of into the night. "Not long now," he spat out, exhaling a puff of smoke.

CHAPTER SIXTEEN

Chrissie was busying herself around the cottage while Jake was at work. It was her day off and she had a lot to catch up on. Since Jake had moved in four months ago she found that she had no time to catch up on the things that she liked to do on her own. Not that she was complaining, she hadn't felt this happy for a very long time. Jake fulfilled her every need. He made love to her most nights, and they worked well together at work, unless he upset her that was! Chrissie was the live wire out of the two of them, and if he annoyed her he would know all about it. But Jake could usually defuse the situation if she hadn't pushed him too far. But if she was being unreasonable, then he would leave her to stew in it. But it was never that long before they were lovingly making it up. Chrissie was still missing Daisy like mad, and she would either phone Daisy at least once a week, or Daisy would phone her mother so they could catch up with one another. Daisy was having a whale of a time in Australia, and had found a job waiting on tables in one of the many restaurants that were dotted around Sydney Harbour. She was enjoying the sun, sand and beaches, going after work with Jasmine for a swim in the warm sea that surrounded them. Today Chrissie was going to work in the garden. Spring was in the air and she needed to do some weeding, plus it was that time of the year again to put her pink wellies on and go slug hunting. The bastards had already started on some of the spring bulbs that were just peeking through the earth of her flower beds. Marmalade went out with her into the garden, following her down to the shed where she got out her wicker basket where she kept her tools and gloves. It was chilly, but the sun was out. Chrissie was going to work in the garden for a couple of hours, then she was going in to sort the ironing out, the one job in life that she hated besides sewing. If Daisy or Freddie ever had a button missing from off a shirt or blouse she would rather buy them a new one than sew it back on again. A bit of an exaggeration, but that's how much she hated those two chores. The smell from the hyacinths were heavenly, and the crocuses that were dotted around in the lawn and flower beds looked magnificent. it was her favourite time of the year with everything waking up from the winter season, and summer time just around the corner. This year she was going to hold a garden party and invite all of their friends, get Jake to light up the barbecue that had not been used for a very long time.

Stretching her back, Chrissie stood up after hearing the bush rustle from the end of the garden. The birds had been disturbed by something and she wondered why. Turning around, she stiffened with fear as she saw a familiar figure appear from nowhere. He was standing by the bush staring at her with those evil eyes of his, smirking.

"At last, Bitch." he said just loud enough for her to hear but not so the neighbours could hear.

Chrissie legs went to jelly as she held herself up against the apple tree to save herself from falling. She couldn't get her legs to move so she could run as he slowly walked up the garden towards her. She had gone into shock.

"Once again, Rosie." he sneered.

She flinched, nobody called her by that name except him. She was known as Chrissie. That was her name now.

"I want to see my daughter."

Chrissie knew that she had to move. She had to get back up to the cottage and get inside before he got hold of her, and press the emergency button on her phone to get through to the police. If she stayed where she was he would kill her. She could see the hate for her in his ice-cold eyes. But try as she did, her legs just wouldn't move. He was getting closer and closer to her, she could almost see the whites of his eyes. He looked insane as he put his hand into the pocket of the shabby grey coat he was wearing, bringing out a pair of rusty handcuffs. Her eyes bulged out at the sight of these as the sheer terror of what he could do to her ran through her body like a sheet of lightning. She thought that she was going to pass out as she swayed on her feet, and it took all of her willpower not to. Then something clicked in her brain. My God, he was going to kidnap and torture her. Or worse still... Kill her. How she got her legs to run under her she'll never know, as she ran screaming so loud up towards the cottage that she thought that her lungs would burst. She could feel the heat of his body behind her, he was so close on her heels. She fell through the patio doors pulling them across with all her strength to stop him getting in as she tried to turn the key in the lock. But her hands were shaking so much that she couldn't get the key to turn as he managed to get his fingers into the crack of the door prising it open. In sheer panic she found the strength from somewhere to give it one more tug, letting out a piercing scream as the key turned. She fell backwards as she saw the tip of his finger drop onto the floor. Stewart kicked at the door violently, howling out in pain as Chrissie ran through into the hallway pressing the emergency button on the phone as she slumped to the floor.

She didn't know how long she had been sat on the floor in the hallway, clenching her chest as she tried to control her breathing. She could hear her name being called and somebody banging on the door. She thought that it was Stewart still trying to get into the cottage, and the shock of it all had brought on a asthma attack. The first one she'd had for a very long time, and she knew that she had to get to her inhaler that was in the kitchen drawer. How she had managed to crawl her way through into the kitchen and pull herself up to reach into the drawer for the inhaler, she'll never know. But after inhaling a couple of deep breaths to steady her breathing, she realised that it was the police trying to get in through the front door. And not the evil bastard who was trying to kill her.

The next day the local newspaper had been full of it, leaving Chrissie feeling so low after reading the headlines:

"MAN STALKS RAPE VICTIM TO SEE DAUGHTER!"

For the next couple of days Chrissie went into hibernation. She didn't want to see or speak to anyone. She spent her time looking out into the garden trying to come to terms with it all. Was it really all over now? Jake took a few days off to be with her, and also to ward the press off as they hung around the cottage. Giving her the space she needed, leaving her to come to terms with what had just happened, but being there for her when she searched him out for comfort. Chrissie didn't want to speak to anyone, let alone the press. She was still getting over the shock of it all. Freddie had phoned asking if there was anything he could do for her, and Natasha had come around, pushing her way through the handful of press outside of the cottage as they yelled out after her asking questions as she made her way up to the cottage to comfort her friend. Chrissie was really amazed by all of the support that she got from her friends, and from the church. Reverand Christian was back from his tour of the Third World, and had visited her giving her no end of support. Simon had sent her a wonderful basket of spring flowers with a card tucked inside of it with, "Please come back soon. Daphne is driving me mad with the linen. She's even worse than you!!!!" on it. That had brought a smile to her face. Tom Noble had come to see her from the police station, assuring her that it was now all under control. They had Stewart locked up inside where he would be locked away for a long time after the trial was over. "Then you can start living again," he'd smiled, squeezing her hand. But would she?

****

Lily had seen a snippet about the coming trial in a national newspaper. Could this Rosie Grimes, now known as Chrissie Brown... be her mother? Lily lived in Bath and knew that she had been adopted from birth. Her adoptive mother told her just before she had died of cancer when Lily was aged thirteen. Rachael thought that it was only right that Lily knew she had been adopted, she was dying and would not be around to tell her if in later years she might want to search for her mother. She had also told her that the reason she had been adopted after Lily had asked her. She saw no reason to lie to her. And she had the right to know why her birth mother had given her up. So when Lily had seen the small snippet in the Daily Mirror of how this woman had been stalked by the man that had raped her many years ago, thinking that the daughter she had with her husband was his. "My God, I could have a sister." was the first thing that Lily thought. Then she saw a photo of Chrissie in the paper, and could see similarities of herself in her. Then she worked out how many years ago the rape had taken place. Twenty-nine years ago. The age she was now. Lily had kept all of this to herself, and said nothing to her father, who was now happily remarried, and living on the outskirts of Bath. She needed time to get her head around it all. She had tried looking her mother up a few years ago, but with no success and had decided to let sleeping dogs lie. But now she had seen this in the paper it had got her curiosity going and she wanted to chase it up. But it would have to be the right time. Not now after all that had just happened to this poor woman. But she would definitely make enquiries and take it from there.

To get back to work had been Chrissie's saviour. All of her working colleagues welcomed her back, but didn't make a fuss of things, and life had gradually got back to normal. Janie was now back at work, and she was keeping the baby. She had gone to see her parents, who at first were upset, but soon came around, saying they would back her on whatever decision she decided to make. So after having a heart to heart talk with Darrel, they decided that they would keep the baby, and Janie would work through until her maternity leave. At the meeting this morning, Mr Grey had gone over the Easter weekend with them, checking that everything was in order, and the Easter Eggs had been ordered in for the egg hunt on the Sunday morning for the children that would be staying there over the Easter period with their families. Simon hated the egg hunts.

"Bloody brats running all over the show," he groaned. "And where was Mr Grey when all of this was going on? "At home that's where," he snorted, turning his nose up in the air as Chrissie told him to stop moaning.

"It's alright for you. You don't have them running around the restaurant and in and out from under the tables looking for a poxy egg that's no bigger than a thimble."

"Simon, you are really getting too old for this job," she teased, giving him a shove along the corridor.

He was up looking around the corridors to see if his staff had collected all of the breakfast trays from off the floors before he got a call from Chrissie, but she was up there checking on the rooms and caught him doing it.

"There's one outside of room 315," she called out after him as he turned and poked his tongue out at her. Jake was just coming out of the lift when he heard all of this banter going on between them, and turned laughing as he heard Simon still mumbling on about something or other as he was going up on to the third floor.

202

"Is she being a pain?" he called out after him, as Simon ranted on about the Easter egg hunt that his staff would have to clear up after all the kids had left the silver wrappers from off the eggs all over the restaurant floor on Sunday.

Chrissie carried on checking the rooms after Jake said that he would be home late from work that evening. Mr Grey had called a meeting between them at six o'clock, and if he knew him and his meetings he would be there at least for a good hour or so, but Chrissie was going over to Natasha's on the way home anyway, so he would probably be home before she was. She had to talk with her friend about the phone call that she'd had on Sunday. It was lunchtime, and she was just in the middle of cooking a roast when the phone rang. Going through into the hallway she picked it up, she was chewing on a piece of crackling from off the pork she was cooking and had to quickly swallow it before saying hello. For a few seconds the line seemed to go dead, and then a young female's voice came on asking if she could speak to Chrissie, please.

"It's Chrissie speaking." Chrissie thought at first it was somebody from work calling her with a problem. But then the voice on the other end of the phone said.

"I'm Lily Small."

Chrissie thought for a moment. She didn't know anyone by the name of Lily Small, and she certainly didn't have anyone working for her by that name.

"Sorry. Do I know you?" she asked, looking down at the phone feeling uneasy.

"No, you don't know me. But I think I am your daughter."

The room swam round as Chrissie flopped down into the chair. Jake who was coming down the stairs saw her face go white and went over to her.

"Who is it?" he asked, "What's wrong?" At first he thought that it was something to do with Daisy. Chrissie's face had gone as white as a ghost, and she was shaking.

"Hello. Are you still there? Shall I ring back another time?" Lily felt awful at just ringing her out of the blue. She could have given the poor woman a heart attack.

"No, please don't put the phone down," Chrissie managed to say as she shooed Jake away.

Jake frowned at her going through into the lounge. He was going to listen on in the conversation. Chrissie looked stressed and after all that she had been through recently, he wasn't having anyone else upsetting her.

"Why do you think you are my daughter?" Chrissie managed to ask without breaking down. The whole of her body was shaking, and she didn't know whether it was through dread or the excitement of her lost daughter finding her.

Lily was feeling the same on the end of the phone. It had taken a lot of courage for her to be doing this. But she wanted to meet her natural mother. She had been thinking about it since seeing the news of the attack on her mother, (or who she thought was her mother) in the tabloid six months ago now, and she had held on this long to reach her. She had found her number in the phone book, and many a time she had picked up the phone and dialled her number, putting the phone down before it could be answered. She had even driven out to where she lived, and saw the beautiful cottage that she lived in, with the roses all around the door and flower beds everywhere you looked. She really had to be hard on herself to stop from ringing on the doorbell. It was only because she couldn't face the rebuff if Chrissie had told her to go away. Over the phone would be bad enough, but face to face she knew she wouldn't be able to take that. She told Chrissie that she had seen the story of the attack on her in the newspaper, and had put two and two together. Her

204

mother (adoptive mother) had told her she had been adopted, and the reason why her biological mother had given her up. Chrissie had tears streaming down her face after coming off the phone. Jake was waiting with a large glass of wine for her after getting the gist of the conversation.

"My God, what next?" She drank the wine in four gulps getting up to refill her glass again. Jake took it from her as she went through into the kitchen seeing the smoke bellowing from her oven. The smoke alarms went off, as Jake threw open the kitchen windows cursing.

"You alright?" he asked after flapping the tea towel around the smoke alarm to silence the noise.

Chrissie took the glass of wine from him, taking another gulp from it before telling him that she had just agreed to see Lily, her daughter, next week, here at the cottage where she would cook her lunch. Had she gone mad? What would she say to her? Jake could see the panic rising in her as he walked over to her.

"My God, what have I done?"

She looked up at Jake for reassurance that she had made the right decision to see her. He put his arm around her shoulder telling her that she had to see her. If she didn't, she would regret it for the rest of her life. Daisy had phoned her later in the evening, and she had been full of the joys of spring, telling her mother what she had been doing over the last couple of weeks. Places she had been to, and the excitement of going to the Sydney Opera House to see A Midsummer Night's Dream, that was playing there. It had taken all of Chrissie's willpower not to tell her about Lily. She really wanted to, but it would have been unfair with her being all those miles away, and she knew that she would be worried about her and she didn't want that. So she would phone her later in the week, after she had seen her. Daisy had been ready to fly home when she found out about Chrissie's ordeal with Stewart, but thank God she had managed to talk her out of it.

She had been in a daze all week, and the week was dragging, even though it was very busy at work. All Chrissie could think of was the meeting with Lily on Sunday. How she was going to react seeing the child she had given away she didn't know. She had managed to swop her Sunday with Dawn, telling her that something personal had come up. Well at least that was the truth. But Dawn did ask her if everything was alright at home. She knew what she had been through this year, and it was unusual for Chrissie to take time off over a bank holiday. Chrissie had told her that she was meeting somebody who she hadn't seen for a long time, which was the truth, and Dawn seemed to be happy with that. When Simon had found out, he had jibed her all week for having the Easter Sunday off, but if he had known the reason why he would have been mortified that he had been teasing her. Jake couldn't say anything to him when he had asked if Chrissie was okay as she had seemed to be down a bit this week. He had been sworn to secrecy, and it would have been more than his life was worth if he said anything at work. He also, thankfully, had managed to wangle the Sunday off, or part of it. He would go in on the early duty, and one of the other managers would come in at twelve to cover. Lily wasn't arriving until one o'clock, so it would give him plenty of time to get home.

Over and over again Chrissie was asking herself how the hell she was going to handle this. What was she going to say to her? What could she say? Honesty was the best policy! Shit that was easy to say if it wasn't you that was in this situation. Did she really want to see her? Of course she did. The truth was, she was scared. Frightened that Lily was going to think the worse of her. She was so out of her safety zone at the moment. But she had to think of how Lily was feeling. Just as nervous of meeting her as she was, and she had to try and remember this while she was feeling so sorry for herself. All of this was running around in her head as she tried acting as though everything was all okay at work. Simon had come down to the office for an afternoon coffee with her, and everything was okay until he started teasing her again about having the Sunday off, and she just lost her cool with him, telling him to piss off. That was so not like Chrissie, and Simon had been so shocked by her outburst that he had gone to see Jake to ask if everything was alright with her. Jake had smiled keeping his lips sealed, but he did manage to reassure him that she was okay. "Give it time. She'll soon be her old self again."

"I don't know if I can do this, Jake."

Chrissie poured herself out a glass of wine before she went over to the oven to check the chicken that was cooking in there. Lily would be there in the next hour, and she felt like a cat on a hot tin roof. She was so wound up that she felt she could burst any moment now. Like an elastic band pulled to its limit.

"You can do it," Jake said, slipping his arm around her waist as he pulled her into him. "She will be feeling just as nervous as you are. Even more so I would have thought. At least you're on your home ground."

Saying nothing, Chrissie shrugged her shoulders as she pulled away from him. She went through and laid up the table for lunch in the dining room area, putting her personal touch to it with the fresh flowers that were stood in the centre of the table, picked fresh from the garden that morning. She'd also used the pink tablecloth, matching it up with her pink-handled cutlery and cruet set. Usually she only got this out for special occasions. Then she went out into the garden. It was a warm September day, and she walked down to her roses, sniffing in the perfume that hung in the air from their sweet smell. Marmalade came through the bush, purring as he came up to her. It was as though he sensed that Chrissie was feeling unhappy as he nuzzled his head around her legs. Chrissie tickled him under the chin before going back up to the cottage, going through into the kitchen and over to the fridge. She pulled out a bottle of wine that was chilling in there, getting a glass from off the Welsh dresser to pour herself some out. But then she stopped herself. Drinking more wine wasn't the answer. She went through to Jake who was sat reading the Sunday newspaper saying that she was going down to the corner shop for some milk and eggs. Jake said nothing to her. The look on her face said it all. She was going whatever he said. But he did tell her not to be long as Lily would be arriving within the next half hour.

Chrissie picked up her car keys saying she would only be ten minutes, then left before Jake could say anymore. She drove down the lane and took the left-hand turn that would take her to the village shop. Why she was going out for milk and eggs when she already had some in the fridge, she'd never know. But she just had to get out of the cottage for some breathing space. She drew up outside of the shop and turned the engine off. She just couldn't do this. She didn't want to meet her daughter. What right had she coming into her life opening up the box that she had locked away so many years now. She wasn't ready to look inside of it. It was still too painful. The guilt she was feeling for giving her baby away engulfed her. But why? She'd had no choice. But then everyone had a choice didn't they? She put her head into her arms leaning up against the steering wheel.

"STOP IT!" She said aloud to herself as she struggled with her feelings.

After sitting there for awhile, she started cursing herself. "Get control of yourself, you stupid cow. You're not the bloody child here." She started the car up looking at the time on her watch. Lily would be there by now, and poor Jake would be feeling very embarrassed with her not being there to see her in. "You're out of order," she said to herself as she drove along over the fifty mile speed limit. Lily was her daughter. Not Jake's. He

208

had already seen her through the dark days, this was being totally unfair to him. The first thing she saw was the red Beetle car that was parked up alongside of Jake's Jeep. Her stomach did a somersault as she drew up behind them, switching off the engine. Everything that she was doing seemed to be in slow motion As much as she tried to hurry herself, the slower she seemed to go. The thought of going indoors filled her with terror. Letting herself in as quietly as possible, she went through into the kitchen, and went over to the fridge where she poured herself a large glass of wine. As she drank it back she could hear the chatter coming from the lounge. Tears came to her eyes as she heard for the very first time in her home the voice of her daughter. She could hear Jake saying that she would be back soon, that she had just gone to the shop for some milk and eggs. She knew that she had to go through into the lounge, but her courage was failing her. Then just as she'd finished telling herself off for being such a coward, Jake came through into the kitchen. He had seen her car parked in the driveway, and put two and two together, knowing she was struggling to come through to see her daughter.

"She's beautiful, Chrissie. Just like you. Come on in and meet your daughter," he said, taking her arm and leading her in through to the lounge.

CHAPTER SEVENTEEN

Lily had lived on her own in a two-bedroom flat for over ten years now, above a craft shop in the centre of Bath, and she loved it. She'd had a couple of relationships over the years, but nothing that had lasted. And at the moment she was living a single life and was enjoying every minute of it. This is what she had told Chrissie after they had got over the emotion of meeting each other for the first time. When Chrissie had entered the lounge, both of them had stood there hovering like birds in flight. Neither of them knowing who should make the first move, and the silence between them had been so painful, it seemed like an eternity to them both before Jake stepped in and introduced them to each other. Shaking Lily's hand seemed so informal to Chrissie. This was her daughter that she was meeting. Not some stranger. "But she is a stranger," a voice in her head said to her as she took Lily into her arms and gave her a hug.

"It's really nice to meet you,"

"And it's lovely to meet you," Lily had said with tears in her eyes.

Chrissie guided her over to the settee, taking a seat opposite her so she could take in her daughter's features for the very first time. She had her large blue eyes, that were brimming with tears, and long fair hair that was tied back in a ponytail. Chrissie couldn't believe how much she looked like her. She could see nothing of that monster in her. "Stop it," the same voice in her head warned her. "This is your daughter. Not him… Let it go." Chrissie felt a shiver go down her spine as she smiled sweetly at Lily.

Jake excused himself. He was going to bring some wine through to celebrate this special occasion before they went through for lunch, that would now be well and truly cooked! The room fell into silence as they looked at each other, taking one another in, and Chrissie knew that she had made the right decision to see her daughter as she felt the surge of a mother's love run through her veins. She couldn't describe how she was feeling right now, only that a gap in her life had been fulfilled at long last, and now she felt that she could move on. So without thinking, she got up and went over to Lily, pulling her up from off the settee, and put her arms around her squeezing her tight. At first Lily didn't know what to do, then realise that she didn't have to do anything as she also wrapped her arms around her mother. Having their arms around each other said it all for the both of them.

It was smiles all around the table as Lily filled them in with her life up to now, telling Chrissie of her adoptive parents, and of how good they had been to her. She told her that her father still lived outside of Bath, and she still saw him regularly. Chrissie sat listening intently. She was beautiful, and lots of her mannerisms reminded her of Daisy, although she didn't look like her. Daisy was more like her father with her colouring and ways. When she had told Lily about Daisy, she had been thrilled, saying that she had always wanted to have a sister, and she couldn't wait to meet her. She was disappointed when Chrissie told her that she was in Australia, but reassured her that she would be back home again early next year, and they would be have a big family reunion. There was so much that they had to catch up on, but it was going to take time. Chrissie was over the moon at meeting her firstborn, but she was feeling really emotionally exhausted by the end of the day. It was going to take her some time to get used to having her around in her life. There had already been a few awkward moments at the table, especially when she had asked about Stewart. "Was he really that bad?" she asked Chrissie, then wished she hadn't when she saw Chrissie flinch at the mention of his name. Jake had stepped in when he saw that Chrissie had been lost for words. The mere mention of his name still made her shudder. But she knew it was something that Lily would want to know about. But right now was not the time to ask her about him. Jake had subtlety changed the subject. But it hadn't gone unnoticed to Lily either as the course of the conversation was changed, laughing at something that Jake had said about something that had happened at work. Lily finally left at 9:30 after having a really great bonding time with Chrissie, asking if she could come to see her again. Chrissie told her that she was off on a Sunday in a couple of weeks' time, so Lily said that she would phone her on the Saturday to confirm it before she came over just in case something came up and she couldn't make it. They hugged and kissed again before she went off in her car, waving until she was out of sight. That night cuddled up in bed with Jake, Chrissie told him that she didn't know if she could talk to Lily about her father. It was still to raw for her to think about it, let alone talk about it.

"Don't beat yourself up about it, Chrissie," Jake said cuddling into her. "The time's not right just now. You've only just met her. Give it time, it'll come."

She turned over in the bed feeling uneasy with herself. She'd felt so fenced in when Lily had started asking her questions about her father. But why? Was she feeling guilty? "Oh stop it. Get to sleep," the same voice she heard before was telling her. "You're making the brain hurt." Chrissie smiled at this, and decided that she would take notice of her inner conscience talking to her. Well, she assumed that it was her conscience

212

talking to her. It was either that, or she was finally losing her marbles.

When she got into work the next morning, she got the surprise of her life when she saw Colin sat waiting for her in the foyer. He had just found out what had happened to her through a friend who had seen it in the newspaper while he had been away on holiday, and this was the first opportunity that he'd had since getting back to go and see her. He didn't start work until 9:30, and knew that Chrissie started at 8:30, so he thought that he would call in to see her on his way in to work. Chrissie picked up her keys from reception from a smiling Shelly who winked at her telling her to have a good day as she looked Colin up and down. Chrissie tossed her eyes up at her, ignoring her as she said hello to Colin, who had come across giving her a peck on the cheek.

"This is a surprise. What brings you here?" She asked, ushering him towards the lift. "I'll make you a coffee once we get to my office," she smiled, getting out of the lift as it came to a halt. Colin followed her along to the office explaining why he was there, and that he'd just called in to see if she was okay. Chrissie thought that was very sweet of him and told him so as she unlocked the office door, saying good morning to Daphne who was outside of the office filling up the trolleys with linen ready for the girls. She smiled at Colin then went back into the linen room when she saw that Chrissie wasn't going to introduce him to her, just dying of curiosity to know who he was, and it wasn't long before Simon was up those stairs and knocking on the office door, opening it up saying good morning to Chrissie, then apologising to her for interrupting. He "didn't realise that she had a visitor," he said. Eyeing Colin up and down. Chrissie could have died. She was going to bloody kill him when she caught up with him later.

"Morning, sweetie," he said as Colin raised his hand to shake Simon's as he smiled up at him from the chair. "You need to be careful when you get up out of that death trap," he said, still taking in Colin's masculine physique.

"He's straight," Chrissie said as she ushered him out of the door, telling him that she would see him later, giving him one of her evil looks as he winked at Colin going out of the door.

When she turned around to Colin to apologise for Simon's behavior, he was laughing.

"Nice bloke," he said, finishing off his coffee.

Then she filled him in on the encounter with Stewart, reassuring him that he was locked away now as his eyes widened. He got up to go when he saw her chambermaids coming in for work, saying that he had to be on his way or else he would be late for work. He didn't realise what the time was. As he got up, the chair leaned sideways almost tipping over. Laughing, Chrissie put her arms out to save him as Colin laughed along with her, saying he could see now what Simon had meant about the chair. Straightening himself up he asked her if they could meet up one evening, already knowing what the answer would be. But Chrissie had been very tempted to say yes, she liked Colin. And if it wasn't for the fact that she was with Jake, she would have taken up the invitation. But she was honest with him and said that she was now in a relationship, so he bowed out gracefully, kissing her on the hand.

"If ever you're free!" he teased.

Jake came on to the scene just as he had kissed her hand, and the look on his face said it all.

"Having fun?" he asked sarcastically. Then looked at Chrissie, telling her that the girls were waiting for their room keys, storming off before she could reply. After saying goodbye to Colin, who hoped he hadn't got her into trouble, she handed out the room keys to the girls with their day list, then stormed down to Jake's office where she tore a strip off him, asking who the hell he thought he was? He didn't bloody well own her. And if she wanted to have male friends, she bloody well would. Then walked out on him before he could catch his breath.

"Whoa, what was that all about?" Simon asked as he walked into the office as she stormed pass him, pushing him aside.

"Domestic," Jake said, asking him what he wanted.

Simon knew by the tone of his voice that he wasn't in the mood for any small talk, so got straight to the point, telling him that he had had a complaint from one of their guests this morning at breakfast. Mrs Cole from room 213 had told him that a thousand pounds had been 'stolen' from her room. Jake put his head into his hands. God, this was all he needed after the scene he'd just had from Chrissie.

"Has anyone checked her room?" he asked, rubbing his eyes.

"Nope," Simon said, putting his hands up into the air.

"Does Chrissie know?"

Simon just raised his eyebrows. He didn't have to say any more.

"Well, I think you should get hold of her and let her in on the saga, then both of you go along to the room and check it with Mrs Cole being present. Let me know when you have found out more. If the money isn't found then we call in the police."

"Okay. We'll get back to you as soon as we've seen Mrs Cole and searched her room," Simon sighed, knowing the reception he was going to get from Chrissie. It was bad enough giving her bad news when she was in a good mood, let alone when she was already on the warpath. He went straight up to her office but the door was locked.

"BOO."

"Freaking hell," Simon yelled out almost jumping out of his skin. "You nearly gave me a freaking heart attack," he said, holding his chest as he turned around to see who it was.

Daphne was laughing her head off. She had sneaked up behind him when she saw him coming along the corridor towards the office, and she just couldn't resist doing it. She knew he would jump out of his skin.

"Cow," he said, half smiling as he began to see the funny side of it.

He asked her if she had seen Chrissie, and Daphne told him that she had just gone up on the floors to chase up the linen porter who had still not come down yet with a trolley load of soiled linen that should have been collected off the floors by now.

"Problem?" she asked walking back to the linen room.

"Whenever is there not a bloody problem in this place, sweetie," he said taking the staff lift up onto the floors.

He found Chrissie on the eighth floor tearing a strip off Tony the linen porter for wasting time talking to the chambermaids, telling him to get his ass down to the linen room where Daphne was waiting for him.

"Great," Simon thought as he went up to her frowning. "Now I've got to tell her about the missing money, she's really going to flip."

"What's up?" she asked him straightening the jacket of her suit.

"You're not going to like this!"

"Try me. The day might just as well go on as it started…. Crap."

Simon told her all about the complaint he'd got this morning from Mrs Cole who was staying in room 213. A thousand pounds had been 'stolen' from her room.

"Oh for Christ sake. What the bloody hell was she doing with a thousand pounds cash in her room in the first place. Why the hell wasn't it put into the hotel safe in the first place?"

Simon just shrugged his shoulders, he wasn't getting into a spat with Chrissie in this mood, he told her that he was going down to room 213, so she followed on behind him muttering away to herself. When they got to the second floor, Chrissie saw Maria who worked on this floor talking to Dawn, and as she got nearer to them she could see that Maria had been crying. Apparently, Mrs Cole had already caught up with Maria, and had almost accused her of taking the money. Chrissie told her to go and have a tea break. She would see to Mrs Cole, and the money would be found as it usually was when something like this happened. It had to be in the room somewhere. Simon had to calm Chrissie down before they went into the room. She was spitting blood by this time. Why was it every time something went missing from a room, it was the poor chambermaid's fault. Tapping her keys against the door, she called out saying who she was, then stood patiently waiting with Simon for Mrs Cole to open the door up.

"At last," Mrs Cole said, letting them in. "I've lost a thousand pounds and it's taken half a day before anyone comes up to see me. Have the police been phoned yet?"

Chrissie and Simon looked at each other. The time was only ten o'clock, so for a start she hadn't been waiting half a day for them to come along to the room. But they made no comment, and Chrissie asked where she had kept the money. Mrs Cole wasn't sure, but she thought she had tucked it into one of her gloves that were in the drawer. Again they both looked at one another but said nothing. Chrissie asked if she would mind if they thoroughly searched the rooms themselves before they called the police in. Then if the money wasn't found they would phone the police straight away. Mrs Cole had grunted a 'yes' and sat down on the bedroom chair while they both went through her 'drawers,' (so to speak), then stripped back her bed that had been freshly made to look under the mattress.

"You'll not find it there. I'm not as stupid as to leave it under a mattress," she said indignantly.

It was getting harder for Chrissie to keep her mouth shut, but somehow she manage to button it, and carried on searching the room for the money. But after going through everything that they could think of, they had to admit that there was no thousand pounds to be found. Chrissie had to ask the question was she sure that she had brought a thousand pounds with her in cash, and as expected, Mrs Cole flipped her lid. How dare they ask her such a thing. Did they think that she was lying?' But Chrissie had to ask her. It was quite feasible for anyone to think that they had brought something with them on holiday, only to find it at home when they returned. That had happened so many times when a guest had thought that they had brought something with them, like a item of clothing, and then had found it when they had got back home.

Chrissie and Simon went and saw Jake after promising Mrs Cole that the police were going to be involved, and could she please be around when they arrived because she would be the first person they would want to speak to. Mr Grey was away on holiday so it was down to Jake to make the decision of what they were going to do. And with no hesitation he phoned the police while Chrissie and Simon went over who had access to keys for the rooms. The police were there within half an hour, and Chrissie took them up to the room where Mrs Cole was sat waiting for them. She excused herself after the police said that they would need to question the chambermaid and any other person who would have had to come into the room that morning. Poor Maria was so upset, but Chrissie reassured her that she knew that she would not have touched that money. IF there was some money in the first place. It had gone around the hotel hotline like a dose of salts, with all the staff talking about it. She told her girls to get on with their work when she found them gossiping with the floor waiters who had come up for the breakfast trays. "Marvelous," Chrissie thought. Any other day I would have to phone down to get the trays cleared. But as soon as something out of the ordinary happens, they're like bees around a honey pot.'

Chrissie made a cup of coffee for herself and Dawn while they had a discussion about room 213. Dawn said that Maria had been very upset, but she had managed to calm her down, and she was now back on the floor working. Chrissie thanked her for that and was just about to go back up on to the floors when she heard Daphne yelling for her.

"Chrissie. Chrissie. Come here quick."

Chrissie jumped out of her chair almost falling over her own two feet as she raced out of the door to see Daphne standing there waving a pillow case in one hand, and a bundle of notes in the other.

Mrs Cole had stuffed her thousand pounds into her pillow case before going to bed that night, Mrs Cole swore blind. She said she 'thought' she had placed the money in one of her gloves. Relief ran through Chrissie and everyone else when they found out that the money had been found safely, especially Maria. The police had not been too pleased with being called out on a wild goose chase, telling Mrs Cole that they thought it would have been sensible if she had kept the money in the hotel safe and not in her bedroom. But she did at least apologise to them all, and gave Maria a large tip, telling her to go and buy herself something special.

219

"What a bloody day," Chrissie cursed, kicking her shoes off while Jake poured her a glass of wine. It was now seven o'clock and she had to meet Natasha and Angie at 7:30 for a meal and a catch up. She was so tempted to cancel it. But then thought again. It would be great to relax with both of them. Get away from the hotel scene for a while and mix with people that were sane, if there were any that is. She was still a bit off with Jake after this morning's episode with him. But that had almost sunk into the background after what had happened today. And he had offered to drive her to where she was going to meet the girls and pick her up again if she wanted him to. So she would put it on the back boiler for now and save it for another day. But she would have to have it out with him. He was going to have to get used to her having male friends besides having female friends if this relationship was going to work. She quickly showered, taking her glass of wine up with her, then changed into a pair of black trousers with a pink polo neck jumper, slipping her feet in a pair of comfortable black boots that she'd had for years, and swung her hair up into a bun at the back of her head. All she had to do now was to slip on her poncho and she was ready to leave. Jake sniffed in the air as she came into the lounge telling him she was ready to go. The perfume she was wearing reminded him of a garden of roses. Following her out into the hallway, he caught hold of her, pulling her into him as he kissed her lightly on the lips.

"You sure you don't want to stay home and have the evening with me?" he asked, nibbling on her ear.

"I'm sure," she said, flicking her warm tongue across his lips as she pulled him out of the door, pushing him towards the car.

CHAPTER EIGHTEEN

As Chrissie walked through the restaurant door, she saw Natasha and Angie deep in conversation, holding hands under the table. She hesitated before going over to them, because as much as she had tried to come around to her best friend being in a relationship with a woman, she was still struggling with it. It was Natasha who noticed her as she walked across to the table, following a young waitress.

"Chrissie, darling." She got up and gave her a hug, kissing her cheeks.

"Hello, Chrissie," Angie said. But she didn't get up, just extended her hand to shake hers.

Chrissie had a feeling that she felt threatened when she and Angie met up. Why she didn't know. But she just got that impression whenever she was around, it was as though she was a threat to her somehow. But nothing could be further from the truth. Chrissie was into men not women. But whatever all the fuss was about she'd never know. It was a known fact that everyone had lesbian or homosexual tendencies in them. Or that's what she had been told! They already had a glass of wine each on the table, and Natasha ordered one for Chrissie as she pulled out the chair for her.

"How's things with you, darling?"

If Chrissie had been on her own with Natasha she would have told her straight away about the meeting with Lily, but with Angie being there, she felt a bit wary of discussing personal things in front of her. So she said that everything was okay, that she'd heard from Daisy and she was having lots of fun, but she couldn't wait until she was back home in the new year. The waitress brought over her glass of wine, which was a large one. Usually she would have a small one, but as Natasha pointed out to her, she wasn't driving home tonight so she could let her hair down. They ordered from off the menu, Chrissie ordering a pasta while Natasha and Angie went for the steak, and as the evening went on, the three of them relaxed down, especially Angie, who had become very talkative, telling Chrissie about the escape of the Great Dane that had been brought into them at the practice that day for some treatment on his ear. His name was Berty, and he was eight years old and was going deaf, so his owner had brought him in for a ear wash hoping that it was just a build-up of the wax in his ears and nothing else untoward. "Just like us humans," Angie laughed. Anyway, he had made a dash for the door when another customer had come in with their parrot, making a beeline for the field at the end of the veterinary garden before Angie and its owner could get hold of his collar. Bounding down the large garden area after him, Angie called out to him, but as his owner said to her, "unless he's right next to you, he won't be able to hear you calling him because he's deaf!" In the field at the end of the grounds were a couple of donkeys that were kept there to graze, and Berty had spotted them, making a leap over the fence to get to them. The owner screamed out after him, but it was of no use, Berty had already got to the smallest of the two of them, sniffing behind its back quarters. Then without any warning... Angie had a coughing fit at this point, and Chrissie and Natasha started banging her on her back asking her what happened next. Taking a drink of her wine, she then went on telling them that Berty had tried to mount the poor donkey who was kicking out her back legs trying to get him off her. The three of them were in fits of laughter when the waitress came over with their food, and she thought they had all gone mad, until Angie explained that she was just telling them a tale from work about a dog and a donkey. The waitress looked at them as though they were mad as Natasha asked her for some mustard before Angie went on to say that they got Berty back over the fence. He'd soon got fed up with being kicked at, and had jumped back over the fence with his tail between his legs. The owner had been so embarrassed by it all, that Angie had to get someone to make her a cup of tea to calm her down, trying to make light of it by saying that perhaps they should get Berty a pair of glasses, then maybe he'll be able to tell the difference between a donkey and a Great Dane. But it fell on deaf ears. Chrissie was laughing so much that her stomach was aching as she ordered another glass of wine. After that, they were very relaxed in one another's company, and after finishing their meal, they went up to the small bar that was in the restaurant area, and carried on enjoying the evening. Angie excused herself to powder her nose, leaving them both to catch up on a few things. She knew how close Chrissie and Natasha were and knew that they would catch up on a few things that they wouldn't talk about with her being there, and she was quite at ease with leaving them together, or though if she was honest with herself, it had taken her some time to get used to them being so close. But she knew now for certain that it had only ever been a platonic relationship between them both. Chrissie was definitely straight. (Whatever that meant!)

"So how did the meeting go with Lily?" Natasha asked.

She had been dying to know and had to restrain herself from phoning her on Sunday. It was Angie who discouraged her from doing it, saying that Chrissie would be mentally worn out after meeting her daughter for the first time and didn't think she would be up to being interrogated.

Chrissie shuffled herself around on the bar stool, getting herself comfortable. "She's really beautiful," she said.

"Of course she is. She comes from you."

As soon as she had said it, she wished that she'd bitten her tongue, and thought about what she was saying before opening her big mouth as she saw the pain shoot across Chrissie's face. Shit.

"It's alright, Nats." Chrissie said, seeing Natasha's frown. "I'm going to have these mixed-up feelings about meeting up with her until I can get over the guilt of giving her away."

"Two brandies please, Natasha ask the young barman as she gave Chrissie a hug. "Now Chrissie darling, I know right now you must be eaten up with what you should have done, and what you should not have done. But at the time you had no choice, and if you want me to be honest, I think that you made the right one. Lily has come back into your life, which has been her choice, and her choice only. Not yours. And it's not going to be easy for either of you, but you'll both get there in the end. I know you will. I've got a feeling in my waters," she laughed, hugging her again into her. "And talking about water, I need a pee."

Chrissie swallowed hard to contain the tears that wanted to flow, laughing at Natasha as she hastily left for the loo. She was right, of course, all that was needed was time. Deep down Chrissie was thrilled that Lily had come back into her life, she was just going to have to get used to having two daughters in her life instead of one. But what worried her most was, could she share the love that she had for Daisy? Could she find that same kind of love for her? When she had first set eyes on her, the surge of a mother's love had flowed through her veins, taking her breath away. But that was before the guilt started to set in. And now she was left with the feelings of love and guilt for her, and dare she say even anger. But she couldn't pass that anger on to Lily. She would have to work on the guilt bit and get over it.....

Oh, God, she hoped so. She'd also been amazed of how much she resembled her with her blue eyes and fair hair, and the mannerisms she had being so like Daisy's had shocked her. Chrissie sighed, she was really going to have to work on her emotions, and she was sure that as time went on she would be able to form a loving relationship with her. She really hoped so.

"Penny for them?" Angie asked, making Chrissie jump out of her skin as she went to order another nightcap. She had been sat there for a few moments after coming back from the loo, watching her deep in thought, and saw the tears building up in her eyes, so she thought that it was time to offer her a nightcap, even though she'd made her jump. "Sorry, I didn't mean to make you jump."

"No, that's okay, I was daydreaming."

"Would you like another brandy?"

"No, I don't think so if I want to walk out of here tonight," Chrissie laughed, finishing off the remains of the brandy that was left in her glass.

"Rubbish. Two more brandies please." Natasha sat down on the bar stool grinning at Chrissie, who was frowning across at her. "Chrissie, darling, Jake is picking you up tonight, so make the most of it. I am, Angie is driving me home," she winked, kissing her on the cheek.

So Chrissie went with the flow, she needed cheering up, and as the three of them sat around the bar, Angie told them of a very funny story about her friend who had taken her dog for a walk. The dog had been called Smudge, and he was a golden retriever. Carol who was his owner always took him into a small wooded area that was near the house for his daily walk. She had let him off his lead to let him run free and to do his business while she enjoyed the peace of the countryside. After about twenty minutes, she whistled for him to come back to her so they could both make their way back home. As soon as he heard the whistle, he bounded through the trees back to her. As Carol waited for him to appear before turning to go back home, she spotted him in the distance with something dangling from his mouth, thinking, "Oh, God, what has he caught now," so she stopped and waited for him to catch up with her, squinting up her eyes to see if she could see what was half in and half out, hanging from his mouth. She let out a yelp when he finally caught up with her with the biggest pheasant that she had ever seen dangling in between his clenched jaws. As she calmed him down from running around her feet, proudly parading his catch, she yelled at him to drop it. Placing it at her feet, she jumped back, suppressing a scream as she watched this body of a pheasant squirming around in front of her. As Carol bent down to see if she could do anything for it, Smudge darted in and picked it up again, running off shaking it around in his mouth. Carol screamed out after him to come back to her, but Smudge carried on trotting towards home with his head held high and his prize possession held in his mouth. When they had finally both reached home, Carol had slammed the back gate closed, and yelled at Smudge to drop what he had in his mouth, slapping his backside with the end of his lead. Dropping it to the floor, she pushed him into the house to get him away from the scene, slamming the door behind him. Then she turned to see what she could do for the pheasant that was now up on its feet with its head lolling to one side. It was making a most peculiar noise and was trying to flap its wings to get away. But then all of a sudden it fell to the ground motionless. Carol let out a small scream as she went over to it thinking that it was dead. Nervously, she bent over to check that it was dead and not still suffering when all of a sudden it moved, making her scream out so loud that it started Smudge off barking as she jumped back to get out of its way straight into a puddle that filled her boots, as it scrabbled to its feet and flew off squawking.

"You've got to be kidding me," Chrissie said, looking totally shocked by what she had just heard.

"No, I'm not," Angie laughed, turning to Natasha who also had the same look of shock on her face.

Then the three of them looked at each other and burst out laughing just as Jake came through the door to pick Chrissie up.

"Hey, who's having a good time, then."

"We are," they all said together, as Chrissie lifted her cheek to be kissed with the other two following.

****

Chrissie was so excited. Daisy was due home in a few days' time from Australia and she couldn't wait to see her. She had got the week off from work so she could be with her to catch up on everything that had happened over the last year while she'd been away. She had really missed Daisy being home with her this Christmas, and even though they had had a lovely time with Lily being there on Boxing Day, where she met up with Natasha and Angie for the first time, it wasn't like having Daisy there with her. When she had phoned her on Christmas Day, they had both cried over the phone, Daisy was really missing being there with her mum for Christmas. It was her first one away. So Chrissie had asked her what she had been doing with her time over there to take her mind off being homesick. Daisy told her mother of the trips that she had made. One was to the Blue Mountains, where she saw the amazing scenery of very high mountains all around her, that had low clouds covering the tops of them, giving the mountains a blue haze. Hence the name, 'Blue Mountains'. And of her week long trip to Shoal Bay in Port Stephens, NSW (New South Wales), where Jasmine's Uncle Brad had an apartment overlooking the bay she had snorkeled and fished the whole week through in the warm sunshine. "It was a holiday of a lifetime," she told Chrissie. And now she was due

227

back and Chrissie couldn't wait to see her. She had cleaned the cottage from top to bottom, and warned Jake what would happen if he made a mess anywhere. Daisy was arriving on Wednesday, so Chrissie had a couple of days where she could get everything up together before she got home. Lily was over the moon that she would soon be meeting her sister, and it was good that over the weeks that Chrissie had been seeing Lily, they had bonded closer together. There was still a way to go yet, but Chrissie was hoping that in time they would become close. She had invited Lily over on the Sunday for lunch. Daisy would need time to get over her jet lag, and Chrissie wanted to have time with her before they were to meet. This was the only downside of Daisy coming home. Every day Chrissie was getting more and more uptight about their meeting. Would Daisy despise her for giving her sister away? Would it cause rift between them? All of this was going through her mind and she just couldn't shake it off. She knew that she was being absurd, but that was how she was feeling. Jake had told her not to be so stupid, of course Daisy wasn't going to blame her. "What blame," he asked, silencing her with one of his passionate kisses that ended up taking away all of her doubts for awhile as he made passionate love to her on the floor of the lounge.

Daisy had been home for two days now, and Chrissie had fussed around her like a bee around a honey pot. God, how she'd missed her. She looked good, wearing a tan that could put a top model to shame. She looked gorgeous. And it wasn't until they had caught up with what they had both been doing over the last year that Daisy brought Lily up. She couldn't wait to see her on Sunday, but in the meantime she wanted to know all about her. Who did she look like? Did she look like her mother? Did she look like her? Whew, so many questions, Chrissie couldn't keep up with her. So she told her as much as she could, telling how she resembled her in many ways, and that she had had a good life. Her adoptive mother had died but her adoptive father was still alive living on the outskirts of Bath. It was Jake that had broke it up, much to the relief of Chrissie, by coming in from work and interrupting them, not realising that they were in a discussion about Lily.

Lily had been on edge all week about the meeting with Daisy. She was dying to meet her, but now the time was getting closer, she was feeling very nervous about it all. How were they going to react to each other? Was Daisy going to find her a threat coming into her mother's life after all these years of having her to herself, or was she going to welcome her with open arms? She was sure that she had lost a stone worrying about it. But Lily so wanted the first meeting to go off well. She really was looking forward to having a sister in her life.

Chrissie had been up with the larks, she couldn't sleep. The time was finally here where her two daughters were going to meet for the very first time and she was a nervous wreck. She had been out in the garden since seven that morning clearing out pots ready for the spring bulbs to go in, still finding those blasted slugs hanging around in-wait for the new growth of plants. Bastards. Jake had got up just after Chrissie, taking her a coffee out with a chocolate biscuit to soothe her nerves. God, what would she have done without him? Jake had offered to move out when Daisy had come back home, but Chrissie was having none of that. He had now become her soulmate, and he was going nowhere. That man had stuck with her through thick and thin, and although at times she could wring his bloody neck, as he could her no doubt, she loved him. Whatever love was.

Lily was due to arrive around lunchtime, so Daisy took her time getting ready by having a shower. She wanted to be relaxed when Lily arrived even though like Chrissie, she hadn't slept much last night. She had lay awake thinking of what was she going to feel for this stranger that was about to come into her life. Was she going to like her, or was she going to be a threat to

229

her? She had been the only child in her mother's life for a long time now, and she didn't know if she would be able to cope with somebody else sharing her mother's affection. But she wanted to see her. She was thrilled when she heard that she had a sister out there somewhere. But now this was reality. Her sister was coming to her home. Did she want that? "Oh, shut up," her inner voice said to her, and finally she had drifted off into a troubled sleep. But now she would be arriving anytime soon, so she had to get herself ready and make sure she was down there to greet her in. The doorbell rang dead on 12:30, and it was Jake who answered the door. Daisy was still upstairs fussing around with her hair, which looked perfect swung up in a ponytail, but she wasn't happy with it. As the morning had gone on, she was losing her courage to meet Lily, and she'd jumped when she'd heard the doorbell ring. Chrissie was out in the kitchen filling up Marmalade's dish with some chicken that was leftover from yesterday, so it was left to Jake to show Lily into the lounge, asking her if she wanted a drink of any sorts. He knew that Chrissie had already hit the wine, and he could feel himself getting really uptight with her. Lily declined, sitting herself down in the chair as Jake excused himself to fetch Chrissie.

"What the bloody hell is going on? Why didn't you answer the door to Lily?" he snapped at Chrissie, who had her head in the fridge.

"What's the problem, I'm just coming?" she said, raising her voice at him.

"The bloody problem is, Chrissie, your daughter has just arrived to meet her sister for the first time and neither of you were there to greet her in. Do you think that's fair when it's her that has come into the family, not you and Daisy?"

Jake knew that he had gone too far, but it was the truth. She didn't see the look on Lily's face when neither of them were there to greet her in.

Chrissie was shaking with rage, but before she could reply to him, he had left the kitchen and gone back through to Lily, who was sat looking around the room. Taking a swig from the wine bottle, Chrissie stuck a peppermint into her mouth, ("you'll soon end up an alcoholic at this rate"), her inner voice said to her as she told it to sod off as she went through to Lily, apologising for not being there when she had arrived. Lily could feel the tension coming from all of them, including herself. And still Daisy had not appeared. Chrissie excused herself, leaving Jake with Lily while she went to get Daisy. She found her sat on the end of her bed, staring out into space.

"Daisy, what are you doing? Lily's here, she's waiting downstairs to see you."

"Well I don't want to see her."

"What?" Chrissie was shocked at the tone of her voice. It was Daisy who had wanted to meet up with her in the first place. But she stayed calm and went over to her, putting her arms around her. "Daisy, I know how you feel. I felt like this the very first time that Lily had come to see me, and I even drove down the road to give myself more time before I met her. But how do you think she is feeling right now? Sat down there with Jake knowing that you have second thoughts of meeting her."

When Daisy walked into the room with Chrissie, Lily got up, but wasn't quite sure what to do or say next until Chrissie introduced them both, pushing Daisy gently from behind to go over to her. For a moment or two they stood smiling at each other. Then shook hands with each other, both feeling awkward as they looked each other up and down. Lily was beginning to wish that she had never come here, and Daisy was feeling the same. What was she to say to a complete stranger? She looked across at her mother, willing her to say something. But Chrissie held her ground. It was down to the two of them now. After what seemed to be an eternity of silence between them, Daisy

made a step forward, and put her arm around Lily, giving her a hug. The feeling of pride that Chrissie felt at that moment at seeing her two daughters hugging each other would stay with her forever. She only hoped now that they would bond with each other. But what if Daisy didn't accept her? She couldn't force her into loving a sister that she had never known. She could only hope that in time they would get to know one another, and eventually would bond together as sisters. But only time would tell…